Praise for Father Andrew M. Greeley and his acclaimed novels...

THE BISHOP AT SEA

Bishop Blackie Ryan has been dispatched to the USS Langley, *where he soon finds a mystery as deep—and as dangerous—as the ocean all around...*

"Father Greeley manages to write a first-rate mystery and at the same time include the major sociological issues facing today's military. The story line is exciting and the treatment of today's issues is sensitive, compassionate, and accurate. It's a great book!"

—Robert J. Spane, VADM USN (Ret.)

HAPPY ARE THE OPPRESSED

In a novel of family sins and secrets, Blackie investigates the Cardin family—heirs to an unmatched legacy of wealth, prestige, and murder...

"Greeley's vivid reconstruction of Chicago's Gilded Age elevates this saga above the level of a standard whodunit."

—*Chicago Sun-Times*

"He has mastered the art of suspense."

—*The Arizona Daily Star*

HAPPY ARE THOSE WHO MOURN

Blackie Ryan is called to a suburban parish to investigate a ghost, but uncovers some far more earthly disturbances—like murder...

"Greeley writes with passion and narrative force."

—*Chicago Sun-Times*

"Greeley is superb."

"A first-rate storyteller!"

continu...

D1040788

HAPPY ARE THE POOR IN SPIRIT

Blackie Ryan investigates the attempted murder of the rich and famous Bart Cain and discovers some long-dead ghosts in the Cain family closet...

"Greeley is a wizard at spinning a yarn."

—Associated Press

"The unflappable Blackie Ryan could definitely become habit-forming."

—*Publishers Weekly*

"Greeley writes with style."

—*Newsday*

HAPPY ARE THE PEACE MAKERS

The sleuthing bishop investigates a beautiful widow suspected of murder...

"Vintage Greeley, terrific entertainment."

—*Booklist*

"Readers will not be disappointed."

—*Minneapolis Tribune*

"Andrew Greeley just gets better and better!"

—*Dayton Daily News*

HAPPY ARE THE MERCIFUL

A Blackie Ryan novel featuring the perfect locked-room mystery—a double murder beyond belief...

"Spellbinding . . . appealing . . . He's a true storyteller."

—*Fort Worth Star-Telegram*

"Keeps the reader captivated!"

—*The Fresno Bee*

"Absorbing and suspenseful . . . another winner."

—*Rave Reviews*

FALL FROM GRACE

A shattering novel of sin and scandal—a woman learns the darkest secrets of politics, the Church, and her own heart...

"Shocking . . . Greeley's characters have plenty to confess!"
—Associated Press

"A page-turner!"
—*People*

"With unerring wit and charm . . . Greeley seems to be doing the impossible with his novels."
—*Detroit Free Press*

WAGES OF SIN

A novel about first love and last chances—a man relives the passion, guilt, and obsession of his youth...

"Fast-paced . . . romantic . . . emotional!"
—*Publishers Weekly*

"The mystery keeps you guessing until the last page."
—*USA Weekend*

"Entertaining and satisfying."
—Associated Press

AN OCCASION OF SIN

Greeley's boldest masterwork of passion, faith, and sinful secrets—a priest's investigation into the scandalous life of a Cardinal who may become a saint...

"An intriguing cliff-hanger to the very end."
—*Pittsburgh Post-Gazette*

"A surprise ending . . . engrossing, entertaining, suspenseful."
—*Publishers Weekly*

"Father Greeley's own special blend of clerical politics, sex, and salvation."
—*Kirkus Reviews*

TITLES BY ANDREW M. GREELEY

Fiction

WAGES OF SIN
AN OCCASION OF SIN
DEATH IN APRIL
FALL FROM GRACE
THE CARDINAL SINS
GOD GAME
ANGEL FIRE
HAPPY ARE THE MEEK
HAPPY ARE THE CLEAN OF
   HEART
HAPPY ARE THOSE WHO
   THIRST FOR JUSTICE
HAPPY ARE THE MERCIFUL
HAPPY ARE THE PEACE
   MAKERS
HAPPY ARE THE POOR IN
   SPIRIT
HAPPY ARE THOSE WHO
   MOURN
HAPPY ARE THE OPPRESSED
THE BISHOP AT SEA
THE BISHOP AND THE
   THREE KINGS

The Passover Trilogy

THY BROTHER'S WIFE
ASCENT INTO HELL
LORD OF THE DANCE

Time Between the Stars

VIRGIN AND MARTYR
THE ANGELS OF SEPTEMBER
THE PATIENCE OF A SAINT
RITE OF SPRING
LOVE SONG
SAINT VALENTINE'S NIGHT

The World of Maggie Ward

THE SEARCH FOR MAGGIE WARD
THE CARDINAL VIRTUES

Mystery and Fantasy

THE MAGIC CUP
THE FINAL PLANET

Selected Nonfiction

THE MAKING OF THE POPES 1978
THE CATHOLIC MYTH
CONFESSIONS OF A PARISH PRIEST
HOW TO SAVE THE CATHOLIC
   CHURCH (with Mary G. Durkin)
RELIGIOUS CHANGE IN AMERICA
THE BIBLE AND US (with Jacob
   Neusner)
GOD IN POPULAR CULTURE
FAITHFUL ATTRACTION

The Bishop and the Three Kings

—— A BLACKIE RYAN MYSTERY ——

Andrew M. Greeley

BERKLEY BOOKS, NEW YORK

THE BISHOP AND THE THREE KINGS

A Berkley Book / published by arrangement with
Andrew Greeley Enterprises, Ltd.

PRINTING HISTORY
Berkley edition / November 1998

All rights reserved.
Copyright © 1998 by Andrew Greeley Enterprises, Ltd.
This book may not be reproduced in whole or in part,
by mimeograph or any other means, without permission.
For information address: The Berkley Publishing Group,
a member of Penguin Putnam Inc.,
375 Hudson Street, New York, New York 10014.

The Penguin Putnam Inc. World Wide Web site address is
http://www.penguinputnam.com

ISBN: 0-425-16617-1

BERKLEY®
Berkley Books are published by The Berkley Publishing Group,
a member of Penguin Putnam Inc.,
375 Hudson Street, New York, New York 10014.
BERKLEY and the "B" logo
are trademarks belonging to Berkley Publishing Corporation.

PRINTED IN THE UNITED STATES OF AMERICA

10 9 8 7 6 5 4 3 2 1

For Wolfgang Jagodzinski, Erwin Scheuch, Ekkehard Mochman, Rolf Uher, Irene Müller, Michael Terwey, and all my colleagues at the Zentralarchiv of the University of Köln.

We three kings of Orient are,
Bearing gifts we traverse afar
Field and fountain, moor and moun-
tain,
Following yonder star.

O star of wonder, star of night,
Star with royal beauty bright,
Westward leading, still proceeding,
Guide us to thy perfect light

—John E. Hopkins, Jr. 1820–1891

Like Blackie and his nefoo Peter Murphy, Ph.D., I admire the charm in the different ways in which English is spoken in our country. I believe that these styles of speaking (including Black English) are part of the rich cultural assets of our pluralistic republic. I abhor the bigoted nativism that insists that everyone speak English exactly the same way. Hence, like Blackie and his nefoo, I am delighted by Cindasue's "hill talk," as she calls Appalachian English, a delight of which she is very well aware, shy and sly leetle mount'in critter that she pretends to be. Thus I reject at the beginning any suggestion that I am ridiculing her or anyone else who speaks the Appalachian dialect. I have used teen talk and Irish talk in other books only with respect. So I use Appalachian talk in this book.

Y'all hear?

Moreover, the idea of the name Stinking (or more properly Stinkin') Creek (Crik) came from a wonderfully perceptive and sensitive book by John Fetterman (*Stinking Creek: The Portrait of a Small Mountain Community in Appalachia*). In his book, the name is a pseudonym for his hometown, whose culture and values he quite properly admires as I do. My Stinkin' Crik is not based on his town or any other real town.

(At the end of the story, I list the books about Appalachian English I have consulted in an effort for verisimilitude.)

The characters, incidents, and motives in this story are completely fictional. The behavior of the Köln clerics, the security systems, and the art workshop at the dom are products of my imagination. Also fictional is the argument that the art treasures should be put in a museum to protect them from pollution. So, too, is Blackie's suspicion that there are no relics inside the Shrine of the Magi. The chancel screen does not separate the shrine and the main altar from the rest of the dom. There is a workshop, but it is not beneath the dom where I have placed it. Moreover, I have restored the parsonage, which was removed in the sixteenth century.

I have made the shrine lighter for the purposes of the story than it in fact is. Anyone wanting to borrow it for awhile had better bring along a crane.

However, the beauty of the shrine, the loveliness of Köln, and the charm of its people are real.

So, too, is Blackie's interpretation of the meaning of the "star of wonder, star of night."

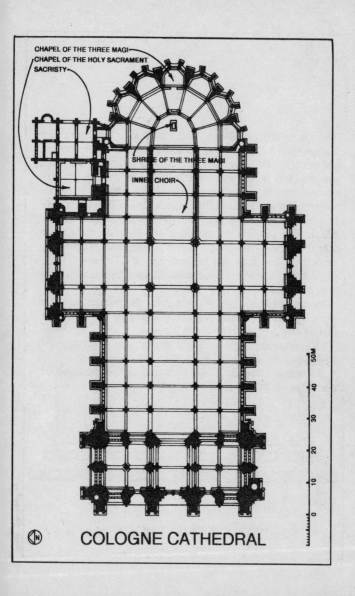

CHAPEL OF THE THREE MAGI
CHAPEL OF THE HOLY SACRAMENT
SACRISTY

SHRINE OF THE THREE MAGI

INNER CHOIR

50M
40
30
20
10
0

COLOGNE CATHEDRAL

SHRINE OF THE THREE MAGI

1

Bishop John Blackwood Ryan

"They've stolen the bodies of the three kings!" Sean Cardinal Cronin, by the grace of God and the strained patience of the Apostolic See announced in his most dramatic tenor voice, pointing his finger at me accusingly, as if I, personally, was responsible for the theft.

He had swept into my study like a crimson tornado, his usual style when he needed a favor from me. His tall, spare frame was clad in a cassock with crimson buttons, and a cummerbund, cape, and zucchetto of the same color. He wore an ostentatious, bejeweled pectoral cross, a gift from his sister and his sister-in-law, Senator Nora Cronin. Some social event of considerable moment must have transpired earlier in the evening.

"Blackwood," he had announced as he seized a full bottle of my treasured supply of Bushmill's Green from its hiding place, "We're in trouble."

I had turned away from the computer and my long essay on "Russian Trinitarian Mysticism As a Love Affair"—a late-evening amusement—to face him head-on: if Milord Cronin said we were in trouble, it usually meant that *I* was in trouble.

"Indeed?" I had said cautiously.

He had filled a Waterford tumbler for me and poured a much smaller amount for himself. Since he did not usually drink a nightcap at all, I had become all the more convinced that I was in trouble. I had glanced at the icons on my wall—I called them icons now that I was into Russian mysticism—and prayed for help. The only one I could count on was the medieval ivory Madonna, which my old fella had given me because it reminded him of my mother. The Johns of my youth—pope, president, and Baltimore quarterback—would be of no use in the present situation. Neither would the newest addition, Clare Marie Raftery Boyle, a young woman who had helped me solve a mystery a hundred years old.

The cardinal had removed a pile of computer output from my easy chair—cathedral financial records in this instance, depressing as always—sank into the chair, sipped from his tumbler, stretched out in satisfaction, and announced the grave robbery.

"Deplorable . . ." I said with a loud sigh as I sipped cautiously from my Waterford. "Which three kings?"

"The three kings from the Orient: Gaspar, Balthasar, and Melchior," he replied as his blue Celtic mercenary-warrior eyes flared with indignation. "What other three kings are there?"

"I would remind you that the current translation of the readings of the Feast of the Ephiphany, which you your-self have approved for use at Eucharistic celebrations in this archdiocese, depict them as astrologers, which may be more accurate but lacks some narrative vigor."

"That's besides the point, Blackwood," he insisted, a frown creasing his handsome face. "The point is, their bodies have been stolen."

"From the archdiocesean cemetery system?"

"No, of course not, from the cathedral in Cologne! This is a very big deal. Outside of Rome and Compestella, the kings were the object of the largest pilgrimages in the Middle Ages. They deserve credit for making Cologne one of the great cities of Europe. To lose them permanently would cause a grave crisis in the church."

"It is the devout and plausible conviction of the Greeks and the Russians that there were twelve of these astrologers. They argue that since there are twelve apostles and twelve legions of angels and twelve tribes of Israel, there must be twelve, uh, astrologers. In its own way, that argument merits some credence, particularly if you happen to be a Russian or a Greek. We, on the other hand, believe there were only three because there were three gifts brought: gold, frankincense, and myrrh. One gift, you see, one king. It is, I must concede, a typical manifestation of the Western empiricism that the Greeks and the Russians abhor."

"How come then that there are only three bodies in the Cologne Cathedral?" He demanded, baffled by my little excursus into scriptural interpretation.

"Is one permitted to observe that it is very unlikely that the bones entombed in that lovely city on the Rhine are in fact those of the wise men, of whatever number, who came out of the East to Bethlehem? . . . Moreover, as I remember, they were stolen from the cathedral in Milan by that exemplary Catholic king, Frederick of the Red Beard. So this is not the first theft."

"That, Blackwood," Milord Cronin informed me, "is totally beside the point!"

I refrained from noting that this was the second time he had accused me of missing the point. In fact, he was well aware that I was deliberately missing the point, because I didn't like what it obviously was.

"The point is that it is close to Christmas."

"Ah," I said. "I had thought that it was the first week in October, fully eighty-five shopping days till Christmas."

"If we don't get the Three Kings back before Christmas, the word will leak out, and all the world will be in Cologne to reveal yet another Catholic scandal. In the days of Freddy Barbarossa, you didn't have Christine Armanpour descending from a helicopter to tell in shocked tones that the Catholic Church had spoiled Christmas."

"Beat the Grinch to it," I said, trying to sound sympathetic.

The leprechaun who haunts my quarters at Holy Name Cathedral had stolen most of my aqua vitae, as he usually does. I decided that it would be pointless to refill the glass: I would not sleep much that night at all. At all, at all.

"You Ryans like to travel," Milord continued, stating what he knew was a total falsehood.

"Patently, we do not. Why leave Chicago, as my sister the federal judge often says, when we have everything here?"

That dictum from the good Eileen is something of an exaggeration. Various members of the clan have traveled to the far ends of the earth for reasons of necessity—kicking, screaming, and complaining all the way out and back.

"Except the bodies of the Three Kings."

"Arguably."

"Claus is a good friend, right?" he continued, circling around our trouble.

He was referring to Claus Maria, Heinrich, Rupert Eugen, Graf von Obermann, the cardinal archbishop of Cologne.

"Arguably," I said again, with the loudest of my West of Ireland sighs.

"We do him favors, he does us favors, right?

"That is the Chicago political tradition."

I sighed again.What he meant was that, if I did a favor for the genial Viking pirate who presided over Köln (to spell it properly), he, Cardinal Sean Cronin, would have a marker to pick up. Such is the nature of the responsibility of auxiliary bishops whose role is roughly analogous of the character played by the excellent Harvey Keitel in the film *Pulp Fiction*: We sweep up the messes that real bishops make.

"So if we can help him get the Three Kings back, he will owe us one very big favor."

"That is the way it works," I assented.

"Besides," he said, swirling around the remaining precious fluid in his glass, "this little puzzle is not without certain interesting aspects."

He had stolen the line from me, patently. I, in my turn, had stolen it from Sherlock Holmes.

"Indeed."

"Oh, yes. The casket with the remains of your three friends is the largest gilded monument in the Occidental world."

"Impressive."

"It would take four, arguably six, men to move it."

"Indeed."

"It is protected by a large, transparent case, which looks like glass but is in fact bulletproof plastic."

"If terrorists wanted to destroy the shrine with automatic weapons . . ."

"Or something like that . . . Needless to say the case is wired with an alarm."

"Naturally."

"Moreover, it is behind the high altar, which they no longer use for Mass, ah, the Eucharist, because we have different ideas of where the altar should be than the Goths did."

"Franks, in this case, though both were Germanic tribes."

"Whatever . . . The whole area around the high altar and the shrine is protected by a wrought-iron fence, which is also wired and is locked unless opened by one of the head vergers of the cathedral."

"A reasonable precaution."

"Finally, they lock the cathedral up at night, unlike this place . . ."

"No one has stolen anything from our cathedral," I pointed out.

I hold the odd position for a priest of our age, that a church building belongs to the people who paid for it and that it should be open to them at all hours of the day and night. A ring of visible light encircles a section in the back of the nave and warnings are posted that anyone who violates that circle will call down upon himself the wrath of Chicago Police Department, the Cook County Sheriff's Police, the Illinois State Police, the Alcohol, Tobacco, and Fire Arms Agency, the Federal Bureau of Investigation, and possibly the Swiss Guard. The warnings exaggerate somewhat, but only somewhat. There are also various electronic wonders, not excluding TV monitors, which preclude the possibility of anyone doing harm to anyone else in our ring of light without the risk of unleashing sounds that would awaken not only the intrepid cathedral staff but most human beings living within the boundaries of the parish.

We have had only a few false alarms.

"They wire their place at night, too. They should, with all the treasures inside. I wouldn't think it is as elaborate, however, as your network of instruments from hell."

"Undoubtedly it is not. No church in the world . . ."

"I'm sure," he held up his hand. "The point is that you have a locked shrine inside a locked fence within a locked cathedral, all of which are not only locked but armed."

"Fascinating," I admitted grudgingly.

"Last week, the priest who comes over to say the first mass . . ."

"Doubtless the pastor, as in this cathedral."

". . . Notices that the shrine is missing. The transparent cage is locked, the fence is locked, the alarm system is still functioning, but the Three Kings have disappeared."

"Most fascinating."

"I knew you'd think so," he said, triumphantly bounding out of the easy chair.

"What did the good clergy of the dom do about their loss?"

I discreetly replaced the financial output papers. One must have an orderly room.

"They replaced it with the fake before they let anyone inside the place."

"Fake!"

"Sure, you gotta have a fake. When they take the real

one down to the basement to fix it up, they put in a wooden one that's painted gold. From a distance, you can't tell the difference."

"Ingenious . . . No one knows about this surrogate and presumably boneless shrine?"

"Be reasonable, Blackwood! Everyone knows about it. When they were doing major repairs back in the seventies, they had the fake in for six months. Didn't bother the pilgrims at all, even if they knew, which they probably didn't."

"All the Kölners knew, however."

"Sure . . . They've talked to the ministry of justice or whatever they call it over there. Everyone is keeping it a secret, however, for fear of publicity. I guess they're having some kind of election."

"The *Polizei* don't know?"

"You got it."

He leaned against my doorjamb, relishing the approaching moment.

"No one claims credit, no one seeks ransom?" I asked.

"Not so far."

"Nor is there a market for gilded shrines with the purported bones of three astrologers."

"Precisely."

"Though there are always the rich private collectors who enjoy knowing that they have something no one else has."

"Creeps," Milord Cronin agreed. "But superrich creeps."

"It is, as you say, a little puzzle that is not without some interest."

"So Claus remembers that you do locked rooms and wants you to come over and have a look around. Strictly private. He doesn't want to upset the Ministry of Interior or whatever by bringing in an *Ausländer*. That means foreigner."

"How can I be a foreigner," I asked, "when patently I am an American?"

"Spoken like a true offspring of the South Side Irish. . . . Anyway, we've got to help Claus get it back."

"So I understand," I said with the loudest of all my sighs.

"One of the young guys can take care of this place. They have more energy, anyway."

"Arguably."

"We have to recover the Three Kings to save Christmas! See to it, Blackwood!"

Then, like a carmine jet that had just turned on its afterburners, he swept from my study, trailing, as he always does under such circumstances, maniacal laughter.

2

"You're going *where*?"

My eldest sibling, Mary Kathleen Ryan Murphy, was exercising her role as senior family matriarch to express surprise, dismay, shock, and horror at the latest folly a male member of the clan was about to perpetrate.

"Cologne. That's a city, not a scent. Though the scent was invented in that city."

"Is it in Thailand?"

The Ryan family knows little geography. The world is coded "Chicago" and "All Other."

"It's in Germany," I said and sighed patiently into the phone.

"Is it anywhere near . . . what's the capital of that place these days? Berlin?"

"It will be soon. For the moment, it is John LeCarré's so-called small town in Germany. A city actually of substantial age called Bonn."

"That's the place. You gotta take Petey with you."

Peter Murphy was her older son, a young man of many admirable qualities, not the least of which was the ability to defend successfully his doctoral dissertation in the anthropology department at The University (of Chicago, but the genitive phrase is rarely used by those associated with that august breeding ground of Nobel scholars). His near record time for this achievement was the result of both great ability and his choice of a primitive tribe to study— Chicago commodity brokers. I thought that he could have done that by talking to his age peers in the various pits before he ever enrolled in The University.

"You're right, Uncle Punk," he had replied with a laugh. "But I had to go to school for four years to learn the jargon."

He had turned down offers from many distinguished universities because they suffered from one very serious handicap: they were not in Chicago. In January he would begin teaching at Loyola University. His dissertation, entitled *Traders on the Run*, would be published in June. Among its chapters, the most comic was about wired federal agents who tried to trap traders into admitting crimes and swept up only harmless small fry.

"Petey?" I said, somewhat bemused.

"Sure. He's got time on his hands. He doesn't start at Loyola till January. He's under our feet all the time around the house."

"Indeed."

"You can tell him you need help for whatever cockamamie scheme Sean Cronin has thought up for you this time. He'll love the idea."

"Arguably."

"You can't tell him that I suggested it, and of course you can't tell him the real reason."

This is the way women of my religio-ethnic background approach life. They assume that you know what they are talking about without telling you. Then when you concede you don't know, they have an opportunity to express wonder at masculine lack of comprehension.

"Which is?"

"Why, Cindasue, naturally."

"Who?"

"Cindasue, you know, the cute little tyke in the sailor suit."

Cindasue McCloud was at the time a petty officer, second class, in what she called "the Yewnited States Coast Guard." The first time she had come to the Murphy house at Grand Beach, all "spiffed up" as she put it, in her summer whites, Brigie Murphy yelled up to her mother, "Hey, Mom, there's a cute little kid in a sailor suit down here!"

The Murphys took to Cindasue instantly, as they did usually to strangers, strays, and, uh, *Ausländer*. Cindasue, who had learned caution in her native mountains, was more reserved at first; but then she, too, fell under the spell of the Murphy magic.

"Y'all are not bad folks," she had conceded, "seeing as how you're no-count Irish Catholic trash."

After that first encounter, however, she was always to my sibling "that cute little tyke in the sailor suit."

Cindasue was indeed a cute kid on her way to becoming a beautiful woman. Additionally, she was an imp and a detective of considerable natural talent. Anyone in that business, as I occasionally am, learns to respect that talent wherever it is to be found. She also spoke fluently three languages, Federal Bureaucratese with her Coast Guard colleagues, Radio Standard English with "real folk," and Mountain English when she was being herself. As soon as she found out that the last-named was popular with the Ryan-Murphy clan, she spoke it all the time with us.

"I thought that romance was long since buried," I said.

"First love is never buried," my sibling said, putting on her psychiatrist's cap. "Personally, I think poor Pete made a mistake that his father didn't make."

"Which was?" I asked, though I knew the answer.

"Not going for it when he had the chance."

"As I remember, the folklore has it that the process went in the opposite direction."

She chuckled amiably, not denying the family legend of how she captured the quiet psychiatric resident from

Boston with whom she had fought daily during her clerk-
ship under his supervision.

"Well, maybe they both missed an opportunity. She
wanted to go to Annapolis or wherever that place is . . ."

"New London, Connecticut, is the site of the Coast
Guard Academy."

"Whatever," she dismissed my factual accuracy as
typical male obsession with the trivial. "And he wanted
to go to The University. Kids aren't like they used to be.
They figure they have plenty of time. Sometimes they
do, and sometimes they don't."

"They are in touch with one another?"

"Certainly not! Brig and she write to each other occasionally. She's some kind of attaché or something in
this Bono place."

"Bonn."

"Whatever . . . He's still in love with her. Trust a
mother's insight."

"Heaven forefend that I would not!"

"Good! . . . You'll ask him to go with you? And try
to take care of them, the poor kids?"

"No money-back guarantees. Does he know she's in
Bonn?"

"*Certainly* he knows."

"So if he jumps at the chance to be my keeper, that
will be a sign he's still interested."

"Shonuff!" Mary Kate replied as Cindasue would
have.

Then she laughed as Sean Cronin would have laughed.
See to it, Blackwood.

What need, I wondered, did the Yewnited States Coast
Guard have for an attaché on the Rhine, hundreds of
miles from the nearest ocean? Maybe they needed a detective to keep an eye on pirates? But the robber barons
had abandoned the Rhine centuries ago, had they not?

Peter Ryan Murphy accepted my invitation casually
enough.

"Hey, that sounds cool, Uncle Punk. I don't have anything else to do, and I think I'm getting on Mom's nerves.''

He did not even ask what I would be doing in the Rhineland—which meant he didn't much care.

What he did care about was another shot at the diminutive and gorgeous young woman with whom he had never quite fallen out of love.

See to it, Blackwood.

3

Peter's Story

"P.O./3d C. L. McCloud of the Yewnited States Coast Guard, Michigan City Station, suh. I'm a-searchin' for two bodies. Have you noticed any unusual bodies on the beach, suh?" The voice was exhausted, the body was short, the green eyes were weary, the face was pinched and red, the navy blue jacket and jeans were soaking wet.

I was about to tell the waterlogged kid on the doorstep that I didn't want to buy any magazine subscriptions when the phone rang. It was my mother, wondering whether I had finished my term paper—left over from summer school and required for graduation next summer.

"The Coast Guard is here looking for bodies," I said, trying not to sound too groggy. "I'll call you back."

"Your mammy?" A green eye considered me with more shrewdness than seemed appropriate.

"You know what mothers are like." I shrugged.

"Shonuff." The kid, dripping wet, edged into the kitchen of our beach house, a businesslike walkie-talkie bulging out of a blue jacket pocket.

I made one more effort to clear my head from the effects of the previous night's six-packs and said, "Bodies?"

"Yassuh," responded the kid forlornly. "I've been a-ransackin' the whole beach since five o'clock this morning, but I can't find none nowheres."

"Smack-dab out of bodies?" I said, showing off the course in American dialects from last year (and an A at that).

The thin shoulders straightened up, like an under-sized linebacker bracing for a blitz.

"I've been instructed to interview civilian residents to ask if they have observed any bodies." The high-pitched voice was pure redneck; the short, cropped auburn hair was dripping water, as were the navy blue jeans and jacket, on our kitchen floor.

"I'll make you some coffee," I said. "No, I haven't seen any bodies. How do you folks expect to find bodies with twelve-foot waves wiping out the beach and rain pouring down for three straight days? It'll just be a chance if you 'uns find any bodies."

"I know all about the rain, sir," said the weary redneck voice in perfectly grammatical Standard English. "Do you mind if I sit down?"

I gestured toward the kitchen table and then made a remarkable discovery as the redneck coastguardsman sank into a chair by the table. Maybe it was something about the set of the thin, tired shoulders. Anyhow, I tightened the belt on my blue terrycloth robe. The coastguardsman was a coastguards*woman*. Or maybe I should say coastguardsperson.

"What's this about bodies?" I asked, puting the tea-kettle on to boil. Whatever gender, the best I could do for the Department of Transportation on a gray, rainy day in late September was instant coffee.

"A civilian craft ran out of fuel just before the gale blew up three days ago, sir." The green eyes watched the teakettle hungrily. "There were five people aboard. Three stayed with it and two elected to swim for shore. The three came aground in the craft the day before yesterday. No trace of the other two."

I found some donuts in the icebox. One of them disappeared as soon as I put it on the table. "Craft, fuel, elect, civilian"—they'd taught this teenage redneck waif to use Coast Guard talk. I wondered if she'd ever seen a body when Lake Michigan finished with it.

"You certainly don't figure to find any bodies in waves like those?" I gestured at the ugly white walls sweeping in at the front of our dune.

Now, as my mammy, Dr. Mary Kate Ryan Murphy, the distinguished psychiatrist, would note, I am at that age in life when anyone of similar age and with a certified set of female reproductive organs excites libidinal interest. So I was libidinally interested in C. L. McCloud, P.O./3d, Yewnited States Coast Guard. Mild libidinal interest. Like wondering what she'd look like if she was not wearing her jacket.

She compressed her thin lips. "May I call my base, sir?" she asked.

"Yas'm," I agreed. I'm an anthropologist, not a linguist, but placing redneck talk is a kind of a hobby. "Southwestern West Virginia, isn't it, way up in the hills?"

I was rewarded with a faint, crinkly smile for my efforts.

"Stinkin' Crik, suh," she returned to Appalachian English. "McCloud's Holler, tell the truth. Ah joined the Coast Guard to get shet of the mountains and see the world out yonder."

"Is Michigan City, Indiana, any better than Stinking Creek, West Virginia?"

"Yassuh." She removed her walkie-talkie. "Not much, though . . . Mobile one to base, mobile one to base. Can you read me, base? Over." She turned away from me, her neck actually turning red.

Reevaluated from the perspective that she was a coast-guardswoman, C. L. McCloud could be rated cute, even pretty, possibly beautiful, but that would be going too far before I had more data.

Base didn't read her until she had fiddled expertly with the machine. Then base came through loud and clear.

"That you, Mountain Flower? Where the hell you been? Over." That voice was pure New Orleans black.

"Roger, base, this is mobile one. I have been interviewing a civilian resident in a home on the beach, the first civilian I've found this morning."

I put the coffee in front of her. Again, the wry, crinkly smile. Definitely kind of cute. Arguably gorgeous. Short even for a woman, but not too short. Take off the jacket, kid.

"He reports seeing no bodies."

"Roger, Cindasue. Call the CO in Cleveland on the phone; he'll give you more instructions. Over and out, Mountain Flower. Stay dry."

She sighed and put down the walkie-talkie. "May I use your phone, suh?"

Somehow, another donut vanished. She was gratefully sipping the coffee. I nodded my head.

She called collect and asked for the CO. "McCloud here, suh. I have been patrolling the beach since five. Yes, suh, I am very wet. I have found one civilian resident who I am interviewing. . . . Yes, suh, a young man about twenty, football-type ape with black hair. Just out of bed, good-looking in a shanty Irish sort of way . . . suffering from a hangover . . ." She flashed the damn crinkly grin again. "No, suh, not my type at all. My mammy done warned me about you Irish papists. Said you were no-count and shiftless." The lips tightened. "Yes suh, yes suh . . . Suh, do you want me to continue the patrol to New Buffalo? Yes suh . . . I was afraid so . . . yes suh, shonuff, I'll try to stay dry." She hung up with another sigh, kind of like the one patented by my uncle, Blackie Ryan, the priest.

"Pete Murphy is the name that goes with the shanty Irish hangover," I said, putting the final donut in her mouth.

"And James McCarthy is the name of that damn male chauvinist hound dog who is my boss," she mumbled through the donut. "All you Irish are alike."

I said something nasty about how a teenage punk

coastguardswoman from out of the hills couldn't hide the fact that her ancestors were Irish, too, an' they probably came over after Culloden Moor an' left the true church.

She replied, unzipping her jacket, that her 'uns had been in Stinkin' Crik thirty years 'fore that Dan'l Boone fella came over the hills. They were shonuff Americans, not biggety 'mgrants.

I complimented her on her study of the drinking subculture of the Irish papists but asserted that we hadn't invented moonshine.

Underneath the jacket, as best as one could observe through a heavy blue sweatshirt, she was more than presentable. I exercised the horny male's right to fantasize about helping her out of the sweatshirt.

She countered in kind that if you have to live with hound dogs you study their moods. I remarked that Michigan City must seem like paradise compared to the mountains where they sure had enough hound dogs. She said, her green eyes shooting fire, that the real hound dogs were better than the human kind, grinned her crinkly grin, which was kind of growing on me, and put out her mug for more coffee.

"Why the rush to find those bodies, Cindasue Mc-Cloud?" I asked, deciding that they were nice young breasts and that she probably could be considered beautiful. "If they wash in at all, it will be after the storm stops."

She was serious again. "Have you seen anyone on the beach at four o'clock in the morning, Mr. Murphy, suh?" The title was not ironic. They sure enough trained her to be polite.

"Dead or alive?" I asked, intrigued.

"Alive." Her eyes were now fixed on my face.

Oh, my God, a redneck girl detective. "Sorry, Cindasue McCloud, girl detective, ma'am, but I'm usually sleeping off my hangovers at four o'clock in the morning. What night?"

"Monday night. The woman in the house with the blue gazebo was interviewed yesterday by one of our personnel. She 'lowed that she woke up precisely at four o'clock and thinks she saw two subjects on the beach.''

So that was what she had to ask the CO about. "And they fit the description of the people who didn't make it to shore?"

She nodded. "Do you know a varmint from Long Beach named Harold O'Connell?"

"Was Harry the one who drowned?" I asked, embarrassed at being out of touch with the news. "I've been doing a term paper..."

"Keepin' yah poah mammy happy?... Would you recognize this hyar varmint if you saw him on the beach at four o'clock in the morning?"

She was boring in like a truck. This Cindasue McCloud, girl detective, was something else. She'd checked me out, too, the little imp. And decided that she could play her cute leetle redneck game for all it was worth.

I found another box of donuts. "Okay, Mountain Flower, let's have the whole story from the beginning. The CO told you it was all right to fill me in. Play it straight, and I'll help."

The eyes narrowed and the sweet little face peered at me for a moment of raw shrewdness. I guess I passed the test, though I'd hate to have been a varmint up in the hills that she was going after with a squirrel gun.

She shrugged her thin shoulders. "My name is not Mountain Flower, despite what that blacktrash J.G. calls me. This ridge runner Harry O'Connell is in slathers of trouble with his father-in-law. He done run off from the family brokerage firm with a whole heap of money— more than a half million dollars in negotiable securities. He also done committed adultery many times with a nurse he met at the hospital when his littleun was born. His father-in-law done told the U.S. attorney's office in Chicago. They were going to drop in 'n' talk a mite with Mr. O'Connell on Monday morning. Then he hears the powerful bad news that Mr. O'Connell and this here scarce-hipped nurse drowned on Sunday afternoon. Name a Moira Walsh. Typical no-count Irish papists.'' She grinned at me. "No one done found the securities, neither."

"So, the guess is that they are on their way to South America?" I said wisely, and then as an afterthought, "And I'm infinitely more virtuous than Harry."

She ignored my defense and returned to Standard English, except she always pronounced *united* as *yewnited*—the correct way, I suppose she would have argued. "The United States attorney's office was very anxious about our finding the bodies. When one of our personnel interviewed Mrs. Blue Gazebo yesterday, Commander McCarthy, using his native wit, thought that maybe the good old Northern District of Illinois was shonuff not telling us everything it ought to. So they allowed finally as how death by drowning was mighty convenient for Mr. O'Connell and Ms. Walsh. So this refugee from the hills and the hollers is likely to catch her death of cold unless, please suh, you give me some more coffee."

I was beginning to think it might be a good idea to fall hopelessly in love with her. For her part, less romantically but more realistically, Cindasue McCloud was trying to make up her mind whether she liked me. She wasn't much to look at, a little tad all bundled up in her sweatshirt and jacket again, but I wanted her to like me. Anyhow, I gave her the coffee. She eyed me speculatively. I thought maybe I passed another test.

"Why would they hang around the beach, Cindasue McCloud? Why not head for South America right away? Should not the Northern District have the feds watching airports instead of wilted mountain flowers slogging through the sand?" OK, I was walking on thin ice. She didn't seem to mind. Hell, the race keeps going because people our age size each other up. I wished she'd take off her sweatshirt so I could do some more sizing. I sat down across the table from her.

"It's the wilted mountain flower's own fault. I observed to Commander McCarthy that if I were running away with a half million dollars, I would lie low for a long time before heading for an airport, even if I had staged a drowning. So I would go to ground, uh, take refuge quite near the place where I landed on the beach, and stay there until . . ."

"A snowstorm covered your tracks."

"Uh-huh. Anyhow, the commander, whose father was one of your corrupt Chicago cops, said I was in the wrong branch of government service, that I had a mind like a corrupt cop, and would I like to patrol the beach and interview residents to establish my theory? He then arranged for it to rain for three days. . . ."

"Why did you leave West Virginia and join the Coast Guard, Cindasue McCloud?" I asked, wondering what she thought about sitting at a kitchen table with a man who was twice her height and weight (well, almost), wearing only a battered blue terrycloth robe.

"Personal questions are irrelevant to my patrol responsibilities, Mr. Murphy," she said primly. Then, relenting, she added, "The Coast Guard guarantees to keep you away from mountains after you're out of high school. If they like you, maybe they send you to college. Now, I must continue my patrol. Thank you for the refreshment."

She stood up, hunched her shoulders like she was going out on a raccoon hunt, and eased toward the kitchen door. I'd scared her. Damn.

"Can I come help? I've always wanted to be a detective." Lame, but the best I could do on the spur of the moment.

"You're not authorized government personnel, Mr. Murphy, suh. If you saw Harry O'Connell any time since Monday night and could tell me . . ."

"Cindasue, I feel sorry for anyone who married into the Haggerty clan, but I never did like Harry much, and I don't approve of larceny. If I'd seen him, I'd tell you. . . ."

She looked up at me, again the shrewd mountain animal, nodded her head as though I had convinced her, and walked out into the sheets of rain. She winced when the first deluge of water hit her. "Thank you very much for the coffee and donuts, Mr. Murphy. The commander of the Coast Guard thanks you, so does the secretary of transportation, and so does the president . . . only''—and she actually smiled very pleasantly at me—''don't try to deduct the expenses from your income tax.''

So I 'lowed to myself that I was in a whole heap of trouble, cogitatin' 'bout fallin' in love with a female varmint from the hollers when I should have been doin' up my term paper.

Then I 'lowed as how my poah ole mammy would dote on Cindasue and would never forgive me for not hog-tying her if she found I had the chance.

By 1:30, I finished exactly two paragraphs about the Irish traveling folk (or Irish Gypsies, if you want to call them that, though they're not really Gypsies) in America.

I gave it up, made two large hamburgers with everything and a thermos of hot coffee, and walked down the slippery stairs to the beach. I noticed that the storm winds (in excess of forty knots, according to KWO from Sears Tower) had knocked over the totem pole at the house next door. It hung drunkenly over two nymphs and fauns in the rock garden, as though it were going to fall against the door on my nutty neighbor's terrace level.

Down on the shore, the ugly white walls were still sweeping in. It was a nice, soggy beach to walk on, with the sand squishing under your feet, if you didn't mind twenty-seven knots of wind blowing straight down the lake from the Soo.

I found Cindasue a half mile down the beach in the New Buffalo direction, a lonely little figure huddling against a battered old boathouse, shivering with the cold and looking all plumb tuckered out. She refused neither hamburger nor coffee.

''Nice of you to shuckle out and bring me vittles.''

I pointed out that if you huddled under the overhang of the boathouse, you only got half the rain you'd get out on the beach.

''How long you out here?'' I asked over the howl of the wind.

"Twelve-hour duty. Me and my big redneck mouth."

"You don't really expect to find them out here, do you Miz Cindasue?" I asked in my best cornpone accent, digging into the second half of my hamburger.

"Look, Pete Murphy, boy anthropologist"—the little bitch had guessed that—"don't patronize me, or I'll go after you with my varmint gun."

Again she started out being angry and turned friendly. I was getting kind of worried.

"Anyway, I figure it has to be somewhere between the crik and New Buffalo. No way you can cross the crik when the waves are rolling in. If they walk down toward New Buffalo, they'd run into the permanent residents. That gives them about a mile and a half of beach."

She continued to munch efficiently on her hamburger. Small girl with a big appetite. And, I filed it away for future reference, a very neat little rear end.

"If they have the kind of criminal minds that you have and are smart enough to think that way ... Harry O'Connell is no prize when it comes to brains."

"The woman is. Woulda worked, too, 'ceptin for Mrs. Blue Gazebo."

"How do you see the case, Cindasue McCloud, girl detective?"

"Well." She dragged the introductory word out and once again paid no attention to my sarcasm. The attractive little petty officer was perfectly prepared to accept the label of detective. "I been figurin'. If I was goin' to disappear round hyar, and if I knew this crazy lake, I'd think, Cindasue, what if the sky clabbers up and the waves turn right smart? I'd take a gander at the beach and not want to climb over that pesky groin in front of you'un's pump house."

"So if you were planning to disappear somewhere near the blue gazebo, you'd have to come ashore between the pump house and the crik ... uh, creek."

"Yassuh, twixt the pump house and the crik ... lessen you get plumb knocked in by them powerful wave things."

She drew a diagram on the sand. "So happenchance that you'd be hiding in one of these eight houses twixt the crik, hyar, and the pump house, hyar."

"That narrows the search, doesn't it? Only eight houses where they might be, if'n your theory is right, Cindasue, girl detective."

"Six. Ah cased your house this morning. And we can eliminate Mrs. Blue Gazebo." She rubbed out the diagram with the impatient toe of an absurdly tiny Coast Guard sneaker.

"*Cased* is not Appalachian English."

"Is now." She smiled at me and my heart stopped stone dead.

"Let's go case the other six houses."

"Ah cain't do that. Ah don't have no federal warrant."

"Can't you watch a civilian poke his shanty Irish nose around?"

"Ah suppose so . . . would you really, Mr. Peter Murphy, suh?"

"For that smile, Cindasue McCloud, I'd do almost anything."

So we climbed over the groin and up the side of the dune, and worked our way through the gardens and the poolsides and the patios on our part of the beach, a-peekin' an' a-pokin' an' a-prowlin'. Have you ever prowled a summer resort in early autumn? It'll give you an idea of what earth might be like the day after the end of the world.

We didn't find nothin'. So, drippin' wet, we stood on a concrete seawall and surveyed the angry lake.

"Ah'm just about ready to holler calf rope." Cindasue sighed. "I'm plumb tuckered out."

"Climbing up all them stairs like a jackrabbit would tucker anyone out."

She had led the way on our a-pokin' and a-prowlin' like a forest creature bounding through the mountains, a slender, fragile leetle varmint whose energy and charm would break your heart. Mine, anyway.

"Peter Murphy, suh, the pump house!"

"You don't think they could be hiding there?"

She charged down the dune to the pump house without bothering to answer. I traipsed along after her and arrived a good half minute after she had thrown open the door and bounced inside.

Thank God the place was empty, save for a powerful lot of spiders.

I took firm possession of her attractive little shoulders and held her against the slimy and rusty green wall of the dim old pump house.

"Cindasue McCloud, don't you dare take a chance like that again, lessen I have to put you over my knee and spank that gorgeous rear end of yours."

"Varmint." She sighed as I kissed her.

I could tell Cindasue hadn't been kissed very often before. She was startled but not exactly offended.

"What for did you do that for?"

"My mammy, who is a psychiatrist, says that it's natural for young men and women to kiss one another."

The good doctor had never quite said that; she never needed to.

"Ya mammy is a shonuff headshrinker?" Her green eyes opened wide.

"Uh-huh. So's my pappy." I touched the side of her face. "And my uncle is a pure quill Catholic priest."

"Does he have horns?"

I realized that much of her redneck act was just that: an act. Half fun and full earnest, as Grandpa Ned would say.

Partly a defense and partly a put-on; Grandpa Ned would like Cindasue.

I kissed her again. She pushed me away, but not decisively.

"Go 'long with you. I'm a decent acorn calf. You got no call to try to hornswoggle me; you're nothing but a sky-gogglin' side-hill slicker, a bodacious fuddle-britches."

I laughed. She didn't.

"Get out of here, ya hear?"

I had scared her. Shame on me. Shanty Irish bumbler. Still, she was close to laughing.

"Sure enough, Mountain Flower." I walked back into the wind, which seemed to have picked up while I was kissing Cindasue. I thought that somehow it was a friendly wind, thoroughly approving of my romantic advances. "But at five o'clock—'scuse me, ma'am, seventeen hundred hours—I'm going to be on our sundeck with something in the way of supper. If you show up, I might just note another tax deduction."

Cindasue McCloud, girl detective, looked at me coldly, almost said something rude, turned her face away, and mumbled, "Can't tell what someone might do at five o'clock if they're hungry enough." She laughed, first time I'd heard it, a kind of bell-like sound in the middle of the woods.

"The Coast Guard," I said, "should not be searching for anything but dead bodies. You sure you don't want company?" I shouted to be heard above the banshee wind as she walked away.

She turned back and shook her head decisively. "I'm jus' moseyin' 'round to the beach lookin'. That doesn't need help. You go back and finish your term paper so your poah old mammy won't have to worry about you."

She must have guessed that, too. Sherlock Holmes at Grand Beach. And I still wondered what she looked like under that sweatshirt.

Anyhow, at five o'clock—oops, seventeen hundred hours—Cindasue Lou McCloud (her full, sure-enough name, and her mammy made corn pone and moonshine up the hollers, and I didn't believe any of it anymore) and I were sitting on my family's sundeck overlooking the seawall, which keeps the lake away from the dunes, eating steak and sipping some of my poah father's best 1961 burgundy. The clouds had finally blown off and the sun sinking toward Chicago turned our lake into a surging mass of expensive diamonds. Cindasue ate the steak and guzzled the wine like both were going out of style.

"You shonuff put the little pot in the big pot for me,

Mr. Murphy, suh.'' She glanced at the vintage year on the almost empty wine bottle, of which she had consumed at least her full share. ''Your pa sure must have a powerful heap of money.''

I said it was better than the mountain dew her father made at the still back by the outhouse. She grinned crookedly and 'lowed as how it shonuff was.

Well, it was getting to be pleasant, what with the blue sky and the burgundy making me feel warm, and Cindasue squinting up at the sun. She talked a lot about the hills. I could see why she liked them and why she wanted to leave. Then the grin faded, and I had the girl detective on my hands again.

''Six houses''—she ticked them off on her tiny fingers—''two with concrete seawalls that would be hard to climb, one with that high-headed ole totem pole, 'nother one with an empty prefabricated storage hut by the side of the pool—''

'' 'Nother one with a shanty Irish football player. Actually a rugby player.''

She held my jaw steady with her right hand and kissed me. Her lips tasted of steak sauce and burgundy.

''Who kisses purty good for a papist.''

I realized I was being pursued by a shrewd hunter with a varmint gun. No, not pursued, hog-tied, 'fore I knew what had happened.

''You're tryin' to seduce me, bodacious Cindasue.''

''Tell me, Peter Murphy, suh''—she changed the subject abruptly—''about that weird old house next door to yours,'' she said thoughtfully, eyeing the tilted totem pole, the rock garden, the nymphs, fauns, and elves, and the ugly, rusty seawall. ''We didn' find anythin' there, either, but it sure is a passin' strange place.''

''It belongs to a crazy lady who is never around. There are all kinds of work persons who come in periodically and do things like trimming the hedges, painting the nymphs, and straightening out the totem pole.''

''Could anyone be hidin' in that house?''

I swear she was sniffing the air like a hound dog.

"Not likely," I said. "She pays the town marshal to look around inside every night. I saw him go in last night."

"Hmm . . . well, it was a nice idea. Give me some more of that dew; it shonuff makes the cold go away. . . ."

So I poured out the last few ounces of the wine. Our eyes must have locked on the door at the terrace level of the nutty rock garden at the same moment.

"What's . . ." asked Cindasue.

"It's supposed to be an apartment she built there for her husband. A couple of rooms in the side of the hill with beads and cushions. At least that's the beach legend . . ."

It was crazy, but we went up to have a look. I didn't even argue. We crawled over the old retaining wall, crept across my neighbor's smoothly cut lawn, and got to the edge of the roof of the apartment. Cindasue had her ear to the ground.

"Don' hyar nothin'," she said, now completely the mountain huntress. "Let's go have a closer look-see. . . ."

I helped her down the face of the retaining wall and jumped down next to her. We were right in front of the door, which was a sure enough damn fool place to be.

The door swung open suddenly. There was a woman, blond and hard-faced, dressed in jeans and a white sweater, pointing a gun at us. Harry O'Connell was cowering behind her, a gun in his hand, too. I wondered, almost as an abstract speculation, whether they knew how to shoot and whether they were going to add murder to larceny and adultery.

Cindasue Lou McCloud did more than speculate. She dived at the woman, hitting her in the stomach with her auburn head, shoving the gun away with her left hand. The gun went off, a bullet whistling a safe distance above my head.

Harry ran over me like a semitrailer, a briefcase in his hand. I never did like the lout. Remembering that I was all-American three-quarter-back, I grabbed an ankle with one hand and tripped him up. I would have had him, but out of the corner of my eye, I saw a gun barrel come down on Cindasue's head. I let him go and jumped the woman, who was pulling the gun back to strike again.

She was, let me tell you, a biting, scratching tiger, a real cave woman. Finally, all-American that I was, I managed just barely to wrestle the gun out of her hands. She took off after Harry, who was scrambling up the hill.

I carried Cindasue into the stuffy cave. It did have beads and pillows just like we had believed when we were growing up. Cindasue's hair was bloody, but she seemed to be breathing all right.

I pulled her walkie-talkie out of her jacket. "Mobile one to base, mobile one to base. This is Pete Murphy. I hope you folks are listening. They're heading for the highway. They're carrying a briefcase with a half million dollars of negotiable securities. Get a doctor here; they've knocked Cindasue out."

"Base to mobile one." The slob sounded remarkably cool. "Can you identify the subjects for us, Mr. Murphy? We will notify appropriate police personnel."

"To hell with police personnel . . . get medical personnel here. Didn't you hear me say they hurt Cindasue?"

I turned the damned thing off. Cindasue was stirring.

I still hadn't solved the mystery of what she looked like with her jacket off, but she felt very nice and soft in my arms. She opened her eyes, focused on me, then looked frightened. Firmly and insistently, she pushed me away. Well, I told myself, you've been given the brush-off before.

An hour later, we were standing on Lake View Avenue behind our house. Everyone was there: the state police, the county police, the township police, and the village marshal. All of them with their red and blue lights whirling. The fugitives had been "apprehended" in the woods, we were told. There was also a battered blue government motor-pool car with a very handsome black J.G., his Coast Guard Academy class ring on one hand and a

wedding band on the other. Cindasue Lou McCloud, girl
detective, looking woebegone and confused, leaned
against the hood of the car.

"You are in real trouble, McCloud." He seemed 'bout
ready to cry. Everyone liked my Cindasue. "You were
not authorized to take subjects into custody. You should
have radioed base before you attempted to apprehend
them."

She shook her head, still dazed. "No, suh, I mean yes,
suh, I mean, suh, the information was that they were
armed and the woman might be dangerous. I was afraid
that they might have radio equipment with which to monitor our calls. If you inspect the apartment, suh, you'll
see I was correct in my surmise. I did not feel justified
in risking Mr. Murphy's life, suh, by attempting communication."

He sighed with relief. None of it was true, and he knew
that, but now he could write a report. He patted her arm.
"Okay, Mountain Flower, I guess we can stand to have
a heroine, though we'd sure as hell hate to have anything
happen to you. We need a redneck around here to beat
up on." He flashed even, white teeth at the two of us.

I wasn't going to be the one to ask why she couldn't
make a telephone call. Or why she endangered my life by
trying to peek into the apartment. I was in love, you
see, and I figured by the time the CO got around to thinking of those questions, either he'd be content with a real
live redneck heroine or Cindasue would have an answer
for him.

Besides, if our friends had seen us looking at the rock
garden from the seawall and were ready for us, they
might never have let us back into my house to make the
call.

So who wanted to argue?

The next week, I was sitting on the beach late in the
afternoon correcting typos on my term paper (which the
professor had told me rated another A-plus, much to my
poah old mammy's delight) and soaking up the eighty-

plus Indian-summer sun. You'd almost forget that there
had ever been a storm. A light, peaceful haze hung over
the mirror-smooth lake, the smell of burning leaves in
the air.

A girl in a green string bikini with a shirttail type thing
over it was walking down the beach. I tried not to stare.
She sat down beside me. I wondered how come I was so
lucky. But honest, only when she began to talk did I
realize it was Cindasue McCloud, girl detective.

"You won't believe it"—she sighed, no redneck accent now—"but it was a waste of time. Mr. Harold
O'Connell's wife and father-in-law are disposed to be
forgiving, especially since they have both him and the
money back. I guess he found out that there was more
to Nurse Walsh than sex when they were locked up in
that horrid cave. So unless you and I want to make a fuss
about assault with a deadly weapon, the whole thing is
dropped."

"They might have killed you, Cindasue," I said pro-
tectively. My question about what the real Cindasue
looked like was now answered. The lines were much
more than satisfactory, better than I had hoped; for to tell
you the truth about my dirty imagination, it wasn't her
green eyes I was looking at anymore.

She was embarrassed by my inspection, but no way
did she turn or blush. "I know what it's like to want to
run away," she said simply, "but it's up to you, Peter
Murphy. If you want to press charges, you are perfectly
within your rights."

"What made you think it might be that house?"

"That bodacious ole tot'm pole. I sez to myself, Cindasue, suppose you're thinking 'forehand that you'd be
out on that wicked lake and are looking for a sign that
you've come to the right beach late at night. What you
goin' to be serachin' for? And I sez back, Cindasue, happen you remember about that ole pole and the cave house
under it. And then I'd say, Cindasue, why not hide for a
few days in that old cave, 'specially since that golly-

whooper of a pole will tell you whar it is, in the stone
dead a night.''

"So you dressed up all fancy in that expensive swimming thing just to come to tell me I ought to give people
another chance and to explain how you solved the mystery?''

She drew a very long breath, a movement that made
my eyes pop and my heart leap. Again, the mountain-
hollow shrewdness in her face. "No, Peter Murphy, suh.
I got all gussied up in this wicked thing to see if you'd
give me another chance. I lost my nerve the first
time. . . .''

It was a pretty amateurish kind of kiss, both of us
being scared stiff, but she felt even nicer in my arms this
time. We both knew we were crossing an important line
in our lives.

I'd held young women in my arms before. But none
whose little heart pounded so fiercely against her ribs till
I soothed it into serenity. And none whose offering of
her whole self was so filled with trust.

"My mammy done warned me," I lied, "about green-
eyed mountain critters that hog-tie you with trust.''

She just giggled and snuggled closer.

"I think we're in love, Cindasue.''

"Shonuff," we said together.

4

Blackie

"Cologne," my excellent nephew Peter Murphy, Ph.D., informed me, "was founded in 38 B.C. by one Marcus Vispanius Agrippa, son-in-law of the Emperor Augustus. It was called Oppidum Ubiorum, after a Germanic tribe called the Ubii who were allies of the Romans and moved from the right bank of the Rhine to the left."

"Remarkable," I observed.

If the worthy Peter Murphy is good at anything, he is good at research. Alas, as the sun rose and our bumpy, rattling MD-11 struggled over the land of our ancestors, I was in no mood to hear the results of his search for information about Cologne (or Köln as the Kölners call it). The Ryan clan of my generation does not like to travel, unlike our parents or the next generation. The ride from Chicago to Grand Beach, Michigan, is the outer reach of distance with which we're comfortable. An obligation to travel from Chicago to the shadow of the Golden Dome on the fringes of South Bend, Indiana, is normally an affront to our comfort, our peace of mind, and our fundamental human dignity. We do travel for one reason or another—business, the renewal of romantic love, solutions to the little problems Cardinal Sean Cronin imposes on me—but we are never happy with the travel itself, especially if it is in a creaky, bouncing MD-11. We could not land soon enough at the airport of Düsseldorf to suit me.

"Uncle Blackie?" The aforementioned Peter Murphy, Ph.D., broke his narrative to ask a question. "Do you really think the bones of the Three Kings were in that catafalque in the Cologne cathedral?"

"I deem it highly improbable," I said with my notorious West of Ireland sigh, which to some sounds like an impending asthma attack. "Nonetheless, the shrine stands as memorial to the stories of all humankind who have the courage to follow their star."

"Hmm."

"How could anyone get that big, gold-covered thing out of the cathedral?"

"Oh, *that*? There are a number of ways that could have been arranged. We'll just have to wait till we get there to, uh, verify my hypotheses."

That academic allusion was enough to satisfy him for the moment.

"In 48 A.D., the Emperor Claudius married Julia Agripina, daughter of General Germanicus, who was born in the town of the Ubii. She made the town a Roman city called Colonia Claudia Ara Agrippinensium, whence the name Cologne. She was the wife of Brother Cadfael in the *I Claudius* series. Poisoned him, if you remember."

"Indeed."

I was not unaware that Derek Jacobi had played not only the lame Emperor Claudius but more recently a clerical dectective from an earlier era. I was nonetheless impressed that one of the younger generation was even aware of the *I Claudius* series.

"It was not a bad place to live. An eighteen-kilometer aqueduct brought fresh drinking water into the city, and there was an underground drainage and sewage system. For four hundred years, it was the northeast cornerstone of the Roman empire."

"Fortunate."

If the respected Peter Murphy noted my closed eyes, he did not let them prevent the continuation of his narrative.

"The German barbarians eventually drove the Romans away from the Rhine and occupied Cologne, though by then they were Christians. They built a lot of churches and appointed an archbishop, who became one of the electors of the Holy Roman Empire along with the archbishops of Mainz and Trier, the Count Palatine of the Rhine, the King of Bohemia, the Elector of Brandenberg and . . ."

"The Elector of Saxony," I finished off the list for him, "of whom the most famous was doubtless the Polish King Augustus the Strong."

"Gosh, Uncle Blackie, you know everything."

"Arguably," I replied, closing my eyes even tighter. "Even that Captain Picard was Sejanus in the *I Claudius* series."

"The Franks chose to make their capital at Aachen or Aix-la-Chapelle as it is also called. Then in 975, a Schottencloister was established, an Irish monastery . . ."

"Doubtless a major contribution to civilization, culture, and religion!"

"Maybe . . . One of the Romanesque churches near the cathedral, or dom as they call it, is Great Saint Martin's, which may be named after our countryman, who was the abbot. The bombs almost completely destroyed it. But they've restored it. In a couple of hundred years, no one will know the difference."

"Impressive."

"For a couple of hundred years, Cologne was in eclipse. Then it became a center of religious pilgrimage when relative peace returned to what had been the Roman Empire. The Shrine of the Three Kings . . ."

"Alleged Three Kings."

"Right . . . The shrine to those who follow their star . . . was the main attraction for the pilgrimage. It therefore played a major role in the revival of the city. . . . We're kind of like those pilgrims from a thousand years ago, aren't we?''

"Arguably.''

"The city has always benefited from its position where the highway meets the river. Even today, two trains cross the Rhine at Cologne every minute.''

"Noteworthy.''

"They began to build the cathedral in 1242 at the height of the city's great prosperity, but they didn't finish it till the middle of the last century. Cologne became a focal point for all the religious wars in the sixteenth and seventeenth centuries and then for the Napoleonic wars after that. This whole area of northwest Germany was a burned-out battleground till after the Congress of Vienna, and then it underwent another one of its periodic revivals. It became part of Prussia, which Cologne Catholics, civilized by years of French occupation, didn't like at all. Still, it prospered till the Second World War.''

In which 90 percent of the city was destroyed by allied bombs. Many historic churches were obliterated, and the cathedral turned into a hollow shell after seventeen bombs struck it.

"Cindasue is in Bonn,'' Peter Murphy added. "She's on the staff of the U.S. embassy there.''

"Cindasue?'' I asked, guardedly opening one eye.

"That Coast Guard petty officer I dated five, six years ago. My mom and sisters called her the cute little tyke in the sailor suit.''

"She talked funny, did she not?''

"Appalachian English . . . when she wanted to. Very bright, very pretty, very independent.''

"I know the type.'' I sighed and closed my eyes.

"We even talked about marriage, though she was only eighteen.''

"Hmm . . .''

"We were both very much in love.''

"That happens.''

"She was offered an appointment to the Coast Guard Academy at New London, Connecticut. She wanted a college education. Couldn't blame her. I wanted to go to graduate school. We agreed that we were too young to get married. . . . Do you think we were?''

"What did your parents and sisters think?''

"They all adored Cindasue. If they had to trade, I think they would have taken her instead of me.''

"Unlikely.''

"I'm joking. Anyway, we broke up. Wrote to each other for a while. Then that trailed off. I got involved with other women, none of whom worked out.''

"That happens.''

"I don't know about her. I presume she had suitors. She was too pretty not to.''

"Was there not a religious difference?''

"That wasn't a real issue. Cindasue thought Catholicism was neat. She thought you were wonderful.''

"Excellent taste.''

"I think she was intimidated by the clan. Felt inferior because she came from Stinking Creek.''

"Americans a lot longer than we are.''

"So she graduated from New London and is now a lieutenant J.G. and an attaché at Bonn.''

"Curious that the coast guard would need an attaché several hundred miles from the North Sea.''

"You never know what the government will do. I'm a little frightened to see her again. I think I blew it. I should have stayed in touch with her. I guess I lost my nerve.''

"There's no reason to believe that we will encounter her, is there?'' I said, opening both eyes to examine my distinguished nephew's face.

"She'll know that I'll be in Cologne.''

"So?''

"Mom and my sisters have kept writing to her. The Ryans don't give up easily.''

"Nor did your father, as far as that goes.''

"I guess. Though the family legend said that he had an easy time of it.''

"So you think she will appear while we're in Cologne."

"Maybe."

"And if she doesn't?"

"Then I'll have to decide whether I want to follow my star, won't I?"

"Arguably."

"Cologne prospered between the two world wars, in part because it had a very progressive mayor."

"Konrad Adenauer."

"He built parks and improved the university and expanded business. He later became mayor again after the war till the Brits fired him, just as Hitler had done. We intervened, and they reappointed him. The city was virtually destroyed. He built it up again and became first Herrn Bundeskanzler of the *Bundesrepublik.* Restored democracy to Germany."

"Admirable."

"Heinrich Böll, the great Cologne novelist, hated him. But he was a little nutty about politics."

"Though he did have the good taste to marry an Irish wife."

"Really?"

"Really. He was very pro-Irish, which was remarkable in a German."

Peter Murphy sighed in imitation of my sigh.

"What do you think I should do about Cindasue?"

"Do you know whether she has other involvements?"

"I doubt it. Nothing serious. One of the women in the family would have whispered it in my ear."

In matters of the heart, the gifted Peter Murphy, Ph.D., was a tyro—like most men. It would never occur to him that he was with me on the trip because what one of the Reformers very unwisely called the "monstrous regiment of women" had conspired against him.

"Happ'n she shows up, you done got no problem," I said, a-slippin into Cindasue talk. "Else maybe you done got a big problem."

He didn't notice my dialect.

"I think she's still too shy to be that pushy."

"Happ'n she do, you aren't a-going to be a-running away?"

"I don't know."

If Lieutenant J.G. C. L. McCloud did appear, I thought, Peter Murphy would have to run pretty quickly if he wished to preserve his Irish bachelor status.

Wisely, I didn't say that.

In fact, I didn't say anything. Secretly, however, I agreed with my Freudian sibling: I hoped the aforementioned junior officer of the Yewnited States Coast Guard did appear. Moreover, she was not without some skills in the area of detection. In the absence of my usual sidekick, Mike "The Cop" Casey, she would be a welcome ally.

What if she solved the problem before I did?

That was unlikely. But in dealing with puzzles, any problem solver was always welcome. Cindasue was admirably disrespectful of me, which was distinctly to her credit.

We were served tea, orange juice, a croissant, and scones without raisins. The captain warned us that the airport was overcast, ceiling at 500 feet. I sighed loudly in protest.

"So, Uncle Blackie," Peter Murphy returned to his narrative mode, "We are visiting a city that is more than two millennia older than Chicago."

Comments like that only impress academics, of which I am one in a nondysfunctional way.

"Though in its present form it is relatively more recent than Chicago."

Peter Murphy, Ph.D., laughed loudly.

"You're incorrigible, Uncle Blackie!"

"Arguably."

Remarkably, the pilot managed to find the Düsseldorf airport despite the overcast, though, it seemed to me, only at the last moment. The MD-11 hit the runway with approximately the same noises that the sanitation department makes in its virtuous early morning efforts to sustain Chicago's image as the City That Works.

A cabin attendant babbled at us in a language that might have been German—or Frankish, as far as I could tell.

Peter Murphy took charge of my passport and landing card, which he filled out with the appropriate information. With deliberately (or so it seemed to me) maddening slowness, the rickety plane inched its way toward the terminal. Finally, to my enormous relief, the pilot turned off the Fasten Seat Belt sign. We had finished another brave experiment in intercontinental travel.

Bedlam broke out instantly in the cabin as passengers yanked luggage out of overhead compartments, nearly decapitating one another, and fought for position to escape the plane. Peter Murphy protected me with some skill. Only one large bag hit my shoulder, and I was pushed out of the way by only two grimly determined German women.

We staggered along the concourse—after Peter had grabbed me when I set off in the wrong direction. Then we entered the arrivals hall, which was filled with nationals of every nation under heaven. My heart sank. We would never escape into the fresh air, even the overcast fresh air.

Then I observed a very attractive young woman with long auburn hair and a dark blue suit in the company of a local immigration officer, the latter dressed in a khaki uniform trimmed in green.

She saw me, grinned, and like the hoyden she would always be, ran across the floor and embraced me.

"Priest!" she yelled, "you done come here a-solvin' mysteries."

"Cindasue," I said as she hugged me. "I assumed you would be here to greet us."

"Shonuff . . . and you a bringin' that no-count polecat nefoo of yours, Dr. Peter Murphy."

She embraced my astonished nephew and kissed him with something like determination. Twice. He turned purple in embarrassment but showed no inclination to resist her assault.

"You shonuff look fine, Dr. Murphy," she said. "With them strands a silver in your hair. Just like your daddy. People hardly notice you a no-count polecat."

"You look wonderful, Cindasue," he managed to say.

"You still a-talkin your Catholic blarney," she said, patting his face affectionately.

Cindasue had improved with time. Maybe she wasn't any taller, but she wore shoes with heels, her hair was long, perhaps she had filled out a bit, she had decorated herself with makeup and earrings, and she was infinitely more poised and sophisticated than she had been at Grand Beach in her "sailor suit." Her green eyes were as lively as they had ever been and even more bewitching now. And the long hair, which now framed her face, turned it from merely pert and pretty to beautiful. Periodically, she would sweep the hair away from her face in an appealingly gracious gesture.

Devastating would not have been a bad word to describe her; appropriately, Peter Murphy was devastated. Which was what he was supposed to be.

She took our passports and landing cards from Peter's hand, gave them to the immigration officer who, with a dutiful smile, stamped them and bowed respectfully.

He exchanged words with Cindasue in rapid German, bowed again, and led us out of the immigration hall and by the customs post.

The young woman had clout. Why, I wondered, was she exercising the influence of the Yewnited States of America on our behalf—particularly of whatever unit of the federal government for which she worked, almost certainly at other things than monitoring the currents of the Rhine? She might just as well have waited for lost love beyond customs. I sniffed an aspect of our little problem that I had hitherto not suspected: the feds were involved! Why should they care about the kidnapping of the bones of the Three Kings?

The immigration officer led us to the lobby and saluted

our escort, she saluted back casually, as though she were perhaps a rear admiral, flashed a brilliant smile, and said *"Danke schön"* to the officer.

He smiled back, bowed again, and responded, *"Bitteschön."*

"We could go to Cologne by train," she said, shifting into standard English, "but I brought a car, and I think it's more fun to approach Cologne from across one of the bridges. Its skyline is nothing like Chicago's, but the cathedral is gorgeous from that perspective."

"What you a-doin' for the Yewnited States of America in Bonn, Cindasue?" I demanded as we ventured into the parking lot.

"Nothin' much, priest. Just sittin in my office, a-minding my own business and a-reading papers all day long."

Somehow she had captured Peter Murphy's right hand.

"About Rhine River currents?"

"Some'in like that."

"And you're assigned to take care of us?"

"Isn't that an amazin' coincidence?" She chuckled.

She found an impressive looking Mercedes sedan with the flag of our republic on the license plate and opened the door for us.

"Cindasue," I said, "you CIA?"

"Don't you go a-saying that, priest," she said, averting her eyes. "I plumb ain't a-workin for Langley, nohow, noway."

I was ushered into the front seat of the car, and Peter Murphy, reduced to total silence by the lovely young woman who had embraced him with such fervor, was exiled into the rear seat.

"You a-workin' for some gumshoe operation, Cindasue," I said, "and they want you to keep an eye on us."

She merely laughed, a richer and more confident and more charming laugh than she had possessed in the old days at Grand Beach.

"Just a-killin' two birds with one stone," she said as she started the car.

5

"Still a center of pilgrimage isn't it?"

Peter Murphy, Cindasue, and I stood in front of the massive Cologne Cathedral under a clear autumn blue sky—the overcast having lifted—and watched the throngs of people pouring into the gray gothic pile. Fourth biggest church in Europe, bigger than any of the other medieval cathedrals. Not delicate by any means but impressive, awesome even, as it reared above the railroad station and the central *Platz* (named *Roncalliplatz* after Pope John), and the Roman-German museum and everything else in sight, like a fiercely protective Roman-German mother.

"Are tourists pilgrims?" I asked my nephew.

"Were not the pilgrims five hundred years ago tourists?" he replied.

Dangerous young man.

"Sure do beat the hard-shell Babtis' chapel down to Stinkin' Crik," Cindasue conceded. "Thez put a powerful 'mount of work in this place. Done a right smart job, too."

"Still a-comparin' Stinkin' Crik to everything else, Cindasue?" I asked.

She laughed, swept her long hair out of her face, and switched into mostly standard English.

"Uncle Blackie, I may not have learned much in the last half dozen years, but I have learned that Stinkin' Crik is no better and no worse than any place else. Just different. Way different from this here place."

So quickly had I become Uncle Blackie.

"Lot of heat'n here," I continued, "Asi'n folk. Seems like they all done brung their cameras."

She laughed again.

"I know you can't help it, Uncle Blackie. And I don't mind, 'cause I know you surely do respect hill talk. Jest so long as you do remember that I the only autentic' hill person in this here town. . . . Now, why don't you go into that briggetty place and look at the shrine while Peter Murphy, Ph.D., and I a-clim'in' that thar tower to the top, all hondred and eighty-five steps of it."

She took Peter by the hand again and led him off to the tower. He went willingly enough. He hadn't said much to her during our ride down from Düsseldorf, mostly because she continued to talk almost as fast as she drove her car. Cindasue was nervous, and Peter Murphy was dazzled.

"Aren't we driving a little fast, Cindasue?" he'd said once.

"Them's kilometers, not miles."

"A hundred and fifty of them."

"Shonuff."

"That's ninety miles an hour."

"Hush, you mouf, chile. Thez no speed limit on these authobahn t'ings. And thez a lot safer than roads leadin' into McCloud's Holler."

So Peter had hushed his mouf.

I doubted that there was any such place as McCloud's Hollow. Cindasue mixed fact and fiction about Stinkin' Crik with reckless abandon. She was, after all, Irish, wasn't she? Even if she kicked with her left foot?

She had been right about the view of Cologne and its Cathedral from the right bank of the Rhine, especially in

the newly arrived sunlight. It was not Chicago from the
Lake—but what is? However, the cathedral, with its ring
of attendant Romanesque churches, especially the huge
Great Saint Martin's, was more of a shrine to the distant
past than the dubious gilt catafalque of the equally dubious Three Kings. It shimmered in the sunlight, its pin-
nacle somehow invoking heaven's protection on the busy
river traffic, the roaring trains, the reconstructed water-
front, and the shops and office buildings and hotels clus-
tered along the bank of the Rhine. It had not protected
the city or even itself from allied bombers, but it had
presided over the postwar economic miracle.

"Wow!" Peter Murphy had exclaimed.

"Sure is plumb pretty, ain't it? You papists shonuff
done build fittin' churches. . . . Should have come across
this here bridge in spring when that ole river was six feet
above flood, Ev'rythin' down there covered with water."

"Not a very broad river, is it?" Peter Murphy asked.

"Broader than Stinkin' Crik," she had replied coolly.

"Not as broad as the Mississippi or the Amazon."

Next to me, Cindasue smiled happily. Apparently, their
relationship was fitting back into its old routine.

"Never done seen them criks. Have to take me there
sometime. By hooker my crook."

"Arguably," he had said.

We all had laughed. I had felt distinctly out of place.
On the other hand, they probably needed me as a sound-
ing board as they strove to reclaim the past. Not for long,
I thought.

No longer than the Coast Guard officer's order that I
inspect the biggetty cathedral while she and Peter Murphy climbed to the top of the tower.

She had parked the car on the lower level near the
cathedral, no easy feat, because like every modern city,
Cologne seemed to have a massive parking problem. In
fact, she had parked in an illegal spot, attracting the almost immediate attention of a cop, also dressed in an odd
combination of khaki and green. He had approached with
his ticket book open and a grim frown on his face.

Cindasue pointed to the embassy license plate, smiled, and waved. The cop had smiled, slowly at first, and then broadly. Then he saluted.

"These here Rhineland Cat'lics sure are nice folk," she had said. "Shouldn't ought to tell you two, but people sayin' onliest folks more friendlier are you papists from that there island out betwix Europe and America. Now then." She had become the federal bureaucrat. "Here's the drill. We're going to look at the dom, then I'm going to buy you lunch at the fondue chalet, then I'll take you to your hotel, then we'll pay our respects to the cardinal."

"Yes, ma'am," Peter and I said together.

The young woman had sniffed. But her marvelous eyes had twinkled.

So she and Peter, hand in hand, had rushed to the tower steps and I had drifted into the nave of the dom.

It was indeed vast. Only Saint Peter's, Saint Paul's in London, and Santiago da Compestella were larger. Somehow its Gothic arches made it seem even larger than the church in the Vatican, which had cost us Germany, though not the Rhineland. I should like to say that the misty light streaming through the windows created a glow that made one want to lose oneself in mystical contemplation. In fact, contemplation would have been no more difficult in the United Center before a Bulls' game or O'Hare International Airport at Christmas. The dom was jammed with people, most of whom were barely aware that it was a sacred place or of what one ought to be doing in a sacred place.

I was attired in my usual bishop's uniform: a clerical shirt without a collar (I always lost them) black jeans, and a Chicago Bulls jacket. Because I am the least prepossessing of humankind (you could get on an elevator with me and not notice my presence) this uniform usually escapes notice. Perhaps I am a creepy middle-aged man who likes to identify with Michael and Scottie and Dennis.

I am noticed only by dogs, little children, and teenage

women, all of whom, for some inexplicable reason, dote on me. Particularly, the dogs, who automatically become friendly, no matter how fierce they are or pretend to be. I have no explanation for this phenomenon save that the dogs seem to like me, perhaps because I like them.

Nonetheless, I seemed to attract substantial attention from the Japanese tourists, ah, pilgrims. They would bow, grin happily, blast away with their expensive cameras, and then grin again, often remarking, "Micher Jordan" before their final bow. The magic name was not infrequently accompanied by the motions of someone shooting a basketball.

Better, I thought to myself, then identifying the city with Ar (as they would pronounce it) Capone and a Thompson submachine gun.

I wandered about indifferently pausing to admire the astonishing collection of paintings, statues, altarpieces, and stained glass windows. The place was a vast and striking museum, a reminder of a thousand years or so of history and art. Not exactly a church, however.

I found the Blessed Sacrament chapel and slipped in. A few old people of both genders and some young couples were engaged in fervent prayer. I joined them, with more or less fervor. I thanked the deity for the great, if imperfect faith, which had produced this outsize Gothic building and all its artistic prizes. I admitted that I found the medieval era difficult to understand and conceded that a wandering Irish bishop a thousand years or so ago would have arguably understood it better. Though arguably not, too. I prayed for all those who had died in the various wars that had been fought along this side of the Rhine, especially those who had been killed in the American and British bombings in 1944 and 1945, which had reduced the city to rubble and the population from over a million to less than 40,000. I also prayed for those who had rebuilt the city and for those who had turned Germany into a working, if less than perfect, democracy. I prayed for the Americans who had died in the war and for all others who had died.

Finally, I requested that Herself help us in our search for the lost shrine and also for my two young charges that they might find Her through one another.

Thus, having made my orisons, I departed to inspect directly the Shine of the Magi, or rather, for the present, its surrogate.

It was behind the main altar, which no longer served as the regular altar for the Eucharist in our postconciliar church. It was every bit as splendid as it was alleged to be: the largest gilt reliquary in the Occident, looking much like a golden Roman basilica, though in fact it was three boxes, one on the top of the other two. Heaven forefend that each of the Magi would not have their own private tomb. The Magi themselves were carved in gold on the back along with the Emperor Otto IV. Various apostles and prophets, all tall men who looked like kings, were arranged on either side on the front. Above it all on what would have been the facade if it were truly a basilica, sat the king of heaven looking down in approval at the whole phenomenon. The shrine was covered with neatly arranged, multi-hued jewels. The Emperor Otto IV had pillaged the glittering precious stones from Byzantium and figured that entitled him to a place near the Three Kings, observing them respectfully. Indeed, the tomb of the Magi was itself a massive, overdone, but sumptuous jewel box 1.53 meters high, 2.2 meters long, and 1.1 meter wide.

Pretty big to smuggle out of the equivalent of three locked doors.

I had to admit to myself that it was one of the most breathtaking works of art I had ever seen—in memory of itinerant magicians and a disreputable theft, possibly many such.

Small wonder that thieves might want to make off with it, as previous thieves had done with the relics inside.

Properly understood, I told myself, it was a monument to something far more glorious: the men and women who had the courage to follow their star.

Should they have existed at all, probably the original

Magi, hardly kings, were a group of ragtag wandering astrologers who had no notion what reverence waited for them in years ahead.

The original had been stolen several times before and often damaged; indeed, the curators—or whatever name they bore—had finished their most recent renovation in the early 1970s. What, I wondered, was left of the original, indeed of the original bones?

Truly, the shrine was well protected, first by a thick, perhaps one-inch-thick, transparent plastic box that covered it completely, then by a seven-foot wrought-iron chancel screen that surrounded it and the old main altar. An alarm node with a wire running from it protruded from the inside top of the plastic box, and wires ran all along the fence, whose posts were too close together to permit anyone but an infant slipping through them.

Ah, well, there is no locked room that cannot be opened by someone who has the ingenuity and the determination to do so.

Fascinating.

"Juberous ole t'ing, ain't it, Uncle Blackie? Pure papist idolatry. Waste o' good money."

I turned to greet my young charges. I had the impression that they had just detached their arms from around one another. I took it as a given that my polecat nefoo had kissed her during their ascent to the tower. Arguably several times.

"The relics," Peter Murphy returned to the results of his research, "had belonged to the dom in Milan for centuries. In 1164, Frederick Barbarossa confiscated them—stole them would be a better word—and turned them over to his Herrn Kanzler for Italy, one Archbishop Reinald von Dassel, who was also the archbishop of Cologne. It's not hard to imagine Reinald saying to Frederick, 'You owe me a favor,' and picking up his marker in the form of the relics. Seventeen years later, a certain Nicholas of Verdun set up a workshop here to redo the reliquary. It was probably finished by 1225, a couple of decades before they began work on this dom. You could say they built the dom to provide a church for the shrine.''

"Shonuff is purty," the J.G. agreed. "Happen it be idolatry."

"It's fake as you well know, Cindasue," I said. "The copy they use when they take the original out to brush it up."

"Could fool me, just plumb fool me. Howsomever, I'm just an ignorant hard-shell Baptis' from West Virginy."

"Three million people come through here every year," Peter Murphy observed. "Some days, 40,000 tourists or pilgrims or whatever. They want to see the shrine even if they don't believe the legend. So there has to be something here that is reasonably convincing."

"Uncle Blackie," she asked, "what you thin' be inside that 'ere t'ing."

"Nuttin', Cindasue. Plumb nuttin'. If there were once bones inside, they've turned to dust. I'm sure no one here wants to open the shrine to find that out."

"Or anyone else to open it," she said shifting to standard English.

"How much does it weigh?" I asked.

"A little less than half a ton," Peter Murphy informed us.

We drifted out of the dom, across the *Roncalliplatz*, down a flight of steps, and into a restaurant that looked like Switzerland—or, more properly, like people who had not been there thought Switzerland looked.

Cindasue insisted that "you peckerwoods oughter not try pickin' up the check." In fluent German, she ordered beef fondue for all three of us and a bottle of red wine from the nearby Ahr Valley.

"Rhine red wines are in general not as satisfying as the white wines, but I think you will enjoy this one. It comes from a little valley just down the road from here. There's a cute little town. I'll take you up on Sunday, lessen we go on a Rhine cruise on Sunday. Then we'll ride up to Ahrweiler on Saturday. They have absolutely scrumptious ice cream up there, which you'll love, Uncle Blackie.''

"Lieutenant Cindasue McCloud, ma'am,'' Peter Murphy protested, "Uncle Blackie and I are here to solve a mystery, not to be entertained, however charmingly.''

"Dr. Peter Murphy, sir,'' she replied airily, "here in the Federal Republic, no one works on weekends. They're a very laid-back people, compared to them folks out on that island in the mid-Atlantic. Thez a workin' all the time and cover it up with their charm.''

"You shonuff been to Ireland, Cindasue?'' I asked her.

"Shonuff. I reckon I understand you varmints a mite better now.''

The two young people bantered with each other throughout the meal, shyly and with rare glances at each other's faces, awkward giggles, and frequent flushed faces. I concentrated on disposing of the fondue, a serious business. The leprechaun who steals half my tiny jar of Bushmill's Green every afternoon had also stolen most of my beef.

"You reckon you want more, Uncle Blackie?''

Prudence triumphed over hunger.

"No, thankee . . . but I do have a question, Cindasue ma'am.''

"Aw-huh?'' she replied skeptically.

"Why does the government of the United States of America send one of its most able agents in this part of the world to act as a minder for myself and Peter Murphy, Ph.D.?''

For a moment, she seemed prepared to deny the assumptions behind the question.

"Ah jest happ'n to be in the office, and my boss come in and say, Lieutenant McCloud, we-uns got a couple folks a-comin' through that someone oughter keep an eye on. You the only one around.''

"I don't believe a word of it.''

A smile tugged at her lips and her eyes sparkled.

"Ah jest happen to see y'all on the list and, knowin'

you ain't German speakers, ah jest say I take care of them varmin's.''

"No."

"Some truth in both things, Preacher Man."

"I want the whole truth."

"Well . . ." She hesitated, debating whether to tell the whole truth. "You like the wine, Dr. Peter Murphy?"

"Shonuff, Lieutenant Cindasue McCloud, but you ain't answerin' the question."

"I know I ain't. Oughter tell the truth, I reckon. . . . The government of the Yewnited States of America is very much interested in the fate of the Three Kings. They foresee a scandal that could somewhat destabilize the government of the Federal Republic. Since the Federal Republic is a loyal and trusted ally, our government does not want this to happen. We have established a liason with the count cardinal, in part because we are afraid that either American or Russian Mafia might be involved. When we learned that some amateur detectives from Chicago are coming, we became concerned. I told my seniors that Bishop Ryan was the best locked-room man in the whole Yewnited States. They said that I might want to assist them.''

"Especially since you are already the liason with Herr Kardinal Claus Maria, Graf von Obermann?"

She ran her tongue quickly along her lips and grinned.

"Besides, I wanted to see whether your nefoo," she rested her hand on Peter Murphy's arm, "looked any wiser now that he's Dr. Peter Murphy."

"And?"

She glanced up at my nefoo and smiled slightly.

"Hard to tell; maybe a tad."

Only then did she remove her hand from his arm.

"Well," Peter Murphy observed, "I can't say that Lieutenant McCloud is any brighter than she was at Grand Beach that first summer. She was the smartest woman I ever knew, even then. Maybe she's a tad purtier.''

Lieutenant McCloud sniffed derisively, but she also blushed.

"And," he added, "I can't recall her being a wine connoisseur in those days, either. They must have courses in that at New London."

So it went.

Cindasue also ordered us three large helpings of chocolate ice cream.

The leprechaun stole some of mine as well as much of the wine from my glass.

In the *Roncalliplatz* once again, I observed that under the caressing October sun, two activities seemed especially popular: Lovers were kissing one another, and skateboarders were risking life and limb as well as endangering the lovers.

One skateboarder, perhaps just barely a teenager, missed me by a fraction of an inch as he jumped a curb and then fell flat on this face. Cindasue shouted at him in angry German and he fled as would one who was in fear of his life.

"Polecat," she informed us, "like to break his durn li'l neck."

"I wonder that this disorder is tolerated in a German city."

"Hit is *verboten* after seven-thirty at night," she said. "This hyar ain't no typical German city, no way. That thar fella Hank Böll allowed as how that of all the armies that a-coming through, only the lame, the jokers, and the wheeler-dealers stayed behind."

"He also said," Peter Murphy added, "that Cologne is a city, but that is not the point. It is also a town, and in a town, one can feel at home, whereas in a city, that is not always the case."

"A lot of famous papists taught hyar," Cindasue announced. "That Albertus Maggot taught hyar. . . ."

"Magnus," Peter Murphy corrected her. "It means Albert the Great."

"And some fella named Duns Scotus is buried over to the Minorite church."

"Franciscan," Peter noted.

"And Thomas Aquinas was ordained a priest in the dom, leastwise the one before this one."

"And the city is a center for arts and the media and insurance as well as manufacturing."

The two young people both were grinning broadly as they played the game that some lovers play so skillfully, topping one another in how much they knew.

"And they plumb heath'n folk. Thar carnival starts on November 11. They don't stop drinking their Könsch beer till Lent, but then, they pap'sts."

"And they only tore down the walls in 1881!"

"You done lost, Peter Murphy," She chortled. "Köln is also called the Holy City, *Heilige Stadt*! No way, no how you done know ta other two."

"Rome and Chicago!"

"You done lost!"

"Constantinople," I said, showing off shamelessly.

Peter Murphy lifted the Coast Guard officer off the ground, spun her once, and kissed her solidly.

"You done won!" he announced as he kissed her again.

"Uncle Blackie," she shouted, "make this hyar big ole mountain bear put me down."

She wasn't serious, so I ignored her plea. He did put her down. She leaned against him for a fraction of a second on the way down, a gesture that sent a message louder than her protest.

"Wal," she gasped for breath, "I better drive you uns to your hotel 'fore Peter Murphy a-turnin' worse."

She drove us to our hotel on the Rudolfplatz just off the Hapsburgerring.

"You uns gotter reckon that thar's a thing here they call *Kölscher Klungel*," she warned us. "Hit means that theyz kinda like to take and do official thin's unofficially, like through friendship networks, if theyz gonna do an-thin' t'all."

"We are not unfamiliar with that in our fair city by the lake," I reminded her. "It's called clout."

"Reckon not," she grinned. "Happen that's why they sent you."

Aha.

At the hotel we were given fifteen minutes to unpack and organize ourselves and then we must be punctual for our meeting with Herr Kardinal. The Germans, she told us, liked everything to be punctual.

Ja, ja.

So the feds were involved. And Peter Murphy's once and future sweetheart was truly a fed. Occasionally, the government recognized talent, despite the package it came in.

The kings, magi, astrologers, however many there might have been, were clearly a big deal.

She checked us in with polite and fluent authority and her wondrous smile, which always generated a responding smile. Smooth diplomat, this junior attaché from West Virginia.

Was she on assignment to the ATF, which was also a Treasury Department agency? They had offices in Chicago, did they not?

"Has she changed much?" I asked Peter Murphy as we rode up to our rooms in the elevator.

"Not much," he said. "And a lot. Stubborn as ever."

"You know any women in our clan who is not?"

He grinned. "As fragile as ever, too. When we were climbing up that damn tower, she apologized for not speaking hill talk too fluently. Said she was out of practice."

In my room, I unpacked my Hewlett-Packard OmniBook 800CS, plugged the modem line into a phone jack, and summoned the local line for AOL.

The first message was to Cardinal@archchi.org:

Through some miracle of grace we have arrived on the banks of the fabled Rhine. No Wagnerian characters in sight, however. I believe that shrine is a fraud. Three kings are doubtless still in Milan. Several obvious so-

*lutions to mystery. We see Herr Kardinal Graf von Ob-
ermann shortly. I will tell him I suspect fraud.*

Blackie@aol.com

The second message went to Mkate@LCMH.com (Little Company of Mary Hospital, for the uninitiate):

Mountain Flower sighted. At airport. Reunion smooth.

Arguably grounds for cautious optimism.

Blackie@aol. com

Only after discharging my primary responsibilities did
I open the drapes to inspect Cologne once again. The
dom loomed over everything, a vigilant and loving
mother at this distance. The mix of small parks, trees,
trams, elegant shops along all three streets in my view,
and a Roman tower gate was utterly charming. It would
be an easy city to like, even without the alleged good
spirits of Cologne Catholicism.

I encountered my academic nephew on the elevator
going to the lobby, both of us with two minutes to spare.

"I gotta admit she's dazzling," he conceded.

"Arguably."

"Even more so."

"Ah . . . You are becoming emotionally involved?"

"Arguably," he responded, stealing my line.

"Indeed."

"Maybe," he said, his forehead furrowing, "I never
stopped being in love with her."

"Such things happen."

"I was a jerk for letting her get away the first time."

"Or possibly a very wise man."

"Possibly," he said slowly. "Anyway, we'll have to

see what happens. I don't know what she feels about me."

"Only because you're blind, deaf, and dumb. . . . Now we must hurry lest we be thirty seconds late for her deadline."

6

"Herr Kardinal, may I present His Excellency the Most Reverend John Blackwood Ryan, auxiliary bishop of Chicago. Your Excellency, Herr Kardinal Claus Maria Graf von Obermann."

"Blackie!" the count cardinal said, embracing me in a massive Viking bear hug."

"Mr. Cardinal," I replied, trying to breathe.

Utterly unfazed by the discovery that the cardinal and I knew each other, Cindasue went on: "And, Herr Kardinal, this is his nephew, Doctor-Professor Peter Murphy of Loyola University in Chicago. Professor Murphy, Herr Kardinal Claus Maria Graf von Obermann."

"Herr Kardinal," Peter Murphy said respectfully, little perturbed by the fact that the representative of the United States of America knew that he was already on the faculty of Loyola University.

"Ja, ja." The cardinal beamed as he relentlessly shook Peter Murphy's hand. "I trust that your parents, Herr Doktor Murphy and the charming Frau Doktor Mary Kathleen Ryan Murphy, are well."

Cindasue rolled her eyes at me, impressed again that

the Ryan family knew everyone—despite its reluctance to travel.

"Very well, thank you, Your Eminence."

"And my brother, Mr. Cardinal Cronin?" he asked me.

"As well as can be expected," I said, stating the admittedly ambiguous truth.

"*Ja, ja,*" Herr Cardinal Graf von Obermann said with a contented smile.

Though he was a typical Rhineland Catholic, Claus Maria Graf von Obermann looked not like a Teuton but like a Viking. It was easy to picture this big, strong man with flowing blond hair and a red face in full armor on the prow of a Viking longboat out on the Rhine, an ax in one hand and a flagon of wine in the other. He could play the role of the aristocrat—which he was—to perfection. Our little ceremony in his home in the Lindenthal district of Cologne (between the first two rings of forested parks that circle the city) had begun with Lieutenant (J.G.) McCloud, bowing formally, murmuring "Herr Kardinal," and kissing his ring, a ceremony that was verboten in Chicago. Thereupon, the cardinal had kissed her hand and murmured (in what for anyone else would have been a loud voice), "*Ja, ja,* Fräulein Leutnant!"

For Cindasue, it had been a long way from the wooden, hard-shell Baptis' church in Stinkin' Crik. I reflected that she must be very good at whatever it was she did to be on familiar terms with the count cardinal of Cologne.

But then she had called the equally flamboyant but far more complex angel to the church of Chicago Mr. Cardinal on first encountering him.

Count or not, the angel to the church of Cologne wore what had become the regular garb of German bishops these days: black suit (carefully tailored around his massive frame) and black shirt with a smooth front and white collar tips like those the Christian brothers used to wear—without a trace of the cardinal crimson. Unlike most German bishops—lean and hollow theologians with faces like platefuls of venial sins—Cardinal von Obermann was both a democrat and a liberal, a humanistic humanist whom Rhineland Catholics, theist and atheist, participant and nonparticipant, devout and agnostic, worshiped.

The other bishop, Frederick Heidrich, present in the dark, ornate conference room (fit for a Viking prince) wore a cassock with purple buttons and a purple cummerbund and the required venially sinful face. He was the Dompfarrer, the vicar for the dom, a role not unlike mine in Milord Cronin's Chicago. He looked down at me from his lofty height with an expression of ill-disguised contempt. Presumably, he had never head of the Chicago Bulls. He was accompanied by Pfarrer Kurt Klein, a stiff, erect, elderly priest—also in a cassock—who might have been a panzer commander or a Luftwaffe pilot during the war. Or arguably one of those Gestapo types who in the films always sneered, "We have our vays!" His eyes were always downcast when there was a question of looking at Lieutenant (J.G.) McCloud.

I gathered that there was no love lost between the cardinal's staff—two very bright young priests dressed as he was—and the team from the dom.

"*Ja, ja,* we will sit down and enjoy our afternoon sip of wine and talk about this unfortunate matter," the cardinal announced. "Rudi, Fritz, some wine for our guests, good Rhine wine of course—unless they would prefer some Moselle."

We arranged ourselves around an oak table of the sort that Otto von Bismark might have used. Lieutenant (J.G.) McCloud sat on the cardinal's left and the Dompfarrer on his right.

"Bishop-Doctor Ryan and his nefoo like Rhineland red," she informed Rudi and Fritz.

Normally, I would not wince at a late-afternoon glass of red, not if there were no Bushmill's or Jameson's available. However, circadian dysrythmia a.k.a. jet lag had caught up with me, and I feared that my aging gray cells were already suffering. Nonetheless, it would have been rude to decline the Herr Kardinal's wine. Fortu-

nately, there were no sausages offered as I had feared
there might be. Only wholesome-seeming German cookies with some kind of nameless fruit within. Knowing
my proclivities, Lieutenant (J.G.) McCloud inched the
plate in my direction.

"*Ja, ja,*" the cardinal began with a sigh that was a
combination of pleasure at his first taste of the white wine
and distaste for the subject matter, "we must talk about
the unfortunate matter of the Magi."

Abandoning Celtic indirection as inappropriate in the
present culture, I said, "Obviously, Herr Kardinal, the
bones of the three travelers are not in the shrine."

Bingo, direct hit. Dead silence.

"The one in the dom," said Bishop Heidrich with a
sneer, "is a temporary substitute."

The men around the table held their breaths. Cindasue
glanced at me with a barely suppressed mountain-hollow
grin.

"And an ingenious substitute at that," I agreed. "Patently, there are no bones in it. I was, however, referring
to the real shrine."

"*Ja, ja,*" Cardinal Graf von Obermann agreed, his
face not particularly happy. "What you say, Blackie, is
true. When the shrine was rebuilt twenty-five years ago,
my predecessor, a devout man, wished to examine the
relics to be certain that they were being treated with
proper respect. They found nothing. Naturally, this fact
was not made public. I learned about it myself only after
the disappearance of the real shrine."

"Were previous generations aware of this phenomenon?" I asked.

Rudi shrugged his shoulders. "I examined all the records, Herr Bishop—I am a historian. I found no trace of
this, but I do not think anyone would have noted it. For
all we know, the, uh, mistake might go back all the way
to Archbishop Reinald. The Milanese might have deceived him, too. For all his faults, he was a devout man."

"Impossible," snorted Bishop Heidrich.

"We must face the fact," the cardinal said with another loud sigh, "that for some time, perhaps a very long time, pilgrims came here to honor remains that were not, in fact, present."

"Also," Lieutenant (J.G.) McCloud broke her solemn silence, "they honor all those who have the courage to follow their own star."

My nefoo kept a perfectly straight face. Doubtless he had fed the line to her while they climbed the steps to the tower.

"*Ja, ja,* Fräulein Leutnant," the cardinal exploded with a genial grin. "That is very good! Fritz! Rudi! We must remember that! The shrine honors all those who follow their own star!"

Bishop Heidrich muttered something hostile to himself.

"And not just a band of ragtag wandering astrologers," I continued. "But that is a good reason, is it not, for keeping the police out of the search, to say nothing of the media?"

"Herr Kardinal promptly informed the Herrn Bundeskanzler," Fritz explained. "Obviously, this is a matter of grave national concern, particularly in a time when an election is near and SDP has for a change a very appealing candidate. The Herrn Bundeskanzler advises prudence. He had some very discreet federal police investigate the disappearance. They found nothing. We await a ransom claim or someone taking credit for the theft."

"Turks," snarled the Dompfarrer.

"Now, now, Frederick, let us not be hasty in our judgments," the cardinal said mildly. Then to me he added, "There are many Turks as you know, Blackie, here in the *Bundesrepublik.* Most of them are good, hardworking men and women. Islamic but, like their home country, greatly secularized. However, recently, as you doubtless also know, there has been a rise of Islamic fundamentalism in Turkey and some of it has spread to young Turkish men and women here. The police have found no hints of such a theft in the Turkish community and the young radicals are of the sort that they would claim credit instantly."

"I see."

"It would be bad enough for the public to learn that the Shrine of the Magi had been stolen and replaced by what the Fräulein Leutnant in her wonderfully direct language calls a fake. But if the thieves should take it apart and discover there are no relics, the uproar would be great. The church and the government would be accused of practicing fraud for nine hundred years."

"By atheists who do not care about the shrine," my Cologne counterpart protested.

"But who nonetheless will make great political gains out of it," Rudi said.

"How much is the shrine worth?" I asked.

The cardinal shrugged his massive Viking shoulders.

"It is priceless, of course, even without the bones, a brilliant work of art almost a thousand years old. But who would buy it?"

"A wealthy art collector who would keep it in secret," I replied. "Japanese, Saudi Arabian, even African."

"*Ja, ja,*" the cardinal admitted. "That is what I fear. Such a person would rather possess the shrine than the ransom money we would pay. Perhaps that is why they have not contacted us. . . . Still, eventually, we will have to admit the theft and confess that the present shrine is, what was your other word, Fräulein Leutnant?"

"Plumb phony," Cindasue said calmly.

"Never," Bishop Heidrich exclaimed. "Never!"

"Now, Freddie," the cardinal spoke again in his soft, reprimanding tone, "we should tell the truth. We should have told the truth in 1970."

"People will no longer come to the dom!"

"If I know tourists," I interceded, "they will find the substitue for the stolen shrine even more interesting than the real shrine. Moreover, as Lieutenant McCloud has so wisely and with such penetrating originality told us, it is really and always has been not a shrine to dead bones but to the living faith of men and women who have the courage to follow their star.''

She had the good grace to turn a becoming pink at that comment. My nefoo supressed a giggle.

"Ja, ja,'' the cardinal agreed.

"Perhaps," said nefoo spoke for the first time, "you could commission novels and stories and plays and operas around that theme. Have a Magi festival every year. That would be a fine tribute to them. Arguably a better tribute."

"Ja, ja,'' the cardinal erupted joyously. "Fritz, Rudi, that is a brilliant idea!''

"Ja, Herr Kardinal.''

"Shonuff," Cindasue agreed proudly.

"How much would the parts of the shrine be worth," I persisted, "if they were taken apart and the gold and jewels sold separately?''

"Several million deutschemarks," Fritz replied. "We very much fear that has happened already.''

As well they might.

"And if our friends come back again and steal the substitute?''

A pall of gloom settled over the room.

"Much less," Fritz said. "As everyone knows, the substitute was made in the 1960s when we were repairing the original. They also know that we use it whenever the real shrine has to be repaired. However, the stones are not as precious and the gilt is merely painted on. It would hardly be worth stealing.''

"Herr Kardinal did not know about the bones of the Magi until after the theft," Rudi observed softly.

"Ja, ja, Rudi, but it is still my responsibility. Sometime soon we will have to tell the truth, the whole truth.''

"It will destroy us," Bishop Freddie said sadly. "The whole world will laugh at us.''

"Better that they laugh at us than hate us again," the cardinal said with a loud sigh. "Now, perhaps you want to hear the story of the disappearance?''

"Arguably."

The Herr Bischof began his recitation in the tone of voice of a Sturmführer reporting to an Obersturmführer. (All right, I didn't like the man. Or trust him.)

"Ja, ja. We close the dom every night at seventeen-thirty. Sometimes we must drive the crowds out. Then we clean up the mess from the day . . ."

"Who cleans up?" I asked.

He frowned in exasperation.

"We have a team of Polish *Hausfrauen.* We do not trust the Turks. They would steal things."

"Like art galleries in Russia and France."

The room grew more tense, though the count cardinal grinned.

"They work very hard." Herr Bischof ignored me. "No one cleans as well as Polish *Hausfrauen.* The mess at the end of the day is disgusting. When they have left, I or one of my staff inspects the nave and the chapels to see whether anything has been disturbed or any damage done. That particular night, I myself did the inspection. As always, there were some things that had been broken, but nothing extraordinary."

"The shrine was untouched?"

"Of course, Priest, it was untouched!"

This bit of rudeness was too much for my usually mild-mannered and soft-spoken nefoo.

"The proper title for my uncle," he said in presentable German (a skill of which I was unaware) "is Herr Bischof or perhaps Herr Bischof/Dompfarrer."

"He doesn't look like a bishop!"

"Neither did Saint Peter or Saint John the Divine, who is his patron, or Patrick of Armagh."

The count cardinal didn't bother to try to hide his amusement. Cindasue, more of a diplomat than Claus Maria von Obermann, suppressed a smile, but her gray green eyes bathed said nefoo with complacent approval that suggested admiration, complacency, and indeed adoration not completely unmixed with desire.

Ah, so that's the way things go, I said to myself. *Excellent!*

What I said aloud was my all-time favorite line: "Call me Blackie!"

Since it was unlikely that any of the Germans present had read the opening sentence in *Moby-Dick*, the line lacked its full impact.

"*Ja ja,* Herr Bischof Blackie," my fellow Dompfarrer went on, "that night—two weeks ago last night—after I had as usual ascertained that all was in order, I set the three alarm systems on and returned to the parsonage. The first priest to say Mass, usually Kurt here, since he sleeps poorly because of his war wounds, turns off the alarm system, then the head verger opens the doors. It is six-thirty in the morning. Kurt . . ."

The elderly priest, who seemed to have been sleeping, sat up straight, and in clipped, military German told his story. Cindasue translated, fluently in my prejudiced judgment. I can, you see, understand German reasonably well for a Chicago Irishman, but I thought there was no point in tipping my hand.

"Father says that he flew an ME-262, the first jet fighter in world, at the end of the war. He was nineteen years old. At first they thought they would win the war. Then we Americans developed the tactic of using 'curtains' of P-47s, swarms of planes only three hundred meters above the ones below them. He knew he was going to die when he saw the curtain sweeping toward him. He was frightened, but as you see, he survived."

The Dompfarrer frowned at his elderly colleague's nostalgia. Herr Kardinal, whose father had been executed by the Nazis for his involvement in the plot against Hitler, listened sympathetically.

"The only time he was more frightened in his life than when he saw the shrine was missing was when he felt the fifty-caliber machine gun bullets tearing into his beautiful plane and his body the day he was shot down. What happened in the dom that night was blasphemous. He sent the verger to find the Dompfarrer and began to offer the Holy Sacrifice of the Mass. . . . He means to preside over the Eucharistic celebration, Uncle Blackie."

"Indeed."

She said it with a perfectly straight face. Nonetheless, she was, as the Irish would say, having me on. Also showing off that she had learned all the fashionable, contemporary Catholic jargon. The young woman was an incorrigible imp.

I noted with approval that the priest began Mass and let someone else fetch the Herr Bischof. Even if the shrine had been stolen, the people in the dom, such as they were, were entitled to a prompt beginning of the Eucharistic celebration.

The Dompfarrer took up the story.

"Immediately I went to the art workshop with three of my staff. The workmen were not there yet, of course. We removed the substitute from the safe in which it was locked and carried it—it is very heavy—up to the nave and placed it in the proper location. The people in the church must have thought we were simply bringing the shrine back from where we store it at night. We locked the safe so that the workmen would not know what we had done. Then I phoned Herr Kardinal and he called Herrn Bundeskanzler, the chancellor or prime minister as you would call him. Later, a high officer of the *Polizei* came to discuss the matter with me. I told him what I have told you."

He shrugged as if to ask what more could he have done.

What more indeed?

"Very resourceful," I said, not meaning it completely. "Might I ask when was the last time you used the substitute?"

"Last January. At the beginning of every year we remove the shrine for cleaning and polishing. Even with the protection of the plastic case, the air in the dom, so many millions of people breathing, tends to tarnish the shrine. We do not deliberately deceive. Our publications say that it is cleaned every year, only we do not say when."

"Even when the substitute is used," Cardinal von Obermann observed sagely, "there is still a challenge to those who come, as the Fräulein Leutnant has said, to follow their own star, *nein?*"

"*Ja,*" I agreed. "And no claim of theft? Or demands for ransom?"

"Not at all." The cardinal sighed mammothly. "We now must begin to fear that it is in some art collector's castle, not in Germany. Perhaps the Russian Mafia stole on, as you would say, assignment. Soon we will have to tell the truth."

An alternative explanation flitted across my mind. A single question would answer it. I almost asked the question, but, as often is the case, the picture of what happened slipped away before I had a chance to give it a name.

"That might be wise, whatever the reaction. First of all, you will have told the truth before the media find out about it, which of course they will. Secondly, you will have the police agencies of all the world hunting for it."

The local Dompfarrer snorted in opposition.

"All the alarms were in operation?" I asked him.

"Certainly!"

"But they did not go off?"

"No."

"How are they turned on and off?"

"By a sequence of numbers on the control board in the sacristy."

"You can enter the sacristy without activating the alarm?"

"*Ja,* but not the nave from the sacristy."

I almost said, "Fascinating," but I thought that would be imprudent.

Rudi and Fritz circulated around the table, pouring more wine and resupplying my cookie plate to undo the depredations of the local leprechaun. Everyone relaxed a little. Cindasue smiled at the two young priests, and naturally, they smiled back. She was still the shy mountain creature slipping through the hollows and the valleys of West Virginia; she'd always be that, but she'd acquired somewhere a smooth, diplomatic persona, thick with charm. It didn't hurt.

"You change the sequence of numbers often, I presume?"

"*Ja,* every three months."

"No video monitors?"

"We have discussed it," the cardinal said. "Now, of course, we are installing them. Too late."

"How many people know the numbers?"

"I don't know them," the cardinal admitted, with his big smile. "I know too many numbers as it is."

"As Dompfarrer, I know them, of course. Kurt knows them. Two other of my priests know them in case I am absent in the evening and Kurt is not saying the first Mass—Pfarrer Rosner and Pfarrer Kluge. They are both to be trusted."

Doubtless, but a good cop would not trust anyone.

Neither in cases like this did I trust anyone.

"I may speak to the police official whom the Herrn Bundeskanzler sent that day?"

I consumed two cookies, lest the leprechaun beat me to them.

"Naturally," the cardinal agreed. "I believe that the Fräulein Leutnant can reach him."

"Shonuff."

"Do you have a solution yet, Blackie?" Cardinal von Obermann asked me with what I thought was almost pathetic eagerness.

"Oh, yes," I said as I always do under such circumstances. "A number of possibilities occur immediately. I do not understand fully why the deed might have been done or how, but I think there are one or two fascinating solutions that I will want to consider."

I assume that the gentle reader of this story has already thought of them, too. I will confess to that gentle reader that at that time, I had only the haziest notion of those fascinating solutions. However, it must be remembered that at the moment, my brain cells had been abruptly and unceremoniously translated across seven time zones and that, arguably, I had consumed too much German red wine in the circumstances. The solutions were there, but I would have been hard put to articulate them or even understand them.

"*Ja, ja,* that is good." The cardinal sighed happily. "Sean Cronin said you would solve it."

That settled that.

The cardinal then explained in some detail the reasons for the current political crisis in Germany. In a burst of generosity and enthusiasm with which the cardinal thought all Catholics must sympathize, Helmut Kohl had welcomed East Germany into the Federal Republic and decreed that the same wage rates would apply to the Neubundesländer as applied in the Altbundesländer—the states from what used to be East Germany would be treated as though they were the same as the states from what used to be West Germany.

Unfortunately, many West Germans felt that they were being penalized for the laziness of the "Ossies" and the latter in their turn resented the diminished social "safety net" that the Federal Republic provided—one of the most generous in the Western world. While the situation of the new citizens had improved dramatically, they were not yet satisfied. And the West Germans were disgusted with what they took to be the poor quality of East German work and workers. Now unemployment was at 10 percent in the Federal Republic, an unheard-of level only a few years ago, and it had become necessary to trim the safety net even more.

"We don't need another major scandal just now," he sighed, "especially a scandal of a missing shrine—one which, as Herr Bischof Blackie has shrewdly guessed, is empty."

Ja, ja.

Father Klein (still averting his eyes from Cindasue) had to show us a tattered picture of his "beautiful plane." It was not exactly beautiful, not like the F-18 Hornet my friend Megan flies off the aircraft carrier *Langley.* Rather, it was a World War II type fighter (such as a Spitfire or Mustang) with a jet engine installed awkwardly under each wing. The priest, looking like he was about fourteen, stood next to the plane, a broad grin on his handsome face. Unlike a lot of veterans of that generation, he was easily identifiable because he had not lost his hair or put on weight.

"*Ja,*" he said, Cindasue translating for him, "I once met the pilot who shot me down. He was a very fine pilot and a nice man. He was happy I was still alive. I'm glad they won, though I did not feel that way then."

A tear or two slipped from Cindasue's eyes.

Herr Kardinal showed us out of the house into the bright sunlight, which caused us all to wince after the darkness in his Viking hall. The house was a pleasant enough villa, but no more elaborate than any of the pleasant houses in Lindenthal and hardly palatial.

"*Ja, ja,*" he said. "You are a fine Catholic young woman, Fräulein Leutnant. You're so kind to poor old Kurt."

"He's a nice man, Herr Kardinal. But I'm not a Catholic. I'm what we call a hard-shell Baptis'. I guess I have to be one all my life."

As always quick on his feet, Klaus Maria von Obermann said, "*Ja, ja,* we must all be what we were and are. That is the nice thing about being Catholic. People do not have to give up what they are. Rather, they bring it to us and enrich us with their own heritage."

"Shonuf?" She glanced at me for approval.

"Shonuf," I agreed, "as your man Jimmy Joyce once put it, Catholic means here comes everyone."

"HCE, Uncle Blackie, Houth Castle and Environs." *So there, smart-mouth priest, I've read* Finnegans Wake, *too.*

My nefoo enveloped her with his deep blue eyes, just as she had done a little earlier.

Fast workers, the two of them.

7

"Do you think, Uncle Blackie," my good nefoo asked as we strolled down the Dürnerstrasse, "that your pompous friend stole his own shrine?"

"It would be consoling to think so, yet I doubt that he himself would have the imagination to conceive of such a plan. Perhaps at the suggestion of a political and religious reactionary he might have been a party to such a scheme to discredit the cardinal and the Herrn Bundeskanzler. According to Milord Cronin, he was slated to be the archbishop of Köln. He had powerful friends in Rome and in the right-wing Catholic groups in Germany. Men like him had been appointed to other important sees. He assumed, as did most Vatican watchers, that he would be an automatic appointment. Some wise angel whispered Claus Maria Graf von Obermann into the pope's ear. The pope remembered his family's valiant resistance to anti-Semitism and followed the suggestion of the angel. Bischof Heidrich might feel that he was cheated. But he is essentially a small man, capable by himself of only small conspiracies."

In front of the cardinal's house, hardly a medieval *Schloss* of the sort that would befit an essentially medi-

eval character like Claus Maria Count von Obermann,
Cindasue had suggested that we walk back to the hotel
because Peter Murphy and I needed exercise to ''un-
kink'' our weary bones. We had come out on a tram so,
as she told us, we would learn how easy it was to get
around the city.

In the interest of promoting the cause of true love, I
agreed, with a pretense of enthusiasm.

The Dürnerstrasse was an attractive street, a newer and
brighter version of the shopping streets with which I grew
up in the premall days. It linked two of the rings that
circled Köln, concentric half circles, the center of which
was the dom. The first ring was the old city wall; the
second was the ring on which our hotel was located, the
limit of expansion immediately after the city wall was
torn down. After that, the city built parklands at each new
ring. We were walking between the park near the university and the Stadtwald—the ''city forest'' at the far
edge of Lindenthal. It was, all in all, an appealing way
to arrange a city.

My nefoo and his lady love walked hand in hand, far
more concerned with each other and their possible future
than the problem at hand. They were ''jest broguein
al'ng,'' according to Cindasue, which meant, I gathered,
ambling along on their shoes.

''Happ'n I gettin' ahead of you all,'' I replied, ''you
two are jest like to start a-bussin'.''

''I'm not a shameless hussy,'' she protested with a
pleased blush. ''I'm as shy as a ring-tailed pheasant.''

We all laughed.

However, as we brogued, slowly, toward the Rudolfplatz, Cindasue at least paid lip service to the stolen
shrine.

''You don't think, do you, Uncle Blackie, that nice
cacky ole preacher man had anything to do with stealing
it? I don't reckon he done did it.''

''Pastor Kurt? I have been considering him. Admittedly, Fräulein Unterleutnant, he seems a nice, gentle
man who lives in the past more than the present. Still,

consider the gatekeeper position he occupies at the dom. He had the keys to get in the sacristy. He knew the combinations for the alarm systems. He could have come over at any time during the night, opened the sacristy, turned off the alarm system, opened a door to the dom, watched while a van pulled up to it and a group of men—four or maybe six—removed the shrine, then locked the door, retired to the sacristy, locked that, turned on the alarm system again, and returned to the rectory.''

''Wouldn't there be a risk that the *Polizei* would see them?'' Peter Murphy asked.

''Doubtless. But let us suppose the incident had been carefully planned. The gang would have learned the routine of the patrol cars. They would have chosen the widest band of opportunity that was available to them to minimize the risk. I assume that Köln night life is not concentrated in that area, Fräulein Unterleutnant?''

''Closest is between the Altemarkt and Neumarkt, lessen you want to go out to the Roonstrasse near your hotel.''

''So then we assume that there is little pedestrian traffic near the dom after the trains stop coming into the *Hauptbahnhof* next to it.''

''Still risky,'' Peter Murphy observed.

''Stealing the shrine of the Three Wise Men is necessarily a risky affair,'' I replied.

''Thez boadacious houn' dogs to done try that. . . . Couldn't any of the preacher men in the parsonage do the same?''

''Certainly. . . . Still, I incline to think that . . .''

Before I could finish what I now admit was a weak case against that cacky (shrewd) old preacher man, a bell, much like mother superior's bell in the Catholic schools of yesteryear, clanged behind me, a woman's voice shouted an imprecation, and Cindasue pulled me out of the way of a rampaging cyclist. Patently, the bricked strips on the sidewalk were for such.

''Durn crumbly storm trooper!'' my savior yelled at

the tall, slender, blond woman in white shorts and blue tank top.

The cyclist stopped and waited for us.

She was at most in her middle teens and pretty.

"I am sorry," she said contritely in presentable English. "I did not know you were Americans. We Germans expect everyone to know all our laws, and there are so many laws. It is very foolish of us."

"My friends arrived only today," Cindasue replied in German, somewhat pacified. "I have not yet told them about the cycle path."

"Of course," the young woman smiled at us and temporarily put the sun out. "I am Helga," she added shyly, still in English.

"I'm Cindy," our Coast Guard person replied with a matching smile.

They were bonding, as women do against the other half of the human race.

Then she introduced us as Herr Professor Doktor Peter Murphy and Herr Bischof Johann Rhine.

Helga glanced appreciatively at Herr Professor Doktor Peter Murphy and decided that he was probably already spoken for. Then she turned to me.

"*Ja, ja,* Herr Bischof, I am so very sorry," she bowed her head in shame.

"On such a lovely afternoon in such a lovely city, I must apologize to you for being in your way."

I smiled my most charming Father Blackie smile. The young woman smiled back at me. We were all friends.

"You are very kind. I must hurry now to class."

"Cindy, is it?" said Peter Murphy.

"Jest for these Germ'n folk. They done have a hard time gettin' their moufs around Cindasue. Not like your Chicago varmints."

"It's either Cindasue or Lieutenant, ma'am?" he replied.

"Shonuff . . . and you didn' have to stare at that brazin' hussy and grin at her like a possum, jest because she has such purty tits."

She punched his chest in punishment, very very lightly.

"Staring, Cindasue," I observed, "is inevitable."

"Grinnin' ain't," she argued. "She sure purty, though. Happen she grow up a few years and she gorgeous. . . . I think we all need a beer after that incident."

We were directed to a sidewalk café with large yellow umbrellas and big shade trees. Our girl guide ordered three beers—Kölsch, the local brand, which she extolled. As beers go, it was palatable. She also ordered for me *Rievekoochen*, which turned out to be a slab of fried potatoes dipped in thick applesauce. It was remarkably good, to my surprise.

"We think you'd better get a good night's sleep, Uncle Blackie," Peter Murphy informed me, apparently explaining this early supper.

"Arguably," I admitted.

"Cindasue just happens to have two tickets for the opera tonight. *Magic Flute.* We thought we'd have a swim at the hotel, go to the opera, and then eat supper at some small restaurant and maybe sample a little of the night life near the hotel."

"The very thought exhausts me," I observed.

"Cindasue has a new swimsuit . . ." he began.

"It's the banjo-pickinest thing I've ever owned," she said enthusiastically.

"I think she bought it just to please me," he said with a grin.

"Hush you trashy mouth," she said fiercely. "I buy my clothes to please me, not some polecat man. Happen this here polecat like it, that his problem."

"But you won't mind if he do?" I asked.

"Course not," she said huffily. "And I'm no shameless hussy. I'll change into my suit in his room with him outside the door. And I won't take some of it off like some of these tarts do here in Europe."

"I am reassured," I said blandly. "Not that I entertained any questions in these matters."

"Nor I," Peter Murphy agreed with a perfectly straight face.

"Humf," she observed with considerable skepticism.

The young woman had a fierce need to assert both her independence and her virtue.

But then, as if to restore balance, she bussed him on the cheek.

"Hey!" Peter Murphy protested. "The woman's attacking me."

She dismissed him with a wave of her hand.

"That Helga woman is a typical Kölnerin," she said. "Not that they all would apologize, but only a Kölner would even think of it. She can laugh at herself and all the rules and regulations, even though she keeps most of them. When she has a kid, she'll seek approval from the local authority for its name, but she'll laugh at it then too. These folks are, for Germans anyway, a live-and-let-live bunch. They laugh a lot and believe in having a good time."

"I hear their Karneval is kind of wild," Peter said.

"Terrible wicked thing. I come up here last year for the first night and went back to Bonn on the twenty-one hundred train. Y'all Arsh Catlics don't act like that 't all, no way."

"More subtle," I said.

"Oktoberfest ah'right," she said. "Woman done have to protect herself every inch of the way."

"Deplorable," I agreed.

"If she want to, that is. . . . Anyway," she continued, "you notice what that there Kardinal preacher man say about being blamed?"

"Shonuff," I said.

"Their big problem is whether to be proud of being German. It runs through everything they do and say. Most of the people had nothing to do with the Holocaust because they weren't even born then. Unlike the Japanese, they don't cover anything up. But they're told that all Germans are to blame for it, and that there is a flaw in German culture, which produced Hitler, and that flaw is still here. Lots of writers, their own and others, say that they still do Nazi-like things. They didn't help themselves when they expelled all those poor Gypsies and sent them back to Romania. Hitler tried to kill all the Gypsies, too. What do you think, Uncle Blackie?''

''If I were Jewish, I don't think I would trust them, not for another hundred years or so. On the other hand, the Germans certainly try to run an open and democratic society and to make amends. I have never found the notion of collective guilt attractive. Moreover, there is a dark side to every culture; witness what we have done to African Americans. Or the antiforeign nativism in our country. I find it difficult to distinguish between the men who are elected to public office with the pledge to punish immigrants and the late Herrn Reichskanzler Hitler. They haven't gone as far as he did, but they appeal to a dangerous, dark side of our culture.''

''Aw-huh. . . . You sure right smart, Uncle Blackie. How come you have such dumb nefoos?''

''They are young, Cindasue. Give them time to mature.''

''Thez right purty, though,'' she said and bussed the only dumb nefoo present on the lips.

''Bodacious,'' he sighed happily.

I tended to agree with him. Moreover, the various signals she was sending in his direction were confusing— at least to him.

''I reckon,'' I continued, ''that we should leave the Germans alone and see what happens. When there was anti-Turkish violence in what used to the German Democratic Republic—three lies, by the way, in that title— the outpouring of protest was massive. I don't think it will ever happen again. But, like I say, if I were Jewish, I'd need a lot more time to be reassured. Or to begin to forget.''

She nodded.

''I agree, Uncle Blackie. They're nicer to the Turks than we are to the Mexicans. You have any more ideas on who took and stole that thar shrine?''

"That is a question I will be unable to answer unless my strength is fortified by another helping of that *rive gauche* thing or whatever you call it."

"*Rievekoochen!*" She laughed. "It mean tater pancakes. Not like our tater pancakes, though."

She engaged in a conversation with the waiter in what I took to be the Kölner dialect. They both laughed. He looked at me and laughed again. However, he did serve up another platter of the delicacy, *mit* sausage.

I declined a second beer; however, the young folks did not.

"The most obvious explanation," I said, trying not to sound like a bishop speaking from his chair, "is that a gang of very skillful and very patient art thieves, acting with inside help, lifted it and sold it to some international criminal group, which in its turn transferred it to a very rich and not too ethical collector. In which case, I would think the international police links should be activated and the person in possession should be pursued relentlessly. That would be very difficult if that happens to be an Arab or a Japanese. A European might be more easily captured. But this is pure speculation at the present. Moreover, I supposed the *Bundesrepublik Polizei* have already discreetly pursued that possibility."

"So?" Peter Murphy asked.

"So, we may very well have a much more tricky and complicated explanation, perhaps one—though this is only a wild guess—involving some of the neo-Nazis."

"Or some of the Greens," Cindasue added, as she signaled for the check. "Some of them folks every bit as bad as the Nazis. And there's always the remnants of the Red Army Faction that linger 'round."

"Or Catholic reactionaries."

I was patently whistling in the dark past the cemetery. I'm sure the thorough cops of the federal police had already quietly and carefully explored those possibilities.

We began to brogue down Dürnerstrasse again. Cindasue slipped into a bake shop and came out with a paper bag. She opened it and permitted me to examine it. Two scrumptious-seeming raisin-cinnamon rolls.

"Happen you like to get hungry 'fore you a-fallen asleep."

She retained possession of the rolls, however, lessen I eat them immediately.

For those of you who may be unfamiliar with me, I do not put on weight when I eat and do not lose it when I fast, as I routinely do during Lent and on other occasions. Nor does temporarily abandoning the creature have any effect.

"Punk, you were born pudgy and you'll never be fat or skinny, no matter what you do," says my virtuous sister Mary Kathleen Murphy, M.D.

Punk is the affectionate diminutive my siblings use. This used to be Uncle Punk with their children, but as they matured, that became the equally acceptable Uncle Blackie. Only my late father called me Johnny. As in "Johnny, we are really the only two sane ones in the whole clan."

"Patently," I would always agree.

"You take after me," he would continue. "They take after their late mother, God be good to her." And my dad's eyes would turn sad.

I would add, "She'd better be."

And Dad would then laugh at the image of God in conversation with the late Kate Collins Ryan, as with an equal partner.

To everyone else, I am Blackie, which is patently my name—except with certain liberated nuns who persist in calling me John which is patently not my name.

The next time they did, I would inform them that John the Divine was my patron, and I felt I was entitled to the whole appellation.

Whence Blackwood (which is how Milord Cronin frequently addresses me)? Family folklore claims that I was conceived the night my mother made a Blackwood convention at the bridge table. I tend to discount family folklore, but my mother was eminently capable of such behavior.

We crossed the Universitätstrasse and entered the last park between us and my bed on the Hapsburgerring.

"You notice, Uncle Blackie, what that there Kardinal man say 'bout done being Babtis' and Cat'lic at the same time?"

"I did, Cindasue."

"He right?"

"It's a perfectly orthodox position, Cindasue."

"You hold with it?"

"Indubitably."

"Could be kinda fun, couldn't it?"

"Arguably, that's the whole idea."

Demonstrating his wisdom, Peter Murphy did not comment on that interchange.

"Happen we solve this here mystery thing, we can talk about that."

"We could if you want to," I said, keeping my cards close to my vest.

Finally, we arrived at the hotel.

"Uncle Blackie," Cindasue began, brushing her hair away from her face, "I fixing to say somethin' for a pace o' time and plumb don't know no way how to say it."

She looked down and shuffled her feet.

"I'm powerful sorry about Uncle Neddy's death. He were a right fine man."

She was referring to my late father, Edward P. "Ned" Ryan.

"Thank you, Cindasue. We miss him, all of us, but he's with my mother now."

"And Aunty Helen, how she doin'?"

Aunty Helen was my stepmother, who had lived with my father about as many years as my mother. She was an admirable woman, and considerably more serene than my mother, who had chosen her as a successor. Naturally.

"It was very difficult for her at first, though she knew when she married Dad that she would likely live much longer than he did. She's much better now."

"She a-fixin' to marry again?"

"I am led to believe that she is, with support from the whole family, of course."

"She a right fine woman."

"She is, Cindasue."

"Y'all a heap of fine folks, you Ryans . . . and Murphys, too."

Tears poured down her cheeks and she hugged me. She also hugged Peter, with, I thought, considerably more emotion.

Thinking that there was something in that miniwake that was important, but unable to pinpoint it, I hurried to my room. Before I collapsed into my bed, I turned on my OmniBook. There were two messages.

The first was from Mkate@LCMH.com:

Punk, I don't want Peter hurt again.

Mary Kate.

I pondered the message. Surely the Hapsburg monarch could never have been more imperial. And herself only yesterday insisting that I had to effect a reconciliation between her son and the cute little tyke in the sailor suit. Ah well, mothers need not honor the principle of consistency.

I replied:

That outcome patently unlikely.

Blackie@aol.com.

The other message, as one might have expected, was from *Cardinal@archchi.org:*

Blackwood

Story about bones missing from shrine is absurd fantasy. We need solutions.

Cronin.

I took great delight in my reply:

Milord. Count cardinal admits absence of bones. Probably important to the solution. Only one solution possible. Best regards to my staff, especially all Megans who are doubtless running parish now better than I could.

Blackie@aol.com.

I went over to the window to draw the drape. The Kölner Dom was golden in the light of the setting sun. It had been hit by fourteen bombs during the war and was in semiruins only sixty-five years after it had been finished. Now, for all its resemblance on the inside to Soldier Field during a Bears game, it stood proud and lovely, a monument to two millennia of glorious and tragic history.

Tomorrow morning upon awakening, I would use the high-intensity lamp visor, which was alleged to exorcise jet lag in two days at the most. Then I would turn my rejuvenated gray cells to work on solving the mystery.

Again, the picture of the solution floated transiently across my weary brain. It faded even more quickly than usual.

8

Peter

"You done like me, Peter Murphy, sir?" she asked as she discarded the hotel robe she had borrowed from my room.

"Done," by the way, is apparently nothing more than a word of emphasis in her version of English. Something like the Standard American "y'know?"

I hope I didn't gulp too noticeably.

"I always liked your physical appearance, Cindasue McCloud, especially in a bikini. Now I like it even more."

Doesn't that sound like a professor?

This particular banjo-pickinest concoction did not differ much in its extent from the one in which I had seen her at Grand Beach so many years ago, save perhaps in— How should I say it?—certain strategic abridgements. However, it matched perfectly the green of her eyes, and the gold stripes emphasized both the abridgements and the lovely flow of her body.

"Ya thin' I kinda feathered out a mite?" she asked dubiously.

I stepped into the whirlpool, thinking about how marvelously poetic "feathered out" was.

"Your body has feathered out more than a mite, Cindasue, and the rest of you, soul and spirit and mind and wit, have feathered out even more."

Not bad for Arsh, huh?

She blushed down to the tops of her marvelous breasts and smiled contentedly.

"You a mighty kind man, Dr. Peter Murphy."

I extended my hand to help her into the whirlpool.

"You shouln't ought to look at me that way, not a'tall."

She frowned as though she were about to explode in a temper tantrum. I had witnessed those before and had no liking for a repetition.

"Cindasue, chile," I said taking her hand firmly in mine and guiding her into the whirlpool, "happen you don't want me to look at you with admiration and desire, you don't get yourself gussied up in that banjo-pickinest thing."

She laughed happily and slid into the swirling warm waters.

"I reckon you plumb right, Dr. Murphy, sir."

She cuddled next to me.

"Sorry. Lessen I such a nasty, nit-brained leetle bitch, I wouldn't have said that."

I extended my arm around her waist and caressed her firm stomach muscles. She sighed contentedly.

"I think you know, Cindasue," I continued, hoping that I wasn't too much the academic, "that I'll always treasure and honor and cherish you."

"I know that, Pete." She sighed, and leaned her head against my chest. "I'm just plumb scar'd of you."

"Scared?"

"When my boss told me that you and Uncle Blackie were coming here on the Kölner Dom case and that he wanted me to keep an eye on you, I liked to died. I was so happy that I'd see y'all agin and scared jest plain blind billiards. I felt jest terrible cruddy. I don't know how to deal with you, Peter dear, but I shonuff like to."

She kissed me gently and affectionately. No one in the

pool seemed to notice. Presumably, the scene had been enacted there often before. I held her closer.

"Would it surprise you, Lieutenant McCloud, that I felt the same way when I realized how close to Bonn Cologne was? I liked to die when I saw you in that airport."

"Junior grade," she murmured into my chest.

We were quiet for many moments, enjoying the pressure of each other's body and the delight to which such touch might eventually lead.

"You a-thinking my boobs are any cuter than they used to be?"

"That's a vulgar question, Lieutenant Junior Grade McCloud. I will not give it a vulgar answer. Your breasts, from what I know of them, and it isn't all that much, save in my fantasies, have always been lovely. Now they're richer and even more enchanting."

"You Arsh sure do talk plumb clever."

"You're Arsh, too, Cindasue."

"Left-footed," she giggled. "Cuter than that leetle brat on the Dürnerstrasse?"

"Such comparisons are even more vulgar," I insisted. "Do you mean would I rather play with your breasts than hers? And the answer is absolutely yes."

"Not right now," she warned uneasily.

"Course not."

Not quite yet, but soon, my love.

Then she decreed we ought to swim if we were to arrive at the opera at curtain time.

Her swimming had improved greatly at New London. She slipped through the water like a trim, graceful, and confident otter.

I thought it was a good beginning to a wonderful night.

I couldn't have been more wrong.

9

Cindasue

If You be a-list'n up there, You know what a mess I be.

The man makes me plumb dizzy. He touches me and fire rushes through my body. He kisses me and my knees get wobbly. He looks at me with such delight I want to take off my clothes so I'll delight him even more. I want him to tickle me and play with my boobs and kiss every part of me. I want to feel his body jabbing up and down inside me while I holler with joy. I want to spend the rest of my life with him in my bed at night.

That's how I feel. Is it trashy or jest the way a woman oughter feel when she's met her man?

Is he like to be my man?

Happen I don't fight him off way I did in Chicago.

Was I right in doing that? I wanted to be independent. I wanted to attend college on my own without his family paying for me. I thought I was right then. Now I'm not sure.

In that whirlpool thing I thought I like to die, I so happy.

I still wanna be independent. I wanna be my own self, not someone else's.

He no dog-beater. He never hit me that way.

I still wanna be independent.
But I don't want to lose him, not at all, no way.
You list'n?
Happ'n you care at all 'bout a no-count redneck like me, give me another chance.
I wouldn't blame if he jest a-droppin' me fer keeps, way I acted tonight.

Blackie Again

"Lieutenant Junior Grade, C. L. McCloud of the Yew-nited States Coast Guard, sir," she said, extending her hand to the weary, cynical-seeming Obersuperintendent of police.

The man with the slumped shoulders and the rumpled dark blue suit crushed his cigarette automatically, stood up, smiled, and shook hands with her.

"*Ja, ja,* Frau Unterleutnant. I have heard about you and your colleagues. The name of Herr Bischof Rhine is not unknown among the European police. It is an honor to have you visit us."

He bowed and clicked his heels. "My name is Ernst Schulteis, Frau Unterleutnant.'

"Fräulein Unterleutnant," she said crisply but with a smile that would have melted a Rhine River bridge.

"Call me Blackie," I added softly, blinking harmlessly through my Coke-bottle glasses, a ploy that made most people think I was utterly harmless, which of course I am not.

"And not Ishmael?" he said with a laugh.

The Herr Obersuperintendent was patently no fool. Even a fool, however, would have brightened at the

sight of Cindasue. She had discarded the professional suit
of yesterday and was wearing a sleeveless lime shift with
a radical miniskirt and a gleaming black leather shoulder
bag that crossed her chest and emphasized the shape of
her body.

The costume would melt the heart of the statue of Kaiser Friederich Wilhelm IV to say nothing of all the live
humans we might encounter in the course of the day.
However, it was intended to melt especially the heart of
Peter Murphy, Ph.D.

Earlier that morning, after rising (most painfully) at
seven, checking the Chicago news on the Net to see what
disasters had befallen the Chicago Bears, I had donned
the intense-light visor for the required hour. It had no
immediate impact on my bodily discombobulation, but
those wiser in such matters than I am said it would take
two days. I thereupon had showered, considered seriously
the possibility of climbing back into bed, barely rejected
that course of action, and stumbled down into the dining
hall of the hotel.

It was charmingly arranged and decorated, like the rest
of the hotel, but my stomach revolted at the vast array
of food from which I might choose: smoked fish, salami
and other cold cuts, a wide variety of cheeses, stacks of
thick black bread and hard rolls (none with raisin and
cinnamon like the two I had demolished upon awakening), croissants that seemed unnecessarily soggy, butter
and jam in plastic wrap, yogurt, small oranges and grapefruit and huge apples, and other material too painful to
mention. There was indeed cereal—cornflakes, rice cris-
pies, and what for all I knew might be Müeslix—but the
bowls into which these might be spooned were much too
small. I thereupon filled two bowls with cornflakes,
added several handfuls of raisins, which I had discovered
near the prunes, poured milk in both bowls, and tottered
over to an empty table. A young woman was instantly
upon me, not as I presumed to reprimand me for the milk
I had spilled but only to ask me whether I wanted coffee.

"Tea," I replied briefly.

"With milk and sugar?"

"As black as midnight on a moonless night," I said, quoting from the *Twin Peaks* TV series.

She chuckled, departed, and immediately returned with an ample pot of tea, a small cup, and a large tea strainer. I promptly poured the tea and discovered to my great delight that it was of the proper strength—just slightly less than would cause a teaspoon to bend.

I was on my fourth (minute) bowl of raisin cornflakes (something with which Kellogg's might want to experiment) and my second pot of tea, when my haggard nefoo showed up. He was wearing jeans and a maroon University of Chicago T-shirt. His hair was tousled, he had not shaven (his father and his brother grow beards rapidly), and he therefore looked like he was still a graduate student. A slob, that is.

Bad night.

"They spilled a lot of milk on your table, Uncle Blackie," he said sadly.

I withheld comment until he was well into his first cup of coffee.

"You look beleaguered," I had observed.

"The woman will drive me out of my mind."

"That is usually the case."

"I don't understand her."

"That, too, is usually the case."

"What is the matter with her?"

"Patently, she wants to be in love and wants to be completely independent and finds it difficult to do both, a task not unlike squaring the circle."

He pondered my analysis and then nodded his head and went off to fill a plate with all the breakfast food that had repelled me.

"Why didn't I figure that out?" he asked.

"Because you're in love with her."

"I sure am. . . . It was wonderful last night until after the opera. I wanted to pay for the dinner because she had paid for everything else. . . . Was that unreasonable?"

"Arguably not."

"She became very angry. The day was her treat and that was that. She wouldn't permit me to pay."

"So you backed off?"

"What else was I supposed to do? She was furious at my suggestion."

"Indeed."

"Then we went to this night club just down the street. It was a pretty heavy place, a kind of *I am a Camera* or *Cabaret* sort of place. Weird."

"And you?"

"Fell asleep."

"Ah."

"She woke me up and said she'd better take me back to the hotel if her company was so boring. I tried to explain that I had not slept for almost twenty-four hours. She kept insisting that she bored me. Could Cindasue bore anyone, Uncle Blackie?"

"Most improbable."

"She wouldn't accept my apology. Then I said I'd ride back to Bonn with her. She said I would not. I said I always took young women home from dates. She said it wasn't a date, and she was quite capable of driving herself to Bonn. She'd done it many times at night before."

"Ah."

The young woman was spoiling for a fight after a perfectly pleasant day with her once and future love. What was amiss here?

"And I said that I still wanted to take her home and she said I'd fall asleep in the car because she bored me and besides how would I get back to Köln? And I said I could take the train and she said there were not many at that hour of the night and that I'd fall asleep and wake up in Hamburg."

"Arguably, she was right."

"Yeah, I know. So she pushed me out of the car, literally shoved me out, and then went off in a cloud of dust. Somehow I blew it, but I don't know why. I'll have to apologize to her this morning."

"Don't!"

"Why not?"

"Wait to see what she says."

"She won't apologize."

"Five dollars says she will."

"You know I can't resist a bet!"

Precisely.

For some reason, Cindasue had become terrified of my harmless nefoo. She would have to deal with that herself. She couldn't have it both ways.

As Peter Murphy was finishing his breakfast (his sisters would have called it "yucky") and I was ill-advisedly experimenting with a soggy croissant and plastic raspberry jam (an intolerable violation), Cindasue had bounced in, keys in hand and arrayed in the breathtaking lime creation I have already described.

She had bussed him, to use her word, enthusiastically, murmured something that was surely an apology, hugged him fiercely, and joined our table. She produced a paper bag and passed it across the table to me. Raisin cinnamon buns, naturally. With real as opposed to plastic butter.

"Reckon'd you would'n like the croissants they serve in these fancy Continental hotels. Peter Joseph Murphy, what's that crud you a-feedin' your face? You'll like to be sick all afternoon. Here's a paper bag for you, too."

He had opened the bag.

"Ice cream!"

"Italian ice cream, the kind you love. Eat it now, darlin'. . . . We see this copper man in a half hour. I like your beard. You look like a shonuff Arsh pir'te. Don't he, Uncle Blackie?"

"I.R.A. gunman."

"I didn't have time to shave," he said apologetically.

"I hope you don't done shave it. You look real cute. And you can glower at people today if they don't help us and plumb scare the livin' hell out of them."

My poor nefoo had looked like he'd been run over by a train. In a manner of speaking, he had. Later, when she dragged us out of the hotel to see the Herr Obersuperintendent, he had whispered in my ear, "I owe you five bucks."

My experiment had been a success. Cindasue was scared of intimacy but still wanted it. It would be a delicate task for Peter Murphy to win her out of her fear. At some point, he would have to confront her about the cause of that fear. Fortunately, he would have many chances to do that, because patently she was deeply in love with him.

"You spoke with my friend Michael Patrick Vincent Casey?" I said to the Herr Obersuperintendent.

He laughed genially.

"He said you might suspect I'd call him."

Ernst Schulteis did not seem like a man who would smile easily. He was perhaps my age, maybe a year or two older, so born after the war. His salt-and-pepper hair was cut short, his faced lined with melancholy, his gray eyes sad because of all that he'd seen. A typical wise and good cop of his age who hovered on the brink of cynicism and perhaps despair over the perversity of humankind.

"You know most of the story already, *ja?*" he asked us.

"We know that the cardinal called the Herrn Bundeskanzler and that the latter told you he wanted a careful, thorough, and discrete investigation. Immediately."

"You know the Herrn Bundeskanzler, Blackie?"

Mike "The Cop" had patently told him to call me that.

"No, indeed."

"Then you have guessed accurately. Those were his very words. *Schnell! Schnell!*"

His office, steeped in the smoke of thousands of cigarettes, was a typical cop office from anywhere in the world. Metal furniture, dirty window facing a blank wall. As depressing as the job. A kind of tomb from which few really good cops would escape alive. The building was a concrete block in the middle of a street of ingeniously constructed medieval houses, with large eaves, in the shadow of Great Saint Martin's. Presumably, genial

Irish sprites still floated around, laughing, as the Irish always tended to do, at the Germans.

"And your conclusions?"

"Someone inside the parsonage must have let the gang into the dom, at least four of them, more likely six. They worked as quickly as they could to remove the shrine. Then they hauled it off in a van. The officer in one of our patrol cars thought he saw a van pulling away from the dom, by the *Hauptbahnhof*, at three-oh-seven. It was dark in color, as best he could remember, but too far away to identify further. Naturally, it did not arouse his suspicions, *ja?*"

"I presume so," I said. "Who let them in?"

"You mean who could open the sacristy door and turn off the alarms, and then open a door to the dom?"

"Indeed."

His face, which was once handsome and still displayed some distinction, had settled back in its usual melancholy mode. He shrugged.

"There are four priests on the staff in addition to the Herr Dompfarrer. Two of them were away at a clerical conference in Koblenz. They might have come back, but that seems unlikely. They took the train down there instead of their cars. That leaves Pastor Kurt Klein and Pastor Hubert Schultz, who is just recently ordained and is not overly intelligent."

"And the Dompfarrer?"

"*Ja, ja.* . . . You don't like him either, Blackie?"

"Not hardly," I said, using a Cindasue term.

"Yet he is not capable of such a thing, not by himself."

"I tend to agree. We have no evidence that any of the priests did turn off the alarm system. Pastor Klein is a strange old man, seems to live in the past. Very *complicated*, if you understand what I mean."

"Unfathomable."

"*Ja, ja.* I don't think he even understood my questions. But then he might have. It is hard to tell."

"He showed you the picture of his Me-262?" Cindasue asked.

"*Ja,*" the Herr Obersuperintendent said, a smile flitting across his face. "That is very good, Fräulein Unterleutnant. You, too, solve puzzles?"

"Jest an appr'ntice to Uncle Blackie."

Little brat!

"You think it was Pastor Klein?" Peter Murphy, looking very much like a growling terrorist now, inquired.

"*Ja, ja,* Herr Professor Doktor. If I had to choose, I would choose him, but on the tenuous grounds that he is the most mysterious of the lot. We have followed him, of course. And all the others. They have done nothing unusual."

"You assume that the gang was professional?"

"Very professional. They were what you would call slick. Probably Eastern European, perhaps from the New States, but their gangs are rarely that industrious."

"No hint of which gangs?"

"We know that a Bulgarian and a Ukrainian gang have been in the Federal Republic recently. They have both slipped away. Interpol is trying to track them down for us."

"You have directed a very professional investigation within the constraints imposed upon you."

"*Danke,*" he said, nodding appreciatively. "The constraints were not a problem, actually. Even if the theft had been public, we would not have been able to do more and perhaps less."

"You exclude terrorists and political groups?"

"They would be so filled with their success that they would have claimed credit by now. As far as I know, no one has done so. The Herr Kardinal tells me that he has heard nothing, and I believe him. The Herr Dompfarrer says the same thing, and I would not believe him, normally, but I can think of no reason why he should lie."

"You a-thinking some art collector has it now?" the Unterleutnant asked.

"That is possible. Presumably, the gang would not

have even attempted the theft unless there was an agreed purchaser and an agreed price. That shadow world being what it is, there could be other bidders and the gang could be demanding more money. We have made very careful inquiries of Interpol and in our own Länder and there is no evidence of any such transactions, though it is a very obscure world. If I had to choose the kind of man who might now be admiring the shrine, it would be Heinz Zellner, who has a large *Schloss* on the Rhine above Bonn. He possesses immense resources, loves to hoard art, enjoys risk, and has great power. We have never been able to get inside the *Schloss*. Those who have tell us nothing. He might be sitting there now, high above the river, chuckling to himself as he admires his acquisition. We have no way of getting in.''

"He is that powerful?"

"*Ja, ja*, he is that powerful."

There was silence in the room. We all realized that we should not ask how a man could be so powerful that the Federal Republic could not search his house on suspicion that he had stolen an artwork over a thousand years old.

"If we had the slightest evidence that he indeed was part of the theft, then the Herrn Bundeskanzler would authorize a search, but," he snapped his fingers, "we have nothing. We will continue to watch the house, of course."

"And he, himself?"

"He is in South America now."

"A nice place to be if a big heist is going down," I commented.

"It would be very easy for the gang to simply drive across the river and down to his castle before anyone knew it was gone," Ernst Schulteis sighed. "However, that is all pure speculation."

"Indeed."

"I reckon," Cindasue said, "that if you could sneak some people into that there house, you would have done it already."

"His security is very tight. Much tighter than that at

the dom. His guards are armed and dangerous. We do not want a gunfight with them, as you can well imagine. Eventually"—he shrugged again—"we may be able to plant a servant in there. But that would be both difficult and dangerous. He is a very suspicious man. Perhaps paranoid. Very right wing. We are sure he funds the neo-Nazis, but we cannot prove it."

"Such men often make a small slip because they become overconfident," Peter Murphy observed, doubtless thinking of the downfall of a commodity baron who had become part of his dissertation.

"Quite correct, Herr Professor Doktor. We expect that eventually he will, and we will grab him quickly. But there might be a long wait."

In my head, a thought was pounding. This was all wrong. The Obersuperintendent had done his best. He was not hiding anything. But something was missing. Or something had been missed. Indeed, I had missed something very important.

"What kind of priestly work does Father Klein do?" Peter Murphy asked, proving that he, too, could spot something that his love and I had both missed.

The chief inspector, as we might have called him, shrugged again and fiddled nervously with the pack of cigarettes in his jacket pocket.

"To my surprise, he works mostly with youth groups. They find him very mystical. I find him merely confused and confusing."

We were all silent for a moment. The inspector removed his cigarettes.

So, he would have access to crazy young people who might do anything for their priest. However, they were hardly likely to be capable of such a well-organized raid.

We thanked Ernst Schulteis and left the darkness of the police headquarters to enter once again the brightness of Martinsviertel, the "neighborhood" around Great Saint Martin's. I was, as usual, the last one out of the office. Schulteis slipped a card into my hand that had both his office number and his home number.

Outside, Cindasue produced large sunglasses with white rims that made her look like a fashion model.

"Well, Peter Murphy, Ph.D., wh're you a-fixin' to buy us lunch today?"

"Well, I was thinking, since I'm not nearly as presentable as you are, we might try that outside café by the Dom Hotel, or maybe one of those cafés down by the river. What about you, Uncle Blackie?"

I sighed in protest at the prospect of having to walk any distance for my lunch and then conceded that the riverbank might be more appropriate.

"It a-fixing to rain tomorrow, so we'd better take advantage of the riverbank while we can. And for supper, Professor-Doktor Murphy?"

She was laying it on pretty thick, I thought.

"I thought maybe the rathskeller beneath the old *Rathaus.*"

"Right fine place, you done good r'search, Doktor Murphy. Now, Uncle Blackie, I'll show you Great Saint Martin's and all the nice places around here, and then we'll go eat. I have an idea how we can invade that *Schloss* Zellner down the river. We can talk about it over lunch."

That's all we needed, a scheme to invade a small fortress.

11

"Whafo you do that fo?"

We had come out of St. Martin's Church, a high-vaulted Romanesque church built in the year 1000 (when Romanesque was striving, without knowing it, toward the Gothic) on the ruins of an earlier church, which in its turn was built on top of a Roman swimming pool.

"This is one of the twelve Romanesque churches you papists done built in this here city," She had begun. "They like to be torn down to make palaces for bishops and such like, cept'n the folks here 'bout done threw the bishop out of town in 1288. Then a couple hundred years later, theyz talk about tearin' them ag'in, but 'long 'bout then, like the early 1500s, the Köln stopped being a trading center and the city were right poor. Never did recover till last century. So they have these wonderful ole churches besides the dom. This here one were jest 'bout destroyed by the bombs. You can see lines on the walls whar the repairs start. It's kinda barren-like 'cause most of its inards were done blown up. You can imag'ne that, 'fore the dom, it was the first thing you seen, a-coming across the Rhine. Now I'll take ya over to Sankt Maria am Kapital, which theyz done built on top o' the Roman Capitoline temple.''

Great Saint Martin's, probably where the Arsh monastery had been, was a striking building on the outside, the result of a brave effort to push Romanesque as high into the sky as you could, but somehow hollow on the inside because it was barren and obviously so new. Yet, in a couple of hundred years, it would seem as old as the other churches, and few people would remember World War II, save as an incident in this city's incredible survival. I marveled at the dedication that insisted on restoring this church while they were rebuilding the city and the dom. Perhaps the Kölners were not a deeply religious people, perhaps they had never been, but they did care about their history and the religious buildings that had been part of it.

So we wandered through the old city, which the Kölners had reconstructed to preserve its medieval buildings with their tall slated roofs, narrow streets, and tiny alleys, and then dotted with little plazas and cafés and gardens and late-blossoming flowers and multicolored umbrellas. It was the kind of medieval town that the Disney people might have constructed—a comparison I would never make when a Kölner was present.

Then my brave nefoo bent over and kissed his lady love with considerable intensity. She had demanded an explanation, a prompt one by the tone of her voice, though not one that registered any serious protest at the event.

"Because I wanted to," he said, "and because you're so pretty and so smart and so funny and so wonderful."

"Oh," she giggled, "is that all? I thought you were a-trying to say someth'n real serious."

"Only that I love you."

This, mind you, in broad daylight under the autumn sunlight with his uncle, the Herr Bischof, watching.

The aforementioned Herr Bischof thought to himself that at the end of the day—as the Brits say—his nefoo might simply have to carry her off with the same deter-

mination that he had just displayed. This strategy, however, would be a long-term success only if we could get
to the bottom of the mystery that was Cindasue.

"Shucks," she replied to his protestation of love,
"that's nothin' new or excitin', is it, Uncle Blackie."

"Deponent," I replied, "further sayeth not."

They laughed. This time, Peter Murphy firmly took
possession of her hand.

"This here monument to papis' idolatry," she continued, as one who had recovered her voice and her self-
control, "is the church on top of the ole pag'n temple I
was tellin' y'all about. Hit's got hitself some nice stuff
and is real purty, but theyz a statute in here ya'll gotta
see."

"You mean idol, Cindasue?" I asked because a leprechaun had seized control of my mouth.

"Nossir, Mr. Preacher Man. Hit ain't no idol."

The statue in question, the Madonna of Limburg, was
quite breathtaking—a young woman carved in wood that
had been polychromed. She wore a red dress, a wide gold
and blue sash, and a white scarf and veil; her hair seemed
to be red or at least auburn, and she wore a big gold
crown that didn't bother her at all. She was apple-
cheeked and smiling at the grinning, redheaded punk in
her arm. He, in turn, was pointing at someone or some-
body in amusement. Arguably at me.

"Wow!" I said.

"He ain't pointing at you, Uncle Blackie. He a-
pointin' at me me and a-laughin' at me. And I like the
two of them so much, I say keep right on a-laughin'. It
not, no way, an idol. Hit's a lovely woman with a grand
brat that, happen I'm lucky, I may have some day or
t'other."

Peter Murphy wisely did not take up that point; instead, he said, "So we Catholics built some statues that
are idols and some that are not?"

"Long as they show real human people I can id'nt'fy
with, theyz no idols. I don't suppose she looked much
like this, did she, Uncle Blackie?"

"Insofar as she was lovely and happy and loved her son and was thoroughly human with a glint of mischief in her eye—of the sort that is not always invisible in your own eyes—she doubtless looked much like this woman. I would imagine, however, that she was shorter, her skin was darker, her hair brown or black, her clothes were not at all so rich, and she didn't wear a crown."

"Yeah, I'd still like to talk to her, which is what you Cat'lics do, ain't hit?"

"Yep," I said.

"There's another one like her over to the dom. It's in the repair shop, so I suppose they'll show it to us this afternoon."

"We will insist."

"Well, let's go down the river, Peter Murphy, lessen your poor uncle starve to death. We're a-walkin' thru some dark and narrow alleys and I don't want you a-harassin' me, ya hear?"

"Wouldn't dream of it."

But he extended his arm around her waist before we entered the narrow passages from the old city to the riverbank. Doubtless, in order to be sure of his grip, his hand slipped toward her delightful rear end. She did not squirm.

I might just as well have been on Alpha Centauri.

We emerged from the medieval network and beheld the Rhine, a radiant blue in the bright sun with multicolored tour boats and sleek, serious freight ships and barge trains slipping by in both directions. Flags of Belgium, the Netherlands, the Federal Republic, Great Britain, Canada, France, Austria, Switzerland, and even Japan flew stiffly in the breeze. No Stars and Stripes, even though we had in our midst a Yewnited States Coast Guard attaché.

"Shonuff is purty," she said.

She then conducted us along the embankment to the café of her choice, in the shadow of Great Saint Martin's, in front of a hotel that announced itself as the Rhen Hotel Saint Marin in Fishmarkt. She ordered four bratwursts, two beers, and one glass of "vine rot," patently the wine and the extra brat were for me.

"I think we oughter raid that thar *Schloss* Zellner," she began after the waiter had departed.

"How?" I demanded.

"Easy. We jest go up there on Saturday or Sunday, tell the man at the door that we hear Herr Zellner has himself a fine art collection and we'd like to look at it, happen no one minds."

"They will let us in?"

"If we ask real purty."

How could such an intelligent young woman come up with such a goofy scheme?

"Cindasue," I said, "I have no objection to looking at the *Schloss* from a safe distance, preferably from a boat on the Rhine. However, if we went any farther, the best thing that could happen to us would be that they would firmly turn us away. Even if by some improbable mistake they let us in and showed us the art, they wouldn't let us see any of the stuff Herr Zellner has had stolen for his amusement. Certainly not the shrine, should it be there, which I tend to doubt. . . ."

"You don't think it's there?" she interrupted. "I do. Where else would it be?"

For a moment, my solution came back and then faded away into the blue waters of the river.

"It's not there," I continued. "Moreover, if again through some incredible mischance, we did see it there, we would all die painful deaths, yours more hellish than ours."

She was silent for a moment.

"You really think they'd do that?"

"You know enough about people like Herr Zellner from your work to know that he's the kind that would delight in torturing people to death, especially attractive women."

She nodded somberly.

"Moreover, even if he does have it, it is unlikely to be in the *Schloss*. He knows that the federal police will be watching him closely. I very much doubt that the shrine has ever left Köln. It has been hidden here, not too far from the dom itself, until it is safe to move it out. It will be a long time before anyone is likely to display it for the amusement of himself and his friends, years perhaps, maybe even more. The satisfaction of the master thief, should there be such, will come not from looking at it but from knowing that he possesses it and no one else does.''

"Or she?'' Peter Murphy suggested.

"Arguably, though women rarely involve themselves in this sort of obsession.''

"Well, what are we going to do?'' Cindasue demanded.

"We are going over to the dom this afternoon," I said, "to talk to the men in the art workshop. Then, presumably, you and my nefoo will have your daily swim. We will next sup at this *Rathaus* place. We will proceed very carefully and take no chances. Is that clear, Cindasue McCloud?''

"Yassuh,'' she said with a sigh.

"Promise?'' I demanded.

"Promise what?''

"That you will take on no solo missions without my permission?''

She grinned.

"What about dual missions?''

"They are included.''

"I promise,'' she said dutifully.

"You, too, Peter Murphy?''

"Absolutely,'' he agreed.

I was not altogether sure that these promises would be perceived as totally binding.

The reader will note that I made no binding promises that I wouldn't do something stupid.

Which was just as well. Before the afternoon was out, I would do something very stupid.

Cindasue excused herself. Peter Murphy followed her lime-covered form as she walked into the restaurant.

"What do you think, Uncle Blackie?"

"Of her crazy scheme? I'd like to believe she's intelligent enough to realize how crazy it would be and change her mind before she tried it. Only I'm not sure of that."

"She certainly doesn't lack courage. . . . But I meant her attitude toward me."

"Patently, she's in love with you. Arguably crazy in love with you."

"What's going on, then? Why does she become frightened?"

"A fascinating question . . . We really don't know much about her, do we?"

"You mean her life before she showed up in that storm at Grand Beach?"

"She talks a lot about Stinking Creek, some of which might not be fictional. But I doubt that there is a McCloud's Holler up in the mountains. Nor does she talk much about her parents, not at all about her daddy and only about her mommy to put on the woman's lips a comment that is almost certainly fictional."

"We've never met them," Peter agreed. "She hardly ever talks about them. We don't even know whether she has brothers or sisters, do we?"

"And as far as I am aware, during the time she hung around the Murphy family, there was never any mention of going back to Stinking Creek to visit. I wonder if, when she joined the Coast Guard, she left for good."

"Could be," he said. "I never thought of her as all that mysterious, but I guess she is."

"She was," I continued, "popular with her Coast Guard colleagues at Michigan City, was she not?"

"They called her Mountain Flower and delighted in her, though I think she gave them a hard time, too."

"Almost certainly she was a success at New London; otherwise, she wouldn't be here with an early promotion. I feel confident that her superiors and colleagues respect her and enjoy her, just as we do. Yet, Peter Murphy, for all her wit and her mountain talk, who is she really? What was her life like before she left Stinking Creek? Why has she never gone back, if my supposition is correct that she has not gone back? Above all, what were her relations with her family, in particular her parents, about whom she never talks? I think the solution of the mystery of Cindasue Lou McCloud lies in Stinking Creek, just as the mystery of the missing Shrine of the Three Magi lies in Cologne.''

''You think she was a sexually abused child?''

''Perhaps, though one must consider that she seems quite affectionate, which can be incompatible with having been sexually abused.''

''Maybe she was physically abused? Beaten by her parents? Might not they have had old-fashioned notions about how to raise children?''

Peter Murphy spoke calmly, almost clinically, but his hands tightened into fits. It would not be healthy for those who had abused his love if he encountered them.

I sighed, and not a fake sigh this time, either. We humans do so many cruel, stupid, diabolical things to our defenseless offspring. It was intolerable that such an appealing little girl as Cindasue must have been should have had her life potentially ruined by idiot parents. Perhaps even devoutly religious idiot parents.

Significantly, a dark cloud temporarily obscured the sun; the Rhine (or Rhein as the locals call it) turned dull gray.

''She wears many masks, Peter Murphy, none of them unattractive. She is, one must surmise, a sophisticated young woman. Yet she would have us believe that she is a shy, diffident, if contentious, child from the hills. She compares the world to Stinking Creek, a village which, for all we know, does not even exist. She engages in her delightful Appalachian dialect and seduces us into talking the same way. Even her contentiousness is an effort to hide her inherent sweetness, which blossomed into full if transient view yesterday. . . .''

''When she talked about Grandpa Ned?''

''Precisely.''

"I noticed . . . I wanted to pick her up and carry her away. . . . Naturally, I wouldn't."

"Not at the present, in any event."

"She overwhelmed me at Grand Beach. She was pretty and smart and funny and affectionate and fascinating. Now it looks like 'fascinating' means mysterious. . . . I suppose we're all mysterious."

"Especially to our lovers," I remarked, hoping I did not sound too much like Polonius.

"I'm not about to lose her again," he said, his face furrowed into a determined frown. "I quit when she went off to New London. Now I'm not going to quit. If not this trip, next trip then. Or the one after. She will be mine eventually, I promise that."

I did not observe that when the object of such implacable resolve, was in love with the subject of the resolve the odds were heavily in favor of success. Instead, I added a warning note.

"Nonetheless, the excessive mystery around her must be dissolved and gently so."

"Gently and lovingly." Peter Murphy nodded his agreement.

Just then, the mystery woman of the hour appeared, her makeup carefully restored.

"Y'all been a-talkin' about me," she insisted. "I can tell."

"If we were, Cindasue," Peter Murphy said, his hand briefly touching her rump, "the words were only of admiration."

"Shucks." She slipped away from his touch, but not hurriedly. "Couldn't been all that many words. Not that much to admire."

She averted her eyes and bowed her head, but one could still see a smile of pleasure on her face.

"Come on, Fräulein Unterleutnant, you know better than that!"

I was not all that sure she did. But the two of us laughed and she giggled and we dug into our bratwursts.

The dark cloud faded off to the east. The river and its

embankment returned to their Technicolor splendour. Cindasue pointed out the sights across the Rhine in Köln Deutz, including the tall Lufthansa building.

"Bonn is the political capital of the country and is now ceding some of its power to Berlin, which is a big mistake, if you askin' my opinion, which no one done. Frankfurt is the financial capital, ugliest city in world. Munich is purty but plumb *boring*. This here Köln place is the cultural capital—television, books, art, music, fun. Howmsoever, sometimes the fun is pretty heavy, like that awful night club place that put you to sleep, Doktor Peter Murphy?"

"It was the Fräulein I was with that put me to sleep."

"No-count polecat," she replied, punching his arm gently. " 'Twere not. You were a-dreamin' 'bout her when you asleep."

"Arguably!" he replied. "I won't tell you what she looked like with all her clothes off."

Cindasue blushed deeply and grinned. "Hush yo mouf, chile, and eat them there bratwurst the nice man done brung us."

We did as we were commanded.

After we had polished off the *Apfelstrudel mit Sahne* (wondrously and arguably sinfully rich cream), we walked along the embankment and then turned up by the German-Roman Museum toward the dom.

We were greeted by a crowd of half-uniformed young men (red and blue jackets and sweatshirts). They carried large flags and sang militant songs. For a moment, I thought I was back in the 1930s or perhaps at the time of Hitler's first putsch in Munich. Next to me, Peter Murphy looked like he was getting ready for a fight.

"Don' pay them no 'tention," Cindasue reassured us. "Theyz jest one of them dumb sports clubs they have here'bouts. They don' mean no trouble. Scared the ole debil out of me furst time I heard 'em."

"They sound like the SS," I said, not totally reassured.

"Hit the other way 'round, Uncle Blackie. The SS sounded like them. These hyar people always been into sports clubs, kinda superannuated boy scouts. They sing and camp and play games, that sorta thing. Them heathin Nazis jest kind of appropriated it. Don't bother folk around here nohow. Nice workin'-class kids, they tell me, a-havin' a li'l fun.''

"They still give me a chill," I admitted.

"Ya look at them, and ya can tell theyz harmless."

She was right. Still, I thought, the SA and the SS probably looked harmless, too, until they put on their brown and black uniforms. Then I thought of the pep rallies at Peter Murphy's alma mater on the fringes of South Bend, Indiana, and decided I had overreacted.

"Y'all see the scaffolding 'round the tower? Theyz always repairing something up thar. Hit's slowly eroding because of pollution. Thez say that the dom will never be finished till the end of this hyar world."

The art workshop was on the lower level of the dom, an old stone expanse, whitewashed to look cheerful under intense artifical light. A half dozen older men in white technician's jackets (which Germans love) were working intensely on canvas and stone, delicately touching up or repairing slight blemishes. Frequently, they consulted computer consoles on the monitors of which a bright image of the artwork glowed. A touch of a function key zoomed in or back off the image. Canvas covers obscured other works, many of which were concentrated under medieval eaves at one end of the room, some of them on dollies for easy movement. At the opposite end, the closed door of an old-fashioned freight elevator indicated that some of the stone carvings on which the technicians were working could not simply be carried up the winding staircase on which we had descended. Conversation was in hushed whispers. No one noticed our arrival. It seemed to be almost as solemn and unwavering a place as an operating room during heart surgery.

"*Ja?*" a large man with bushy white hair and a red face demanded of us, with a half frown that could easily be replaced by a full smile.

Cindasue, charm turned on all the way, informed him

that she was Fräulein Unterleutnant McCloud and that she and her colleagues had an appointment with Herr Donatelli.

"*Ja, ja,*" he intoned as the full smile appeared. "Il Signore is in his office. I show you."

The name Nicolo Donatelli suggested a tall, aristocratic Florentine, calm, aloof, precise. In fact, Il Signore was a short, rotund, ebullient fellow whose origins could not have been any closer to Florence than Naples. His voice was just under panic level and his sweeping gestures endangered the statuettes that littered every flat space in the room. The walls were covered with excellent prints of the work of Italian painters—Were there any other?—and, as a concession to sunny Italy, there was a single slit of a window behind his desk, on which were spread blue prints several layers thick, from which one could see the patch of blue that prisoners call the sky.

He welcomed us profusely, kissed the hand of the Signorina Teniente, and dusted off three hard-backed chairs for us.

He launched into a lecture on the importance of the workshop, which, he assured us, went back to the days of the immortal Nicholas of Verdun, almost in this very place. Here the great shrine had been built, here it had been repaired many times in the last thousand years, here restored again after the bombing, here they had completely rebuilt it in the 1970s. It was terrible that it had again been stolen. He did not understand how that could have happened, but (with a monumental rise and fall of his shoulders) that was not his work. His work was to keep the art of the dom in good repair. It was, frankly, an impossible task. Everything was so old. Pollution, particularly from the breathing of all the tourists (in his tone that was a dirty word). He had urged that all the old works be retired to an air-conditioned museum that the (ugh) tourists might visit and view through transparent windows. They could make substitutes for the dom itself. Tourists were too dumb to know the difference. No one (wave of his pudgy hands) listened to him, especially the

Dompfarrer (smirk of dislike). Sometimes (light of approval in his eyes) the Signore Cardinale seemed to agree.

"Come, let me show you one of our finest pieces."

He dashed out of the office with the three of us trailing behind.

"He shonuff hog-wild," Cindasue commented, "but he cute."

"Girls always think Italian men are cute," Peter Murphy grumbled.

His lady love simply snorted.

His movements for the first time gentle and cautious, Il Signore tenderly removed a canvas cover from a polychrome statue of the Mother of Jesus, surely the one about which Cindasue had told us.

"Is she not lovely?" he demanded, like a father with a new girl child. "She is the Madonna of Milano, stolen the same time these barbarians stole the shrine. She disappeared in the beginning of the thirteenth century, but this replacement was made in 1280. Even replacements become old after a time."

The young woman, in robes of dark red and blue and gold, with a crown and a halo of stars attached to her, was lovely. Small wonder that the bare-chested (and crowned) child was reaching for her face with his right hand while his left hand held the world like it was a twelve-inch softball (in which we Chicagoans do not believe, taking it as only somewhat less than gospel truth that a true softball is the sixteen-inch Chicago softball).

"She's gorgeous," the idolatrous Lieutenant McCloud said softly, her wicked green eyes aglow with admiration. "I'd like to have known her."

"One notes," I said somewhat irreverently, "that in her right arm there is a scepter as well as a long rosary. The scepter might well serve as a dangerous weapon should anyone threaten that adored son."

"He done died jest the same."

Peter Murphy took her hand.

"The colors we can restore," Il Signore whispered, as

if anything louder would profane this glorious image. "We do that frequently, more often with each passing year. See the image we have made from a medieval painting?" He flipped on a computer switch. The Milan Madonna came to life on its screen.

"We may not know exactly what pigments the original creators used, but we can imitate them better than any of the previous clumsy attempts. However, the problem is the wood itself. Eight hundred years is a long time for a tree trunk. The wood rots slowly, but less slowly now with millions of tourists breathing their foul air on her."

I thought of the ivory Madonna in my study back at the Chicago Dom. The ivory Madonna was a good deal more flippant and disrespectful than this one or her sister over in Sankt Maria am Kapital.

"If I understand you correctly, Signore, you think that all the works of art in the dom should be transferred to a museum and replacements placed in the dom?"

"But of course! We will have to do that eventually in any case, perhaps in as little as ten years for some of them. This poor young woman and her healthy child will survive only one more restoration, perhaps two. Then, alas, she will be fit only for the dustbin."

"You would tell the, ah, tourists about this change?"

"Naturally," he replied, covering the Milan Madonna with loving care. "There is no reason to deceive them. We tell the whole truth: To preserve the originals, we had had to place them in a special museum, which they may visit if they wish. Most will not wish. What difference does it make to them if they see the original or a substitute, especially a good substitute that only an expert could distinguish from the original? All they want is a nice postcard to send home. That we can print for them from our computers, *nonne vero?*"

As he jumped from language to language it turned out that Cindasue could also speak fluent Italian—Milanese Italian at that—*La Lingua Toscana in Bocca Romana*. There seemed to be no limit to the young woman's talents.

"Indeed," I said.

"*Revera,*" Cindasue informed Donatelli.

"The Dompfarrer," he said as he led us back to his office, "will not hear of it. He does not believe that God will permit our treasures to deteriorate completely. . . . As if God had nothing else to do but to work miracles to protect the treasures from his own stupidity."

Inside the office, I took a closer look at what I had thought were prints. In fact, they were paintings. Imitations, all right, but excellent ones. If I had not known as a matter of fact and personal observation that Mona Lisa was in the Louvre, I would have thought she was on the wall here underneath the Kölner Dom.

Interesting.

"You feel that the imitation of the shrine up in the nave would fool almost everyone except the experts?"

"But of course. Even the experts would need very precise magnifiers to be sure. You see, Monsignore, we are not as gifted as my namesake from Verdun. We could not have conceived such a magnificent work. Nor probably could we even have served on his staff of assistants. But we have the skills and the tools to reproduce his masterpiece in a twentieth of the time it took him."

"Impressive. . . . So you are unworried about the theft of the real shrine."

"I deplore it," he said waving his hands. "It is unconscionable! It is one of the great treasures of the history of human art and a great monument to religious faith. It can never be replaced. Still, our little substitute up there serves its purpose well. It could serve that purpose for a long time."

"If the thieves wanted to conceal their crime, could they not have moved the surrogate into place?"

"Perhaps they would have if they could have opened the safe. However, as far as we know, only Signore Cardinale and the Dompfarrer know the combination. . . . The Dompfarrer is a fool! He thinks that his security system is foolproof. *Stupido!* Many men have keys to the sacristy. Many others know the combination for the alarm system. Ha! I myself know it! Anyone could have come into the duomo that night and taken the shrine! I myself have told him many times, and he dismisses me with a sneer! He is a Fascist pig! We Italians, unlike these stupid Germans, know a Fascist when we see one!''

So that made it easier for a lot of you to vote for the Neo-Fascist party in the last election?

''Do I understand you correctly, Signore,'' Cindasue zeroed in on his most crucial remark, ''that only the cardinal and pastor man know the combination to the safe?''

''That's what he says! Everything else is so sloppy here that many may know that, too. I tell them that they should have alarms throughout the cathedral, that they should be activated and turned off from somewhere besides the sacristy, and, above all, that they should have monitors everywhere that a guard could watch from a central location. But there is no guard, except at the door of the parsonage, and he sleeps all night. He could earn his living by watching the monitors!''

Not unlike the system we have at my Chicago Dom.

''He is a fool,'' Nicolo Donatelli raved on. ''As well as not being a real man. The Signore Cardinale should look at what happens in the parsonage . . . not the old pilot, but the others!''

''You're suggesting a lavender parsonage, Signore?'' Cindasue inquired.

''I suggest *nothing*! I know what I see with my own eyes! I will say no more!''

The man trembled with rage and fear as he blurted his half-denial.

''Could you make any suggestions to us about who took the shrine or where it is?'' I asked.

''If you ask me—and you did—I would say that the Dompfarrer and his friends would know. They will do anything to destroy Signore Cardinale and Signore Herrn Bundeskanzler, too.''

''Neo-Nazis?'' Peter Murphy finally got a chance to say something.

Donatelli rolled his eyes, lifted them heavenward, put

his finger over his mouth, and said, "Not too different."

"If it looks like a duck," Peter Murphy said, lifting a phrase out of the American political past, "and walks like a duck and talks like a duck, pretty fair chance it is a duck."

"Si! Si! Si!" Donatelli exploded in approval and clapped his hands.

Fräulein Unterleutnant, in a rare lapse of self-control, jest plain giggled at her lover's comment.

"If you want to know about the duck, you should talk to Frau Strauss," he said winking mysteriously. "She was the secretary here for many years, a lovely and competent woman. The Dompfarrer fired her because he thought she knew too much. She could tell you many things."

"Strauss?" Cindasue asked.

"Si, die Frau vom Franz Peter Strauss. She is called Helena. They live in Ahrweiler. He is the only Franz Strauss in Ahrweiler."

"Benissimo, Signore, and *grazie."*

Who, I asked myself, *is in charge of this investigation?*

12

"Well, that was interesting," Peter Murphy observed as we walked out into the sunlight, "wasn't it?"

"Uncle Blackie," Cindasue asked, putting on her sunglasses, "you notice them paintin's in that there room?"

"Oh, yes. Fakes, patently, because I have seen the real ones in other museums, not excluding that barrel-head Madonna, which is from the Uffici in Florence. Howsoever, Teniente, they are very good fakes. It takes considerable skill and not a little talent to make fakes that good."

"We'd have a hard time finding out what is real inside the dom," Peter Murphy observed, "and what isn't real."

"Do you believe that he really can't take and open that there safe down there nohow?"

"He is a charmer, Cindasue, but I don't think any of us would necessarily believe a word he says. On the other hand, many of his comments have an inherent plausibility. He has created more leads for us, but he also has muddied the waters."

"Do you think he has a business in fakes on the side?"

"I would not doubt it, Peter Muphy. The temptation

to do so would be very great in his circumstances.''

"Everything in the dom could be fake?''

"Arguably. Though I think he would be very cautious. He would have to deceive the bishop, the cardinal, and his own staff.''

"Y'all wait right here in this spot, front of the dom, while I take and call this here Frau Helena Strauss.''

She strode with competent military efficiency, a picture of determination and ability. The attractiveness of the rear view was not thereby diminished.

I hate to admit such a fault in a member of the clan, but I believe that Peter Murphy whistled softly in admiration. I felt it would be bootless to reprimand him.

She flipped open the tiny cellular phone that she had secreted in her purse and made several calls.

"She shonuff do take charge, don't she?'' Peter Murphy remarked admiringly.

"It saves us a lot of work. Besides, are any of the womenfolk of our family any different?''

"She'd fit in well, that's for sure. That's why they're all conspiring against me.''

"Indeed!''

"You don't think I had any choice about coming along with you on this trip, do you Uncle Blackie?''

"I do not recall you raising any fuss about the matter.''

"Not hardly,'' he said with a happy smile. "Gave me an excuse to do what I wanted to do. She sure real forw'rd, ain't she now?''

"And yet very frightened.''

He nodded solemnly. Then she came rushing back, under full sail.

" 'Twar shonuff easy. The woman, who sounds very nice on the phone, said she happy to talk. Sounds like she done meant it. None of your usual German formal caution. I was like to take you up there tomorrow anaw'y. Happen you want some ice cream, Uncle Blackie?''

"It is not beyond conceivability that I might.''

"Wouldn't be healthy, though, to put off a chocolate fix for you chocolate freaks till then. Lessen you don't want to, we could amble down the river a pace and a-visiti'n a chocolate museum.''

"A chocolate museum?" we both exclaimed.

"Shonuff!"

There is indeed a chocolate museum in Köln, on an island in the river a brief walk south of the dom. It looks something like a boat and celebrates a Köln chocolate company. It is long on technology and short on participation. You see how chocolate is transformed from the picking of the beans to the placement of the candy in boxes. In an American chocolate museum, should there be one, you'd actually pick the bean yourself, mix the chocolate and pack your own box. In the hypothesized American museum, you could probably make off with several boxes free. However, the German style was to give us all a piece of chocolate and direct us to the store. I had forgotten to bring my wallet (still on jet lag, I fear, despite the benign influence of the high-intensity light). I pointed this out to Peter Murphy who, at my direction, purchased several boxes and a dozen or so bars.

"Uncle Blackie," he said with unpardonable lack of respect though complete historical accuracy, "you forget your wallet even when you are in Chicago."

I declined to respond.

The chocolate was quite good, though there is no such thing as bad chocolate. Moreover, one can dip a small cookie into a chocolate well and nibble on it while at the same time admiring through a vast glass window the dom. Pure *Kölnsch.*

"Thez got two adjectives here," Cindasue explained. *"Kölnsch* and *Kölner.* The first hit be dialect and they use it for the beer and the water. The second is more formal and they use it for banks and the dom. You uns done never, nohow, call it Kölnsch Dom or they a-putting you in jail."

We strolled back down the river to the dom and then turned on the Hohestrasse, which was the main street of the old Roman city and now a pedestrian mall. At the

Minoritenstrasse we turned again and came to the Franciscan church.

"This hyar fella, Scotus, buried hyar," she informed us, "thez say he Arsh. Purty place."

"They haven't restored it much," Peter Murphy added.

"How you know? You never been thar!"

Inside, we all knelt to pray. I lit a candle in honor of John Dunne the Irishman and bought a couple of postcards to send to a few theologians. Cindasue lit a candle, too. Both my nefoo and I had sense enough not to ask for what she was praying.

There was one more obligatory stop before we returned to the hotel. We crossed an elegant-looking mall on which, unlike the late and hardly lamented State Street Mall, throngs milled around, not all of them tourists, and then turned on to something called the Glockengasse. The reason was obvious: on the hour, a glockenspiel on top of a formal-looking house chimed out a vaguely familiar old German song.

"This hyar place," our girl guide informed us, "called House Number 4711 cuz Napoleon and his gang of polecats abolished street names when they hyar. It didn't work. But 4711 and eau de Cologne became synonymous. Theyz make that smelly water in thar."

"Eau de Cologne?" Peter Murphy asked.

"Yassuh, they done call hit Kölnsch Wasser, and you oughter buy some for your mammy and your sisters and for Aunty Helen."

"Yessum," he agreed.

"And, Uncle Blackie, you oughter buy some for your sisters."

"And that lovely young woman who answers the bell at the rectory," Peter Murphy added as we walked into shop."

"Who that?" Cindasue demanded with a mock frown.

"Megan, of which there are four. Also other parish personnel. I would be in grave disrepute if I failed to do that."

That thar smelly water was flowing from a fountain inside the store, the ultimate in a high-end quality shop. Cindasue told us that its origins were in an Italian formula made in France for health purposes. Folks drank it so they'd be a-feeling better.

"Too expensive to drink now," Peter Murphy muttered as he signed his credit card bill.

"At the end of the day," I told him, "tally up the expenses, and I'll have the sum transferred to your bank account."

"At the end of the trip," Cindasue warned.

They both giggled. Total lack of respect.

The aforementioned nefoo bought his lady love a very large bottle of the smelly water.

"Peter Murphy, suh, ya shouldn' oughter do that."

Outright falsehood, in my judgment.

"You should never say anything like that, Cindasue. Better that you say, 'Thank you very much, Pete Murphy. You're a dear sweet boy and I love you.' "

Her wicked green eyes twitched for a moment.

"Thank you very much, Pete Murphy. You're a dear sweet boy and I love you."

Whereupon she kissed him. I had lost track of the number of times that had occurred during the day.

We then strolled back to our hotel.

"Uncle Blackie," she said, reverting to hill talk, "you notice that thar shade that's a-followin' us?"

"Jeans and a white shirt and a goatee?"

"Yup!"

"He's not all that swift a shade, Cindasue."

"Who could he be?" my nefoo asked.

"He could represent almost any of the parties to whom we have talked in the last two days. I may ask our friend Herr Obersuperintendent Schulteis to ascertain who he is."

"Happ'n he's not one of thars."

He disappeared into the crowd when we arrived at the hotel. He would, however, be back. An amateur. There might be professionals out there, too, that neither Cindasue nor I had spotted.

In the parking lot under the hotel, Cindasue removed a small sports bag, which I assumed contained her swim clothes, and a neatly wrapped package.

"We'uns gonna go a-swimmin' agin, Uncle Blackie. You probably need a bit of a nap."

I had another idea, a foolish one as it turned out. However, since I had absolutely forbidden my young charges to engage in foolish behavior, I had no intention of telling them about it.

"And, Uncle Blackie," the Fräulein Unterleutnant continued, "here's a present for you."

I adore presents. They represent the Surprise, which I take to be the Ultimate Present. I tore off the wrapping with eager fingers.

My two companions giggled again.

Three German-style clerical shirts, like the kind the Herr Kardinal had worn. One of them was even edged with a thin touch of episcopal purple.

"Cindasue McCloud," I said, "I must grant you a special indult in this matter. Ordinarily, only women in my family are permitted to indulge in the patent folly of endeavoring to make me look chic."

"Ya oughter wear one of those when I say so, like when we agoin' to the cardinal's house for Mass and supper tomorrow night."

"Ah," I said, pondering the shirts, which patently were the proper size. "I had not heard of this engagement."

" 'Cuz I haven't told you yet. The message was at my office when I called them after talking to Helena Strauss. Now, ya oughter wear one of them funny lookin' things when we interviewin' people. It'll impress them a heap."

"Better that I seem invisibile and innocuous to them."

"Uncle Blackie," my nefoo informed me, "you haven't been invisible or innocuous for twenty years."

They both giggled.

Palpably they were wrong. However, on this mission,

I had better honor the wishes of the Fräulein Unterleutnant, who was of course opposed to every manner of
papist superstition and idolatry!

They went to Peter Murphy's room to change for their
swim. I went to my room to check my E-mail. There
were two messages from Chicago, one from Milord Cardinal and the other from Milady Mary Kathleen. Both
were succinct and identical:

Well?

I replied first to the cardinal:

*We progress the old-fashioned way, slowly and care-
fully. I fully anticipate success.*

Good enough for him!

And then to the good Dr. Murphy (the kind of doctor,
as she says in an effort to put me and her son in our
proper places, that does good for people):

*We are not without progress. The young woman has
chosen to act like she is already one of the family by
dictating my attire, as foolish as that effort may be. I
believe she and your son are swimming together in the
hotel pool, adequately attired, I presume, though in Europe you never can tell.*

Good enough for her, too.

Then I sent a note to Mike ''The Cop'' (Mcasey
2400@aol.com) in which I asked him what I took to be
a pertinent question.

Then I put on a ''disguise'': brown slacks, a gray sport
shirt, and a blue windbreaker. I also removed my glasses,
which, since I acquired unifocal contact lenses, had become unnecessary, save for image purposes. Finally, I
donned a somewhat rakish beret. In the mirror I was absolutely unrecognizable.

It would be unwise of me to permit the lieutenant junior grade to know of the secret of my contact lenses.

I then made a phone call, noted an address on a sheet of hotel paper, and jammed that into my pocket. I even remembered to put my wallet in my pocket and enough change to pay for a tram ticket. I added to my other pocket an elaborate map of Köln.

I then departed on my trip of folly.

The odd thing about it was that I expected to find nothing.

At the desk in the hotel, I inquired about a tram to Rodenkirchen upriver from Köln. The pleasant and charming young woman drew me a map and wrote out instructions, presumably understanding that I could never remember them or even read them in my own handwriting. She also told me what tickets I should purchase at the tram kiosk outside the hotel.

Remarkably, I was able to make the trip without incident, a pleasant enough ride through what I would have called the "South Side" of Köln. Rodenkirchen, it turned out, was a suburb not unlike Evanston, though when I neared the Rhine, the large villas reminded me more of Winnetka. They were, I thought, perilously close to the river when it was high. Water gates along the embankment suggested that the floods did, in fact, frequently threaten these homes. One could look downriver and see the bridges of Köln—Rodenkirchen had its own bridge— and the spire of the dom. On the upriver fringe of the town, I came upon the Köln villa of Herr Heinz Zellner.

I had, of course, carefully watched behind me for any trace of the shade. Either he was waiting at the hotel or had been deceived by my ingenious disguise.

I had forbidden Cindasue to undertake her raid on the *Schloss*, but I did not preclude investigation of his intown home.

It was an imposing if unattractive place on the ridge above the embankment with a massive wall around it and an ominous-looking water gate, a stone Alpine house with eaves and sloping roofs and elaborate gables. The man may have great taste in art, but this was strictly nineteenth-century romantic kitsch.

I wandered around the wall. There was no sign of activity and no sign of security systems. Unfortunately, the only place where I could see inside the wall was the fancy wrought-iron gate, which looked like a contrivance out of *Doctor Faustus,* a gate perhaps to the antechamber of Hell.

I peeked through the gate and noted with considerable interest a dark green van parked in the driveway.

Wasn't that interesting?

I examined the gate carefully. It was certainly not wired. Presumably, Herr Zellner kept nothing valuable in his town house. Probably never spent the night there. Or if he did, he would have a phalanx of guards to protect him from various left-wing groups that might desire to take actions in the name of the "people."

I watched the house carefully for some moment. There was no sign of human presence. I pondered the possibility of scaling the wall. It would put my very life in peril for what was a minor matter. Perhaps the gate?

Not a chance. I would certainly impale myself on one of its spikes.

I opened the latch on the gate. Nothing happened. I pushed the gate gently. Astonishingly, it swung open. No alarms, no guard dogs, no black-clad gunmen with Uzis. I pushed it all the way open. Still no sign of resistance.

I walked through the open gate.

Nothing happened.

Technically, I was not breaking and entering. I had not broken anything and as yet I had not entered anything, except a big, tree-filled front yard.

I closed the gate carefully, leaving it ajar in case I had to make a hurried exit.

My first stop was the dark green van.

I cautiously tested the back door of the van. It was open. For a master criminal, this was inexplicably careless. Perhaps he was arrogant enough to have become overconfident. No one except a madman, he may have thought, would be crazy enough to enter the yard of Herr Heinz Zellner. Arguably he was right.

I eased the door open far enough that I could inspect the inside of the van. Nothing in it except a pile of canvas covers like those in the art workshop beneath the dom.

Indeed.

Moreover, the van was permeated by the smell of musty paint, yet the covers bore no trace of it. It was hardly a truck for painters and decorators.

I closed the door and pondered the general situation. Would this be enough to unleash Ernst Schulteis's federal cops?

Maybe.

Yet I should still poke around a little more and see what else I might find.

Madness, you say?

I won't argue with that.

So, flitting from tree to tree like a teenage gumshoe, I examined the premises. The garage was locked, as were all the doors I investigated. However, no alarms went off when I pulled at the doors. I slipped around the house and looked through each ground-floor window.

All I saw through slight openings in the drapes was heavy furniture, dark drapes, and somber paintings of political leaders who clearly antedated the present century, though one of them might have been of the late Kaiser. No Nazis.

I pondered the possible penalties for breaking in. I have on occasion picked locks, though always in a virtuous cause.

However, a team of benign and determined angels prevented me from engaging in that folly.

I decided that this was the time to redeploy my forces.

That decision, alas, was a bit tardy because at that point, the first Rottweiler appeared. He was very large, very powerful, very determined, and very angry. His mouth was open and his powerful teeth were covered with froth.

There was not even time to say an Act of Contrition.

Instinct forced me back on my angry dog response.

I held out my hand, palm up, and said, ''nice doggy,'' though I assumed he could not speak English.

He stopped abruptly and glared at me, not sure what was going on.

''Good doggy,'' I said.

I held my hand closer to him.

He sat down and licked the hand.

I patted his head.

''Real nice doggy.''

He wagged his tail enthusiastically and slobbered over my hand.

Then his mate appeared. She seemed even more angry than he had been.

''Nice girl,'' I said and held out my hand.

She slid to a stop and growled. She didn't like what was going on.

Yet in a moment, she was wagging her tail and slobbering over me, too.

Oh, yes, there was a God in heaven who looked after mad dogs, Englishmen, and Blackie Ryan.

Then the two of them cavorted around playfully, showing off for me. They rolled over on their backs, chased one another, and returned to me for pats of approval.

I bestowed these enthusiastically and told them ''nice boy'' and ''good girl.''

Perhaps they did speak English.

I assumed that there was someone inside the house who had released them. I ought to redeploy with considerable haste.

Patting them both affectionately, I eased my way toward the gate. They accompanied me with friendly docility.

''Good-bye, nice boy, nice girl,'' I said as I closed the gate and flicked the latch into place.

Immediately they pulled out of the influence of whatever spell I had put on them. They attacked the gate with enraged vehemence. They barked, they howled, they ranted, they bared their ferocious teeth.

I lamented the fact that humankind could change such nice doggies into fanged monsters. Nonetheless, I redeployed down the street and around the corner as quickly as my shaking legs could carry me.

I plunged ahead aimlessly until I came upon a confectionery shop on a little platz near the center of the town. I fell into a chair at an outside table and ordered in broken German a dish of chocolate ice cream *mit Sahne,* holding up three fingers to indicate that yes indeed I wanted *drei* scoops of ice cream.

"Mit Sahne?" the woman asked in astonishment.

"Ja, ja! Mit Sahne!"

No one seemed to follow me. Perhaps a solitary housekeeper had unleashed the dogs, but had been reluctant to leave the premises. Perhaps my picture was on a tape inside the house, but I had seen no cameras on the outside. Apparently, mutt and mutta were the only security mechanisms. Either there was nothing worth stealing or Herr Zellner was confident that no one would dare intrude on his privacy.

In any case, I put on my windowpane glasses, removed my beret, and turned my windbreaker inside out so that it was now red instead of blue.

Did mutt and mutta—nice boy, nice girl—speak English? That was highly unlikely. Apparently, whatever about me charmed dogs, even Rottweilers, had nothing to do with the content of my remarks.

"You're no Saint Francis of Assisi, Punk," my sister Eileen Ryan Kane had once remarked after seeing a performance like this at Grand Beach when a lab attempted to knock me over, not because of malice but because of exuberant delight at finding yet another human who, she thought, wanted to play.

"You eat too much to be Saint Frances," she added. "What do you do to them?"

"Charm them. Patently."

Whatever it was, I thanked the deity and the team of angels that was usually assigned to me when I did stupid things for sustaining the charm in the most awkward of circumstances.

As I finished my ice cream and tea, I realized that I had to restructure my orientation, that is, find out where in the world I was and how I was to get back to the Hapsburgerring. I removed my map, studied it intently, realized that I had it upside down, turned it over, and finally found Rodenkirchen. It was impossible to determine from the map where the *Platz* was or how I would get to the tram stop from there.

As I was struggling with this insurmountable problem, two teenage women, no older than fifteen, watched me stealthily.

"You are American?" one of them asked politely.

"You are lost?" the other inquired with equal politeness.

Yes to both questions.

"Where do you want to go?"

"Can we lead you there?"

"Is our English correct?"

I told them that I wanted to find the tram for the *Hauptbahnhof* (where I would change for the tram to our hotel), that they could certainly lead me to the tram stop, that their English was very good indeed, and that the angels must have sent them to rescue me.

They listened solemnly until I got to angels and then, as their kind are wont to do, giggled.

There was some reason to giggle, as it turned out. The tram stop was right around the corner.

I was not, therefore, lost. The problem had been that I did not know I was not lost.

We talked about rock and roll until the tram came. From my work with others of their age at the Chicago Dom, I had at least some semblance of what was required to sustain the conversation.

I thanked my angel twosome for their kindness and praised their city as the most friendly city in the world besides my native Chicago (I did not add Dublin because that would have confused matters), rewarded them with candy bars that I happened to have in the pocket of my windbreaker. They accepted the gifts with solemn nods of their heads and wished me *"Auf Wiedersehen, Herr Pfarrer"* as I boarded the tram. I must have smelled like a priest, whatever that smell might be.

I asked Herself to take good care of them for me in gratitude for their generosity.

The ride back to the hotel was uneventful, though a layer of clouds had spread over the *Stadt* and the river. North Atlantic weather at last returns. Slowly, I recovered my serenity or what in my case passes for serenity.

As luck would have it—or as providence ordained— the third of my trinity of magic occurred on the tram. A young mother with a squirming boy child sat down next to me. The brat stared at me rudely. I made a face at him. He grinned and gurgled. I made another face. He squirmed out of his mother's lap and jumped into mine.

"Hans!" his mother protested feebly.

I smiled to assure her that it was all right, indeed to be expected. He curled up in my arms and promptly went to sleep. His mother sighed in a mix of exasperation and pride and murmured something in German that might have been the equivalent of "I don't know what he will do next."

He awoke as we approached the stop next to the main station, ignored me, and eagerly stretched out his arms for his mother. She grabbed him as though she wanted to be sure that he had not rejected her completely. For a moment of contented peace, it was a Madonna and Child picture.

"Danke," she said to me with a radiant smile.

"Bitte," I replied in the tone of one who did this sort of thing every day.

I wondered what would happen on that inevitable day when a brat decided that she (more likely) wanted to go home with me instead of Mama.

Back in my room, I promptly called my good friend, Ernst Schulteis.

"Schulteis," he sighed into the phone.

"Father Ryan."

"*Ja, ja,* Blackie, *wie geht's?*"

"If some of your agents would wish to examine a dark green van next to Herr Zellner's Swiss bungalow out in Rodenkirchen, they might find inside it evidence that some work of art has been in it recently."

"*Ja?*" he said, instantly alert.

"This might give you some reason to search the house, and that, in turn, some reason to justify a search of the *Schloss* up the river."

"*Ja?*" he murmured thoughtfully.

"*Ja,*" I replied.

"You say a dark green van?"

"Precisely."

"*Very* interesting. I will consider what you have said *very* carefully."

"Also, should any of your merry men venture out to Rodenkirchen, they should be advised that there are two fairly serious Rottweilers out there that they must deal with."

There was silence for a moment.

He was certainly trying to figure out how I had ascertained these facts.

He did not ask. He did not want to know.

Wise man.

"We can tranquilize them easily," he said evenly.

"They are in fact rather nice dogs once they calm down."

Again, silence.

"*Ja, ja,* Blackie. I will let you know what might turn up. *Danke.*"

"*Bitte.*"

Now it was time for me to avail myself of a hasty shower and join the two young lovers for supper at the rathskeller as I had promised. I felt no obligation to tell them how I had violated my own rules.

13

Peter

"Law, this hog-killin'est whirlpool in whole wide worl'," Cindasue informed me as she snuggled closer to me. "I want this here thin' for the rest of my life."

I figured from the context that "hog-killin'est" was a superlative—something like "the best." She never did explain what any of her funny words meant. I was supposed to pick it up from the context. "Law," meant the Lord, whom she was praising for the whirlpool.

Part of the fun in this green-eyed imp was figuring out what she was talking about.

Would it pall on me through the years?

I very much doubted it.

"You mean the whirlpool or me?" I asked.

"The whirlpool, natch'rly. . . . Ah can always find a jasper man to be a-huggin' me in the pool."

"Not as good a hugger as I am."

She looked up at me and laughed.

"Don' know 'bout that," as she snuggled yet closer to me. "You ain't no hound dog, though. I sure do feel comfortable in them arms of yours."

"I hope you don't misunderstand what I mean: I want to take care of you forever."

"I reckon I know what you a-saying. It sounds right nice. Everyone needs someone elst to take care of them."

"Cindasue . . ."

"Yassuh?"

"Do you ever go back to Stinking Creek?"

She stiffened in my arms.

"Why for you ask that for?"

"I never hear you say anything about it save in the past. Don't you have friends and even family there?"

She pulled away from me and covered her chest with hear arms, though the top of her bikini was securely in place.

"I got me shet out of that place and I ain't never a-going back, ya hear?"

"I do."

"I don't wanna talk about hit."

"I thought you liked it."

"I did once," she said. "I don't anymore."

No more mountain talk. Now all radio standard English.

"Why not?"

"I said that I don't want to talk about it."

"I heard you, Cindasue. I won't press it now, but we'll have to talk about it sometime. And about your family, too."

"No. Never."

"I see."

Which I didn't.

She glared at me and then slipped back into hill talk for a moment.

"Why for you jarrin' and mouthin' at me about it?"

"Because I love you."

"That's what you *say*."

"You know it's true. You know that I mean it."

"Hmmf," she snorted and shivered despite the warmth of the whirlpool.

She continued to glare. Then she burst into tears and threw herself back into my arms.

"Pete Murphy, you darling man, I know we will have

to talk about Stinking Creek and a lot of other things. Not this minute, though.''

I considered my response. I almost insisted that we had to talk about it this minute. Dumb idea.

''Fair enough . . . Before Uncle Blackie and I go home?''

She nodded her head and laid her face on my chest.

''Shonuff.''

''Good.''

''I have to get all my ducks lined up before I try to talk.''

''All right.''

''Promise me one thing?''

''What would that be?''

''You won't hate me when I do?''

''Cindasue, I can become angry at you, but I would never hate you.''

''My head tells me that. Always has. My heart is afraid.''

''I promise.''

''I believe your promise.''

A peaceful minute passed.

Then she bounded out of the whirlpool and jumped into the swimming pool.

''You jest done get too intimate in that thar thing. Oughter cool yourself off.''

I didn't know whether I had won or lost that encounter. At least we had put the issue on the table. I would not let her take it off.

14

Cindasue

Oh, Lawdy, theyz jest done plumb figur'd me out. It's that preacher man. He sees ev'rything.

This hyar Peter Murphy fella is a-closin' in on me. He real shonuff relentless. I aint goin' get away from him.

That makes me like to feel wonderful. I'm goin' have to tell him all about me.

I wanna and I don't wanna.

I have to tell him the whole thing.

I never do that.

He'll be a-makin' me.

If I want him, I'll have to do it.

And I do want him. Oh, God, you know that I want him. I'm tired of playing this silly game with him. I want to stop fending him off every time he gets too close to me.

He's in there taking his shower now, while I'm supposed to be reading his dissertation.

Just happened to bring it along, he says.

Yeah, and chickens have lips.

I want to take off my robe and my swimsuit and run into the shower and hold him in my arms and blurt it all out.

But I can't and I won't. Not today, anyway.

This dissertation shonuff is bright. He's one smart man. I can't hide from him forever.

And I don't want to.

Help me, God, please help me.

And don't You go a-tellin' me that you sent that durn preacher man along to help!

I know You did, drat hit.

— 15 —

Blackie Again

I did not dress in my clerical shirt, Germanic style, because I had not been so instructed by Cindasue. Moreover, I did not think either American or Germanic clerical dress would be appropriate in a rathskeller. So I settled for a presentably pressed gray sport shirt. I did concede a point to propriety (and to Cindasue) by donning my black suit jacket.

I flipped on my OmniBook to see if anyone on the other side of the ocean wanted to communicate with me. There was a message from the cathedral rectory.

Bishop Blackie,

Don't worry about anything. The parish is in great shape. We won't let any mistakes happen. It's a lot more peaceful here when you're on vacation. Have a nice time in Germany or wherever you are. Cologne is the place where they make that wonderful cologne, isn't it? Don't forget to bring back some for us.

The Megans

All four of them had conspired to send the message. I pondered a moment.

Megans,

The suggested purchase has already been made. They call this city Köln but they call the water eau de Cologne. On the other hand, the label on the vials I will return with—God and the angels reminding me—is called Kölnisch Wasser. Don't ask me why.

During your reign at the cathedral, please refrain from removing the building to the parking lot across the street.

Father Blackie

The second message was from Mike "The Cop." It was what I thought it might be. Quick work. I printed it out on hotel letterhead using my portable printer, smaller and lighter than a carton of cigarettes—and infinitely less deadly. I then stuffed the printout in my jacket pocket and descended to the lobby where Peter Murphy was sipping from a cup of tea. Wisely, he had ordered a pot and a second cup and some cookies. Tea is at its best when cookies have been dunked into it. Peter Murphy poured me a cup of tea.

He had shaved and was dressed like a young commodity broker, blue blazer and gray slacks. No tie, however.

"She insisted that I take the first shower. Said she wanted to read the dissertation."

"Ah . . . she gave it her *nihil obstat?*"

"She said it was plumb intelligent, that I had spent too much time in the shower, and that she hoped I had taken a cold shower. She was grinning when she said it, however."

"And you replied that she was the one who needed the cold shower?"

"Something like that . . . that thar gal, she jest pumb forward, bold as brass."

"I wouldn't doubt it."

"I asked her if she ever went home. She said that she has not returned to Stinking Creek since she left it and never will. Wouldn't tell me why."

"Naturally, you asked her why."

"She refused to talk about it. We had a bit of a spat in the whirlpool. Then she admitted that we had to talk about it. Said she would, but not today. Before you and I went home."

"I should hope so."

"She's scared that I won't love her anymore when she tells me her story."

"You assured her that such a prediction was highly unlikely to be accurate."

"I said it wouldn't happen. Couldn't happen."

"And she replied?"

He signaled the waiter, a gentleman of Turkish origin, I suspect, for more cookies.

"She said she believed me, but she was still scared."

"Most unusual."

"What's going on, Uncle Blackie?"

"Patently, there is some skeleton in the family closet of which she is mightily ashamed. Yet it does not affect either her innocence or charm."

"She's tormented by something, Uncle Blackie."

"Oh yes."

I gave him the printout from Mike "The Cop." He read it aloud.

Blackie, I checked with the attorney general of West Virginia. There is no city, town, village, or hamlet in the state named Stinking Creek. Not even a "crossing," whatever that is. Stay out of trouble. Annie sends her love and the same message. Mike.

"Huh," Peter Murphy grunted as he stared at the page. "This is sure enough weird."

"You must pursue her, Peter Murphy, like God pursues us, implacably but tenderly."

"I'm trying, but God doesn't want us the way I want Cindasue."

"Arguably more so."

He glanced up from the paper and looked at me.

"God is probably more restrained than I am."

"Arguably less."

"That's fascinating theology, Uncle Blackie."

"Merely scripture, properly understood."

At that point, the subject of the discussion bounced around the corner from the elevators.

"My land, you-uns are plumb gussied up. Happen I known that I'd brung along another dress and left it in your room, Peter Murphy."

"You look gorgeous, Cindasue," he said, touching her face. "You could bring along all you need and stay in my room."

"Preacher Man, you make that there bodacious polecat nefoo of yourn stop a-talking suggestive remarks."

"That exceeds my power."

"I'd have another bed moved in," my nefoo assured her, stretching his arm around her tiny waist.

"Lotta good that would do. . . . Come 'long, now, y'all, we have time for a bit of chamber music before supper. So let's traipsy over to that there Heinrich-Böll-Platz and listen to this here Mozart man."

The Heinrich-Böll-Platz was behind the Roman-German museum in the shadow of the dom. It was a combination of three concrete museums with slanted roofs to gather in the natural light. It stood, looking up at the dom as it were, in modernistic defiance. No doubt which would last longer. In the basement of one of the museums was Philharmonic Hall, to which we descended. Doubtless because of Cindasue's repeated admonition that we walk faster, we made it just before the sextet appeared on the stage. The hall could contain no more than two hundred people, a nice-sized crowd for chamber music. The atmosphere was nowhere near as intimate or romantic, however, as the chamber music room at Orchestra Hall. That fact did not prevent my two companions holding each other's hands and leaning very close together as the room filled with Mozart, whose music was almost as bewitching as Cindasue's eyes.

I confess that I listened to Wolfgang Amadeus with only one ear. The other was tuned to my thoughts about what Ernst Schulteis would do with my information. It was inconceivable that he would not send his people out to inspect the van and the house. Did they need search warrants to do that?

Possibly.

But, being cops, they would have the means to find out what was going on upriver that would not alert any of Herr Zellner's influential friends.

Would our friend Ernie, as I decided I would henceforth call him, then go to the Herrn Bundeskanzler and demand permission to search the *Schloss?* If he moved quickly enough, he might well find a hoard of stolen art.

The Shrine of the Magi?

Possibly.

Chamber music concerts are wonderful in that they rarely last longer than seventy-five or eighty minutes, not like a Mahler symphony, which is similar to Texas—big and windy and goes on forever.

Cindasue was weeping as we rose to leave the hall.

"That poor dear man," she sighed, "he a-writing such hog-killin'st music and then he take and die when he's only a bit older than this here polecat nefoo."

"Six years older," Peter Murphy insisted.

"Your gray hair like to make you look older," she sniggered.

"Silver."

So the evening went. The two of them mixed banter with the exchange of adoring glances as lovers always do. I would have been embarrassed if I thought they were aware of my presence. But I was as irrelevant as a stein of beer.

I was also a bit long in the tooth for the rathskeller

crowd, but not so much so as to stand out. In any event, the eyes of everyone in the room were not on me but on the green-eyed witch who sang drinking songs in German, English, and Appalachian and danced up a storm with her handsome and attentive escort.

We left about ten because Cindasue said that my nefoo had to drive her back to her apartment and still catch the 23:30 train back to Köln.

"Won't give him much time for lollygaggin' 'round, will it, Uncle Blackie?"

"A wise but I suspect an unnecessary precaution."

Peter Murphy rolled his eyes. One day he had been forbidden to ride back with her. The next day he had been ordered to.

They did have the courtesy to accompany me to the hotel before they went off on their minor tryst.

I adjured Cindasue to drive carefully because fog was moving down from the Nordsee. She "allowed" that she "shonuff" would.

I warned myself that I had begun to sound like a parent.

There was a message waiting for me at the desk. I should call Herr Schulteis any time. The number was his home number.

I punched it out on the phone in my room.

"Schulteis."

"Hi Ernie. Blackie."

"Blackie," he said, *"ja, gut, gut."*

"What gives?"

"We made an exploration of Herr Zellner's van in Rodenkirchen and found that there had been art in the van. We took this as probable cause, as I believe Mike Casey would say, for exploring the house. The frau in charge let us in when we established that we were police."

"The man must think he's invulnerable to have such a weak security system there."

"Ja, ja. The two hounds are sleeping serenely and will do so for several more hours."

"And you found?"

"Lots of art, some of it very sophisticated imitations. Nothing worth very much, except for one or two pieces, which look very much like stolen art on our Interpol lists, though they, too, may be imitations. He may well have thought that there was nothing in the house worth protecting. But, as you suggest, he does believe he is invulnerable."

"Indeed . . . You will talk to the Herrn Bundeskanzler?"

"*Ja, ja.* I will ask for permission to search the *Schloss* . . . But in Germany on weekends, nothing is accomplished. I will not have permission till Monday."

"That is lamentable."

"We have taken the frau into protective custody. Herr Zellner is in Sicily at his villa there. He will not return till Sunday evening. With good fortune, we will surprise him on Monday morning. In any event, we will surround the house discreetly tonight so that they will not remove anything. If they try, that will simplify matters for us."

"Sunday afternoon," I insisted, "before he returns. Then, if you find anything, you can arrest him at the airport."

"*Ja . . .*" he said slowly. "I would risk my career, but that makes little difference. I will try to reach Herrn Bundeskanzler. He has no love for Zellner."

"One more thing, Ernie. Signor Donatelli at the dom, is he not an accomplished forger of paintings?"

"*Ja,* very accomplished. Also very careful. In our judgment, he is relatively harmless. But I do not trust him or believe him. He could easily fool Heinz Zellner, whose avarice far exceeds his sensibility."

After I had hung up, I pondered the situation. No harm would be done if Zellner's collection of stolen treasure was liberated. I doubted that a man of his influence would do time in prison. Still, his wings would be clipped.

Yet my instincts told me that Ernie and his merry men were not likely to find the Shrine of the Magi in that *Schloss.*

16

Peter

I had hardly expected that I would get anywhere near her apartment, much less inside it. While Cindasue hungered for bodily union, probably as much as I did, if not more, she was also terrified of it or perhaps of what it would represent.

Moreover, if she had asked me into her apartment, I would have probably fled in terror.

I did not expect, however, that I would be reduced to romancing her in the car in the parking lot of the Bonn *Haupbahnhof.*

However, she certainly did not resist my exploratory caresses.

"You ain't nuttin' but a male polecat," she informed me as I touched one of her lovely breasts.

"You just plain pole-kitten," I replied.

"Stop makin' up words," she sighed.

"Cindasue," I began.

"Yessah."

"There isn't any town or village or hamlet or crossing in West Virginia named Stinking Creek."

She pushed my caressing hand away, but gently.

"Course not. There a McCloud Holler, though."

"I see."

"If you really were a smart nuf social scientis' you'd know all about Stinkin' Crik from the book that thar fella took and wrote."

"Fetterman."

"You shonuff read the book?"

"I shonuff did. A couple of years ago in graduate school."

"So what did you think about me?"

She caressed my face lightly, as if to say she wasn't angry if I wasn't.

"I figured you were from the same town that he was, or you just appropriated the name because it was more colorful."

"Uh-huh . . . Real name his town wors'n Stinkin' Crik."

"That's your town?"

"Nawsuh, t'ain't. Mine is an oth'r place. Hit's a lot like his and a lot like what I say about hit. Have a differen' name, though. Happen you want to find out 'bout hit, you could ask the Yewnited States Coast Guard."

"I won't do that, Cindasue."

She moved my trembling fingers back to her breast, which felt enormous and full as I slipped her bra farther away from it and took possession of the whole treasure.

All of this, mind you, was going on in the dark and with her lime shift still mostly in place.

"You fingers shonuff tremblin' Peter Murphy, suh."

"I don't want to hurt you, Cindasue."

"You wouldn't ever do that," she sighed complacently. "But you a-pryin' into my life someth'n terrible."

I pulled her into my arms and absorbed her in the most passionate kiss I had yet essayed with her. She responded in kind. My fingers teased her firm nipple as I kissed her.

"Shonuff," she sighed when, by implicit mutual agreement, we released one another. "That war a right excitin' kiss."

"You didn't try to fight it off," I said as I gasped for breath.

"Din't get much choice. 'Twas nice, though."

"Sure was."

"I hear the train a-comin'. Jest in time. We better walk out to the platform."

"Yassum."

She clung to me as we went to the platform. The train pulled in with a roar.

"I like trains," she informed me. "We uster to have one that was a-comin' through Stinkin' Crik. Not no more . . . My Stinkin' Crik, Mr. Peter Murphy, suh."

We were holding hands on the platform.

The platform guard yelled something that seemed to suggest I'd better get on the train. She kissed my cheek.

"Peter Murphy, suh, you can take and kiss me the way you did in that thar Mercedes car any time you want."

"That's the best news I've heard in a long time."

"Less'n the sitiaytion isn't appropriate."

"Not in front of Uncle Blackie?"

"Nosuh, not 'all, no way, nohow, ev'n if he knows we doin' hit."

I boarded the train and fantasized about the feel of her in my embrace most of the way back to Köln. Passion would overcome her reluctance to tell her story, I told myself. At least I hoped it would.

The train was virtually empty. Not very many people returned to Köln at this hour of the night.

She didn't seem to mind too much that we had poked a little bit into her past. We could probably figure out the whole story if we found out the real name of her hometown from the Coast Guard and set Uncle Mike to work on digging the story out.

That wouldn't be right. I'd have to tell her that in the morning. I'd learn about her story in her own words, no other way.

The true marvel, however, was that a woman would feel such passion for me. It made no sense. Yet I could ride on that fact for a long time.

17

Cindasue

Law, that kiss were somethin' else. I've never been kissed that way 'fore.

I'm still a-riding on the clouds. Never reckon'd a man would like me that much. He shonuff do.

He a great kisser. Nice a-playing with me, too. He so powerf'l strong and powerf'l sweet, too.

Face it, Cindasue woman, you belong to that thar polecat. He's got you all hog-tied up. Happen he wants to make love to you, you'll just plumb let him.

He won't, though, till we be married. He's jest a durn polecat gentl'man.

I'm glad he is.

Hit's time I be a-marryin'. I ache for a man inside me. And then a li'l one, too. If I not be marryin' him, then who else?

I'll have to tell him everythin'. Soon. If he still wants me after that, he can have me. I'm so scar'd he won't want me.

18

Blackie Yet Again

I found Peter Murphy in the dining room of the hotel at nine o'clock, after my second round with the high-intensity lights. He was shaven this morning and wore jeans and a light blue shirt. Quite presentable, but he also looked like he had not slept all that much. I had put on the German priest shirt and had uncovered a brilliant scheme. I would wear it around the cathedral for a couple of days, striking terror in the hearts of all involved from Cardinal Sean Cronin on down.

He had collected the required cornflakes with raisins for me and poured some tea upon my arrival.

"Want some fruit juice, Uncle Blackie?"

"That would be very nice."

"Grapefruit?"

"Why not?

It was raining outside, water coming down in furious curtains. We were in Northern Europe—indeed, in a state called North Rhineland-Westphalia. So we should expect bad weather, just as in Ireland.

I divined by his melancholy aspect that things had not gone well on the return drive to Bonn. There is no one who can look more melancholy than a black Irishman.

"Obviously, I came home on the midnight train," he said as he placed a large glass of grapefruit juice in front of me.

"Indeed."

"We didn't even get to the door of her apartment."

"You expected to ?"

"No. We waited for the train in her car."

"Indeed."

"I sprang the Stinking Creek business on her."

"And her reaction?"

"She pointed out that I was a social scientist and I should have read Fetterman's book and should know that it was a pseudonym for his hometown."

"As it is also a pseudonym for her hometown?"

I, too, had read the book, a marvelous defense of Appalachian culture and lifestyle.

"As a matter of fact, she says that it is not. Her town is like the town in the book and all the things she's said about it are true, but its name is not Stinking Creek."

"Fascinating."

"So that's where it stands. She promises to reveal all before we go home. What can I tell you?"

The last sentence shows the influence of New York talk in American social science.

"Not exactly a romantic evening."

"It wasn't all bad on that account."

"I rejoice to hear it."

"I'm worried about her."

I thought to myself that well he might be worried about her. There was some ugliness in Cindasue's past that was a barrier to their love and must be exorcised.

"Whatever has happened, Cindasue is still Cindasue, a young woman who most of the time is pure delight."

"She said that we could find out her hometown from the Coast Guard if we wanted to badly enough. And I said that we wouldn't do that and I'd wait till she was ready to tell me."

"Excellent!"

"I think I won't ask her anymore until she's ready to

tell me. The deadline both she and I know is before you and I go back to Chicago."

"And if she doesn't tell you then?"

"I won't leave here till she does."

"Again, excellent. You have set down the guidelines, and she must adhere to them."

"Will she, Uncle Blackie?"

Tough question.

"If you insist persistently enough, she will."

"She really loves me. Passionately."

"Patently."

"That blows my mind."

"Better get used to it."

At that point, Cindasue sailed into the dining room, an umbrella and rain slicker in one hand and dress bag in the other. She was, as they say in the naval service, coming at flank speed.

"The rain's a-clearing up," she said. "We'uns going to have two more larrupin' days. . . . Darlin', would you take this garment bag up to your room? Gotta dress spiffy-like, happen you have dinner at the count cardinal's house." She kissed him, lingeringly I thought, and sent him on his way.

"I jest hang on to this here rain stuff. Don't always believe them weather people."

"Wise," I said.

She took off the rain slicker and tossed it on the chair next to me.

"Happen I can have a jar of yo'r tea?"

"Certainly," I said, filling a teacup for her.

"Reckon my jularker told you 'bout our leetle problem?"

"In very general outline."

"He's the lastiest beau I ever done have, Uncle Blackie."

This was a superlative I had never heard before.

"A keeper, huh?"

"Pow'ful keeper."

"I am not surprised."

"I'll tell him everything 'bout me, Uncle Blackie. I gotta. I don' wanna, but I gotta, lessen I lose him altogether."

"Whatever you must tell him, Cindasue, will not change who you are or his love for you. Bank on it."

"I shonuff hope you're right, Preacher Man."

"Ya done hung hit up real good?" she asked Peter Murphy who returned at that moment.

"Lastiest hung-up ever!" he replied with a broad smile as he pecked at her lips.

"Uhm . . . don't distract me, you jularker. . . . We should be a-doing serious work. . . . And you didn't use that superlative right, either. . . . OK, you both look presentable. Let's get to work."

After that outburst of work ethic, she returned his kiss with subtantially more affection than he had originally offered. Then, her face flaming, she turned on her low heels and led us toward the Benz that was waiting outside in the doorman's charge.

"I think she might love me, Uncle Blackie," my nefoo stage-whispered in my ear.

"Arguably."

Her neck flamed even more brightly; she tilted her nose higher in the air, and snorted derisively.

Thus did we start for the Ahr Valley.

Somehow, I ended up in the backseat. At this stage of the developing romance, it was where I belonged.

Before Cindasue started the car, she engulfed my nefoo in a smile of such sweetness that it touched even my normally indifferent heart. He saw only the end of it. It was his face's turn to flame. Cindasue could no longer hide her love, now repressed for some seven years. Moreover, she no longer wanted to hide it.

I closed my eyes to rest them on the way to the Ahr Valley. I had the impression that erotic love had not caused the good lieutenant junior grade to have any less a heavy foot.

"Wake up, Uncle Blackie," Peter Murphy informed me subsequently. "We're approaching the valley."

"We made it very quickly," I replied. "Mostly Cologne flatland till we got up here."

"You done read hit in the guidebook," our leader replied with as happy a laugh as I had ever heard from her. "Ya done seen the parliament building in Bonn when we were a-driving by?"

"Glass house on the river. They should never have decided to leave it for that ugly place in Berlin. I noted with interest we did not have even a quick glance at your apartment building."

The last comment was a guess, but I thought not an unreasonable one.

"You a-fakin', but you're right good at it."

I sighed loudly at her suspicions, which of course were perfectly reasonable.

The Ahrtal was upon us almost at once. The road turned, and we abruptly entered the valley cut through the hills eons ago by the fast-moving stream. It began in the hills behind Bonn and then raced down to the south and turned toward the Rhine below Remagen, the place of the bridge where the U.S. First Army defused explosives in March of 1945 and crossed the Rhine, thus upstaging that great phony Field Marshal Bernard Law Montgomery and the whole British Army and nation.

The sides of the valley, plunging sharply toward the river, were covered with vineyards. If one could ignore the highway and the cars and the occasional signs and gasoline stations, one could imagine a medieval scene.

"Theyz done finished the vintage season and the wine tasting is a-going on now, mostly hit be over. We drunk some after we talk to this here Frau Strauss, *nein?*"

"You're the boss, ma'am," Peter Murphy answered for our clan.

Both of them seemed to think that his remark was very amusing. Would they continue to find each other amusing after a couple of decades together?

Arguably.

The valley became more striking the farther we penetrated into it, on occasion reminding me of the high valleys in the Rocky Mountains of Montana.

"Hit be Ahrweiler," Cindasue announced as we pulled up in front of a very old church with an onion dome on top. "We a-parking here and walking into the old town."

"They're wine tasting already," Peter Murphy observed, pointing at the booths in the little *Platz* in front of the church.

"Later," she said in the voice of an officer of the Yewnited States Coast Guard who was accustomed to giving commands and others obeying them.

"Yasum."

"We perhaps would be well advised," I suggested meekly, "to go into that thar papis' church and pray for the success of our searches for various stars."

The boss lady glanced at her watch and admitted we could have a minute or two. She prayed longer than either of us, however.

As we were leaving, the local pastor, in cassock, approached us. He was of the vintage of Pfarrer Kurt from the Kölner Dom. He bowed and smiled respectfully.

"*Ja, ja,* Herr Bischof," he said respectfully as he kissed my ring, an unheard of and generally intolerable event. However, when in Rome . . .

I complimented him on his lovely old church, his beautiful valley, and his wondrous town (of which I had hardly seen any yet). Cindasue translated for me. The pastor beamed proudly.

"He wants to know where you are from in America, Herr Bischof," she informed me.

"Tell him I am a simple and humble auxiliary bishop from Chicago."

Her green eyes glinted with skepticism. She told him a good deal more than that, including the irrelevant fact that I was the Herr Dompfarrer in Chicago.

"*Ja, ja,*" he smiled enthusiastically. "Chicago! Michael Jordan!"

He made the requisite gesture of shooting a basketball.

"*Ja, ja,*" I agreed as we shook hands again, "Michael Jordan!"

"Der greatest!" he announced.

We took our leave.

As I have said before on occasion, better Michael than Al Capone.

We turned a corner and entered Ahrweiler itself.

"Ain't hit be the lastiest ole town ever?"

It was, indeed. It looked like a set for a Disney film, a slightly crooked cobblestone street of quaint, pretty little dollhouses, attractive shops, and tiny hotels. The tourists, the cameras, and the souvenirs in the windows of many of the shops, the sidewalk cafés with umbrellas advertising Cinzano, the strings of electric lights arching over the street (perhaps part of the wine festival) did not distract in the slightest from the charm.

One had the feeling that it was not what it was in 1150, but that the preservation of the town nonetheless was natural enough and not the result of some developer's chintzy plot. The people had made the town modern and yet preserved it, partly for profit but partly because it was theirs and they wanted it to be something like the way it always was.

"Lots o' folks commute from here to Bonn and even Köln. They reckon the ride is worth hit to live in this hyar purty place."

"Arguably, it is."

Even more lovely side streets branched off, unspoiled even by shops and tourists. Our boss lady led us down one of them.

"This hyar Helena Strauss person lives down this street. Both you polecats beh've right, ya'all hear?"

"Yassum."

"According to my guidebook, these houses date back to the twelfth and the thirteenth century," I observed.

Cindasue, who was leading us as always, turned back toward us, her green eyes glinting with mischief.

"You admit you have a guidebook, Mr. Preacher Man?"

"Doesn't everyone?"

"See!" she said to her jularker.

The houses were very small. Medieval folks, not having television, radio, computers, video recorders, and other of life's necessities, needed less room, much less room, than we moderns do. However, the stone cottages whence our ancestors departed (often with great sorrow) from the west of Ireland were even smaller.

Cindasue knocked on the front door of a neatly painted white house with blue trim and two flowerpots, ablaze with mums, on the door stoop.

A woman opened it promptly.

"*Guten Morgen,*" she said with a polite smile. "I am Helena."

"*Guten Morgen,*" we all replied.

"I'm Cindy," our leader informed her. "This is Bishop Ryan from Chicago and his nephew, Professor Peter Murphy."

Helena kissed my ring. I sighed softly to myself. There was no helping it anymore. My mistake was to bring the ring—with its three swirls from New Grange—along on our pilgrimage.

Cindasue watched Peter Murphy closely to see if he was staring at Frau Strauss. He wasn't, so she glanced away. My nefoo winked at me and proceeded to enjoy his staring when Cindasue wasn't watching.

Frau Strauss led us through the doorway, past a mountain bike, and into a small parlor. She asked us to sit down and then brought from an even tinier kitchen a tray with coffee, tea, and a plate of raisin cinnamon buns "from our own bakery."

"Some Americans like tea," she informed us.

Both Peter Murphy and I admitted that we were among their number.

Frau Strauss was a handsome matron in her middle forties, tall and, ah, statuesque in jeans and a black turtleneck sweater, though with a very slender waist. Her face was mostly unlined and firm, a neatly sculpted circle with deep blue eyes that almost immediately demanded one's attention. She seemed to assume that the face and figure were enough: she wore no earrings or makeup.

The windows in her small parlor were also diminutive, but a sliding glass door had been installed in the back to bring light in most of the day and to create the illusion of more space. The room itself was adroitly furnished in light colors. Some discreet religious prints and a large crucifix adorned the wall. In various strategic places, there were very skillful photographs of a young man and woman in their late teens and a tall, handsome, blond man. There was also a distracting picture of Helena in a two-piece swimsuit on a beach somewhere. Outside, the carefully tended garden, modest in size but alive with mums glowing in the sunlight, assured one that winter was still at bay.

"You shonuff have a beautiful home here, Helena," our Cindy said.

"Danke, Cindy, it is small, but we have worked hard on it. There are three bedrooms upstairs, one comfortable and the others perhaps a little small for our children when they return from Frankfurt, where they are in university. My family has owned this house for at least three hundred years. My husband and I always planned to return here when we retired and open a bakery. When I was dismissed from my employment in Köln, we decided not to wait. Our bakery is now very successful. It is just down the street. It is called Strauss's."

"I can believe it is very successful," I said, wolfing down a second roll.

"Danke. My husband is a very good baker. He is at the store now. We work there together most of the time. It is very pleasant to work with one's spouse. Sometimes," she colored slightly, "it is distracting."

I would imagine so.

I thought to myself that I would never fire from the dom in Chicago such an attractive, tasteful, and intelligent woman, especially since her husband was a baker.

"As you understand, Helena," our Cindy began, "Bishop Ryan is here to ask some questions on matters that are of great interest to the Herr Kardinal. We will promise you complete confidentiality. We will only quote

you to the Herr Kardinal with your explicit permission
and then only after receiving from him an explicit promise that what he learns from us will never go any farther.
Is that acceptable?''

"*Ja*, Herr Kardinal is a very good and honest man.''

Our Cindy looked at me.

It was time to get to work.

"You worked at the dom for many years, did you not,
Frau Strauss?

"*Ja*, for ten years. I began when my daughter was
seven years old. I was the senior assistant. That meant I
was responsible for all the secretarial and bookkeeping
staff there.''

"Was it pleasant work?''

"In many ways. At first, Herr Dompfarrer was a complicated man, but as long as you worked efficiently and
did not expect gratitude, he was tolerable.''

"And then?''

"When the old cardinal died, he thought he would be
next Erzbischof. The older priests supported him, many
of the right-wing Catholics who had great influence in
Rome said confidently that the matter was settled: he
would receive the appointment. The very conservative
papers supported him as did some, but not all, of the very
conservative politicians. Other papers compared his cam-
paign to a blitzkrieg—the irony was lost on him. There
was much fear that he would indeed become the next
Erzbischof.''

"But his blitzkrieg failed?''

"Naturally. He forgot that he had often angered Herrn
Bundeskanzler because of his foolish criticism. He also
forgot that the pope knew of his statements, which many
thought to be anti-Semitic. Finally, he forgot that the
pope would strongly approve of Herr Count Bischof von
Obermann's denunciations of anti-Semitism. So he
failed.''

"And then?''

"He hid from everyone for several days. Then he
changed, quite dramatically. He was cruel to everyone.

He plotted to bring down Herrn Kardinal. He schemed often with the very conservative papers. There was constant attack on Herrn Kardinal."

"The cardinal knew about it?"

"Naturally. He merely laughed. He would say something like, 'Freddy, your friends are after me again, aren't they?' and he would laugh even louder. That made Herrn Dompfarrer even more angry."

"I would imagine that it did."

She smiled and departed to the kitchen so as to repair the damage done to my sweet rolls by the leprechaun, which had managed to ride down to Ahrweiler from Köln.

"Uncle Blackie would never fire that woman," Peter Murphy whispered loud enough so the two of us could hear, but not loud enough for Frau Strauss to hear.

"I should hope not," our Cindy sniffed.

"So, what happened then?" I asked as I began eating another roll.

"He hated tourists. He wanted to close the cathedral to them. He enjoyed throwing them out when the Holy Sacrifice was about to begin. The old Kardinal would not permit that. But when the new Kardinal came, he began to chase the tourists out even when there was not a Holy Sacrifice. He would close the dom at three in the afternoon. He would chase out young women who were not modestly dressed."

"What did he mean by modesty?" Cindy asked.

"*Ja, ja,* shorts that he thought were too short or halters or both. He did not like women, especially if they were young and attractive."

"Sounds like a hard-shell Baptist preacher man to me." Cindy was for a moment Cindasue again. "Theyz clergy where I was brung up."

"Well, you are at least a good Catholic and know that the body of a woman is not evil."

"Yassum."

"What did the Herr Kardinal do when he learned of these measures?"

"He laughed," she said, her dark eyes glittering, "and forbade them. He said in my presence, '*Ja, ja,* Freddy, God made those bodies, so I don't imagine He is upset by them, *nein,* Frau Strauss?'

"I said nothing, naturally.

"Then Herr Dompfarrer said that their bodies were occasions of sin. Herr Kardinal winked at me and said that nonetheless, they would not be barred from the dom as long as he was Kardinal. So some stories about scandalous dress in the dom appeared in the conservative papers."

"Fascinating," I offered. "And then?"

"I do not like to say this." She sighed. "But then he brought younger priests into the parsonage. Men who did not really seem to be men. I do not mind men looking at me so long as it is respectful. But these men did not look at me at all. Or any other women. We were pieces of furniture they ignored. They looked instead at choirboys."

A remarkably candid woman.

"Homosexuals?" our Cindy asked.

"*Ja.*"

"Pastor Kurt?" I asked.

"Oh, no. He is such a sweet man. He has been at the dom for many years. He is complicated, too. We have all seen pictures of his *Zwei Sechs Zwei* many times. He mourned for it like a man would for his spouse who was killed in the war, like my mother did for my father."

We paused briefly in memory of that suffering.

"He is very popular with the young people," she said with a smile of approval. "They find him very amusing and very holy and do not mind the pictures of his airplane. When these young priests came to the parsonage, he kept his own young people away from them. They would not have cared for the young women, anyway. This offended Herrn Dompfarrer. He tried to replace Pastor Kurt, but Herr Kardinal forbade it absolutely."

"The count cardinal did nothing about these matters?"

"He does not like confrontations. Besides, he had no

proof. Perhaps he did not want accusations that he was punishing Herrn Dompfarrer for his blitzkrieg."

"Not a happy place to work?"

"He screamed at me many times." She lifted her gorgeous shoulders. "I would return to my Franz at his bakery and weep in his arms. He would say we should go to Ahrweiler now. I would say that I could not abandon my colleagues."

"Did you ever witness any overt homosexual behavior?" I asked.

She was silent.

"I must speak candidly to you, Herr Bischof. . . . *Ja,* I did see it once."

Her eyes filled with tears. Our Cindy, who had patently bonded completely with this marvelous woman, reached out and took her hand. My nefoo smiled proudly.

"I know that priests are human like everyone else. I know they have their needs and sometimes these needs are not healthy." She sniffed and our boss lady gave her a tissue.

"One night when I was working late—too late—I went to the dom to pray. From the lobby outside the locked doors, I heard screams. I rushed around to the sacristy to turn off the alarms so I could protect whoever needed protection. I opened the sacristy door and rushed into the dom. In front of the main altar, two of the young priests were assaulting two boys from the choir. Against their will. I did not know what to do. I watched in horror. Then they were finished. They laughed cruelly and threatened the boys if they told anyone. I left and went home to my Franz and wept all night. He said I must challenge the Dompfarrer about this, this horror."

"And you did," Cindy said as if it were a foregone conclusion.

"Naturally. The next morning I demanded that he dismiss those two priests, talk to the victims, and report it to the herr cardinal. He screamed at me. He said I was an evil woman, that I was a trap for men, that I tried to seduce everyone. He dismissed me and ordered me out of the parsonage. . . . You must excuse my tears.''

"That's all right, Helena," Cindy put her arm around the woman's shoulders.

"I cry whenever I think about it. I will never forget it. . . . Well, we came down here and bought a bakery that was failing. It has become very successful. We are happier than we have ever been. I realized only after we left Köln how miserable my life had been when I worked for that brutal, evil man. . . . My husband is a wonderful baker."

"He is certainly that," I agreed wholeheartedly and then waved her off as she began to go to the kitchen to bring yet more.

"*Danke,* I think so too."

"Did you ever try to tell the count cardinal about these matters?"

"My Franz and I discussed it often. We were afraid. Bischof Heidrich has many powerful friends. Heinz Zellner, for example. We have no power at all. They might have crushed us. Perhaps we are cowards . . .''

"You are *not,*" Cindy insisted. "If you were, you wouldn't trust us."

She provided another tissue.

"*Ja, ja,* that is true. My Franz said I should trust you."

"Frau Strauss," I said firmly. "I would like to be able to tell the Kardinal what you have told me. I will not do so without your permission and unless he promises me before I tell him that he will tell no one else. Then he will have his proof and he may act on it if he wishes. May I do so?"

"Naturally," she said firmly.

"I know him reasonably well," I continued. "I feel quite certain he will act and act decisively."

"I hope so. . . . It is all so ugly."

"He's given up on his plots against the cardinal, hasn't he?" our Cindy asked as she slipped back into her chair.

Drat it, young woman, that was my question!

"Not at all. I talk often with some of my colleagues who suffer greatly because they cannot leave their jobs.

He talks often about his new plots, in the hearing of everyone. Only recently he said that now he had the perfect plan and that the Herr Kardinal would soon be removed.''

Bingo!

Maybe.

"How recently?" Cindy continued.

She was good, all right. No wonder they had her sitting down there in Bonn. She was also correct that a woman should take over the conversation.

"A few weeks ago."

"Did your colleagues have any idea what it was?"

"No, but they said he was very proud of himself."

Fascinating, but the pieces still didn't fit together as they should. We were missing something.

"Signor Donatelli?" Our peerless leader asked.

Helena Strauss waved her hand.

"He is naturally a forger and cannot be trusted. There is, however, no malice in him. He hates the Dompfarrer and the Dompfarrer hates him. But they need each other."

"He knows all that goes on at the dom?"

"*Ja,* he knows everything and more things that don't actually happen."

Her tears banished, Frau Strauss laughed happily. She was enormously relieved to be rid of the burden of horror that she carried.

"May I ask one more question?"

"*Ja,* as many as you want, Herr Bischof."

"Call me Blackie."

"What a cute name!"

"My uncle," the good Peter Murphy intervened, "is the Dompfarrer in Chicago. He would never fire you."

"You must come to Chicago," I added. "You and Franz would be most welcome."

"I have never been out of Germany," Helena said. "I would like very much to go to Chicago some time."

"We may have something to invite you there for soon," Peter Murphy said, going far over the boundary of the outrageous. Cindy, as we had to call her until we left the Strauss house, turned red again, but she did not seem unhappy. Poor child, we would have to rid her of fears soon: she so much wanted to be Peter Murphy's wife.

"But your question, Herr Blackie?"

"Just plain Blackie," Cindy interjected.

"Have you seen Heinz Zellner at the parsonage?"

"*Ja,* many times."

"What kind of man is he?"

She shuddered and turned pale.

"He is the most terrible man I have ever seen: short, fat, bald, with beady little eyes, huge frightening hands, and a terrible sneer. He looks at women like he would crush the life out of us as slowly and painfully as possible. He rubs those awful hands of his together as if he is preparing to squeeze someone to death. He leers at us as though he knows which one of us will be his next victim. He is pure horror. It is said that he was once a concentration camp guard, but that cannot be proven."

"He is a good friend of Bishop Heidrich?"

"*Ja, ja,* he didn't use to be before the new Herr Kardinal came, but now they often conspire together."

Two interesting guys.

We rose to leave. Frau Strauss shook hands with my nefoo and myself and hugged Cindy. At the door, Peter Murphy raised a final question, the first he had asked in our conversation.

"Excuse me, Frau Strauss, you said you were the bookkeeper at the parsonage," he began with a diffident smile and all the very considerable Celtic charm he possessed. "Did the Herr Dompfarrer make any contributions to dubious organizations?"

Bingo!

Both his lady love and his uncle—the card-carrying detectives in the team—had missed that one.

Frau Strauss leaned against the door, hands behind her back, head bowed—a position that greatly enhanced her appeal.

"*Ja,* that is a very good question. I was afraid that someone would ask it. . . . You will tell the Herr Kardinal what I say?"

"Only if you want us to," Peter said, now carrying the ball.

"*Ja,* I must and you must. . . . He sent many checks, hundreds of thousands of marks, to neo-Nazi and anti-Turkish and skinhead groups. He warned me that I would die in agony if I told anyone about it."

"I guarantee that nothing will happen to you," I promised.

My friend Ernie would put a permanent guard on them, if need be. But I thought that would not be necessary.

However, a sense of palpable evil closed in on me. We were involved with thoroughly depraved human beings. Moreover, we had yet to arrive at the ultimate layer of their depravity.

19

"Well," said Peter Murphy as we consumed our huge and elaborate dishes of ice cream, "I guess maybe I was a little more than just a spear carrier that time, huh?"

"Peter Murphy, chile," Cindasue, as she now was once again, said, squeezing his hand, "you not jest a spear carrier, nohow. You plumb brilliant, ain't he, Uncle Blackie?"

"Arguably."

. "You noticed," my nefoo continued, looking very pleased with himself, "the unusual matter of the alarm system?"

He was imitating Sherlock Holmes on the matter of the barking dog, a line that had once led to a solution of a little puzzle I had been trying to unravel. The late Monsignor Ronald Knox dubbed such a structure a "Sherlockismus."

"The alarm system did not go off when she went into the dom," I said, playing along in the name of family loyalty.

"That's what was unusual. She went through the sacristy door, to which she had a key to turn off the alarm system, but she did not have to turn it off. She did not say she did and careful recorder of facts that she is, she would have mentioned it if she did. One concludes therefore that she had the key and knew the alarm system. That it was already turned off suggests that the young priests who were raping the choirboys had done so.''

"You nefoo shonuff brilliant, ain't he, Uncle Blackie?''

She was not yet family, but she was motivated by other and deeper loyalties. Besides, Peter Murphy was brilliant, though neither Cindasue or I could afford to admit explicitly that we had missed not one but two important points.

"Arguably, Cindasue. What conclusion do you deduce from these phenomena, Peter Murphy?''

"That the dom leaked like the proverbial sieve. Anyone and everyone might have been able to enter it whenever they wanted. The security system was a farce.''

"We did not ask the bewitching Frau Strauss how she had come to possess a key to the sacristy or to know the combination,'' I observed. "She indeed seemed to take it for granted that she would know. They might just as well not have had a security system. Any object of art could be removed from there at any time.''

"And many of them may have been taken.'' Peter Murphy was on a roll and he was not about to stop. "And our Italian friend might have substituted imitations.''

"Arguably,'' Cindasue agreed.

My lines were no longer sacred. These young lovers thought nothing of making fun of poor old Uncle Blackie.

"What do you think, Uncle Blackie?'' She turned to me. "Did the Dompfarrer conspire to steal the Shrine of the Magi, with the help of Heinz Zellner and Signor Donatelli?''

"Perhaps . . . yet there are one or two problems remaining that preclude us from drawing such a firm conclusion.''

"Like why there has been no public revelation of the theft—which there would be if they wanted to bring down the cardinal?''

"Precisely."

My nefoo would doubtless carry a lot of spears from this ingenious young woman for the rest of his life if he were able to solve the mystery that had captured her. There would be many less pleasant ways to spend a life, especially because she would permit him to make any useful contributions of his own and praise him inordinately for his insights, though never so excessively to make him feel she was patronizing him.

"So we have to find the shrine itself?" Peter Murphy concluded.

"Oh, yes, that's why we came, and that now would appear to be the key to everything else we have learned."

"She a shonuff main lady," Cindasue said thoughtfully. "Brave-like and terrible purty, too. I hope I look like that if I linger on till I'm that age."

Peter Murphy hugged her.

"Ma'm, theyz a whole heap of kinds of beauty. You're like to be jest as beautiful as she, 'cept'n in your way."

"She shonuff have purty breasts."

A rule of thumb for the uninitiate: no woman is ever satisfied with her own breasts. Never.

The corollary is that no man is ever dissatisfied with the breasts of a woman he truly loves. Ever.

A third observation. No matter how much the party in the previous sentence insists on his point of view, the party in the antepenultimate will not change her point of view.

It takes perhaps thirty years in the priesthood to understand that process.

"I'm hardly an expert on that area, Lieutenant McCloud," the gallant Peter Murphy went on, "but, on the basis of my all-too-limited observations, so do you."

"You embarrassin' me somethin' terrible, Peter Murphy, suh; but you still a plumb sweet boy."

"Jularker," I said.

It was necessary, I decided, to set in motion a rapid investigation and reform of the dom. Tomorrow would not be too soon, especially if my friend Ernie Schulteis

were able to launch his raid on the *Schloss* Zellner tomorrow night or Monday morning. Thus it might be said
that the count cardinal had been aware of the problem
before art stolen from the dom was discovered in the
Schloss.

If, in fact, there were such art there. Or, as seemed
more likely, clever imitations.

And the Shrine of the Magi?

Voices in the back of my head continued to insist that
the shrine would not be in the *Schloss,* that I knew very
well what had happened to the shrine, and that, if I were
not such a fool, I would realize what I already knew.

Patently, the reader has figured it out long since.

We finished our ice cream and strolled down the purty
streets of Ahrweiler. I ducked into a model airplane shop,
to the surprise of the young lovers who waited for me
outside. I emerged a few moments later with a plastic
bag that contained two boxes.

"Whatcha got in that thar bag?" the Unterleutnant demanded.

I removed the two boxes.

"An Me-262!" she said.

"And a Republic P-47 Thunderbolt!" Peter Murphy
added.

"You shonuff sweet, Mr. Preacher Man!"

"Possibly . . . Our good Pastor Kurt is, as we know, a
very complicated man. It may prove useful as time goes
on to see which way the complexities go."

"I'll carry it, Uncle Blackie, so you won't lose it,"
my nefoo offered.

An act of total disrespect, though arguably prudent.

As we walked back toward our car and the wine-
tasting booths, we passed a scene that appears every day
in most countries of the world: a group of early adoles-
cent males playing basketball, several of them wearing
Chicago Bulls paraphernalia.

We watched them for a few moments. Then Cindasue
asked if she might have a shot or two.

The punks thought that the notion was a real hoot—a

girl wanting a shot. They did not know what kind of a
girl it was. Still, since she was pretty and older than they
were and they were relatively nice boys for pubescent
males (whose brains are at all times overflowing with
lascivious imagery), they threw her the ball.

She retreated to three-point range and drowned her first
effort in the net. Impressed, they threw it back to her for
a second effort. Natcherly, she hit again. And three more
times before she missed her sixth try. The punks cheered
enthusiastically for each basket and groaned when she
finally missed. She waved good-bye, and they cheered
again.

"Oughter quit when I ahead," she murmured, extremely pleased with herself.

"You play basketball, Cindasue?" her jularker asked,
rather stupidly, I thought. Patently, she played basketball
and quite well.

"I done learn all that thar martial arts stuff, too. Don't
you be a-forgettin' that, Mistah Peter Murphy, suh, happen you want to take and get real fresh."

"I won't dream of it," my nefoo replied with a big
smile.

"You played at New London, Cindasue?" I asked.

"Natcherly . . . like to have a lot of small classes. Any
woman could lift a basketball was on the team, e'en you
a leetle mite."

"Point guard, I presume?"

What else?

"Howdja done know hit, Mr. Preacher Man?"

"I knowed."

"I wasn't first string till I was a junior," she said with
patent false modesty.

"Is your real name," Peter Murphy asked, "Cindasue
or Cindy?"

"Happen you know me real well, hit's Cindasue. Else-
wise hit's Cindy."

"Folks down to the embassy?"

"Mostly they call me Cindy; but the ambassador and
mah boss and mah close friends, hit's Cindasue to them.

Natcherly. Y'all can call me Cindasue like always, 'cuz that's mah real name.''

That settled that. She not only was an enigma, she delighted in being an enigma—and sometimes found herself a prisoner of the enigma.

"You were pretty good at marksmanship, I presume?''

"Whafo you ask that fo, Mr. Preacher Man? You done know that I'd be the mostest marksperson in that whole New London place. I'm from McCloud's Holler. We learn to shoot up thar, 'fore we're toilet trained. I set all kinda records up to New London. Made 'em polecats gape. Warned 'em to be a-messin' with Cindasue 'cuz I'm a dead eye. Scare 'em right good, too. Course, Coast Guard folk don't never have to shoot. Anaway, you should call hit markspersonship.''

"I'll remember the warning," Peter Murphy replied lightly.

"Shucks, Peter Murphy, sir, I'd never be a-shootin' a nice jularker like you, 'lessin you got more fresher than I think you knowin' how to be.''

Fortunately, we arrived at the wine-tasting booths at that time.

She refused to sample the wine as she was a-drivin' back to that thar Köln place. She permitted Peter Murphy and me to sample four different kinds, happ'n they be white or red.

Peter Murphy appealed that decision on the grounds that the sample glasses were so small. She granted the appeal.

I continued to find the *Roten* more appealing. My nef-oo bought three bottles of the red that we both agreed was the best.

"Can't hardly git that thar stuff in Mericay,'' she warned us. "Iffin you stay here longer, we could take and mosey over to that Moselle Valley place.''

We both agreed that would be a nice idea, I for reasons of politeness and Peter Murphy for reasons of his pursuit of our leetle point guard.

Nonetheless, I felt certain that our time to solve the

mystery of the locked dom, which was, it turned out, very badly locked, was running out on us.

We climbed back into her dark blue Benz.

"Y'all too dizzy from all that thar firewater to drive," she informed us. " 'Sides, Uncle Blackie has to be a-restin' his eyes ag'in."

Out of respect for the privacy of the young lovers, I did just that.

When the boss lady informed me that we were back at the hotel, I did not bother to pretend that I knew it already. She said that I could go upstairs and take a nice li'll nap while she and my nefoo lollygagged in the swimin' pool.

I did not nap, however. First I called Ernie Schulteis, who reported that he had as yet been unable to contact the Herrn Bundeskanzler, but he hoped he might be able to do so before the day was over. I urged him to persevere. Then I requested discreet protection till further notice for our friends up in Ahrweiler. I would explain later. He agreed, much as John Culhane in Chicago would have, without asking any questions.

I then checked the E-mail. Demands for progress from Milord Cronin and Milady Murphy.

To the former I replied:

The evil is serious and deep. We have yet to reach the bottom, but I expect that we will shortly. Early middle next week if nothing untoward happens.

The promise of accelerating progress was not completely true. I had no idea of when we would be able to wrap up the mystery.

To Milady Murphy I responded with something more closely resembling the whole truth:

Peter Murphy continues to play his cards with remarkable skill, patience, and persistence. Mountain Flower not completely hog-tied yet but a-getting thar.

She was point guard on basketball team at New London.

The final message was, as I had presumed it would be, from The Megans. It was terse and to the point:

What size Kölnisch Wasser?

My reply was such as to infuriate them:

Wait and see!

Thereupon I glanced at the Web page *New York Times* to determine what was officially happening in the world. Nothing much, it turned out.

Then I turned to the real purpose of this alleged napping period: I must figure out what I knew about the mystery of the missing Shrine of the Magi, who themselves had been missing from the shrine for a long time, if indeed those itinerant soothsayers had ever existed.

I remark in passing that I believe it highly likely that there is some truth in the story of both the star and the Magi. Like the other infancy stories, if one is to believe the best scholars on the subject, it emerged in its present form from the liturgical dramas, arguably children's dramas of the early Christians. So the Epiphany plays in the primary grades of every Catholic school on the planet are even older than the written Gospels. The important themes of the story, which are what really matter, is that Jesus came for all and that we all must follow our stars. I suspect that the medieval pilgrims would have agreed if it were put to them that way. However, when one explains stories, one erodes much of their impact, a point that theologians often miss.

What did I know? I began to put answers on the computer screen:

1. I knew that the dom was a sinkhole of corruption.
2. I knew that the Kardinal was a good and liberal man

with powerful political instincts that made him hesitate to move on his enemies.

3. I knew that a right-wing billionaire with odd tastes in both avarice and lust was involved with the corruption.

4. I knew that the lay staff saw much of the corruption, were scandalized by it, and were afraid to report it.

5. I knew that the security system was so filled with leaks as for all practical purposes not to exist. There were no locked rooms, only the appearance of locked rooms.

6. I knew that, however, it was still no easy task to carry such a heavy object as the shrine out of the dom in the middle of the night. Several people had to be active in the process.

7. I knew that the director of the art workshop, the linear successor of M. Henri de Verdun, was an accomplished forger.

8. I knew that the enigmatic and perhaps half-mad Pastor Kurt was extremely popular with young people and arguably half-crazy, though perhaps only crazy like a fox.

9. I knew that the dom parsonage had become a lavender house in which choirboys were raped by priests.

10. I knew that the bishop who was the pastor of the dom, a role not unlike mine, was a hate-filled conspirator determined to bring down the count cardinal and that he had recently bragged about a plot that would certainly do that.

11. I also knew that his treatment of Frau Strauss was ample reason for dispensing with his services.

I considered my list on the computer screen and played with the P-47 and the ME-262 as I did so.

Actually, I knew nothing at all. I had no idea who had taken the Shrine of the Magi or where it was. I had a lot of information but no clues. I would tonight warn the count cardinal of dire consequences of further inaction.

I might know tomorrow whether Herr Heinz Zellner had in fact made off with the shrine. Then the mystery would be solved and we could go home, most likely with Cindasue still not quite hog-tied, to use her term.

Somehow that seemed too easy.

If Zellner had the shrine, why was the information not leaked to the press? As a point of fact, if Bishop Heidrich knew the shrine was missing, why had he not told his far-right-wing journalist friends? Unless my impressions of our conversation at the count cardinal's house were completely mistaken, he, too, was surprised by the disappearance.

Something was missing. Had there been a conspiracy that somehow had been short-circuited by another conspiracy?

I gave it up completely and decided I had better rest my eyes a little bit more before we headed out to Lindenthal for our Eucharist, supper, and confrontation with the count cardinal. By all the rules of Chicago politics, I would postpone the last-named till the end—over coffee and Baileys Irish Cream, which I personally would bring. I erased my foolish notes on the screen.

20

Cindasue

Lawdy, I don't ever want to get out of this here shower. It's not as warm as a man's body, but it's still warm and soothing and I need warmth and soothing right now.

I sent him down to the lobby to wait for that thar preacher man. I didn't want him to see me in my outfit till I come down all gussied up right and proper.

I wish I could disappear into the bowels of the earth. That's pretty silly, ain't it?

I wish I could hypnotize myself and wake up the next day and it would all be over. Either way.

Well, I gotta tell him one way or another. I promised that I would, and we-uns done keep our promises.

I ask every other minute whether he's like to stop a-lovin' me? Maybe, maybe not. You push me, ah say I don' think he's like to stop a-lovin' me. I'll be the happiest woman in the world.

But what if he does? What if he don't love me no more?

I'd like to die.

He was so nice down to the whirlpool thing today. All gentle and tender and lovin'. No passionate stuff at all.

Like he knew jest what kind of lovin' I needed. He done know me pretty well, that's God's truth.

Your truth, I mean.

Wal, I'll tell you somethin,' Lawdy, I ain't gonna give him up without a fight. Uh-nuh.

Tell the truth, when we were all alone down there at the end, 'fore I jumped into the pool, he sorta got most of my bra thing off and touched and kissed my breasts somethin' wonderful. I loved it. He knows now how much I want him. No gettin' away from hit. Don't wanna get away from hit. Don't wanna get away from him. He done licked my nipples so sweet that I knew I was like to die.

Wal, thank you that you done brung him into my life. He is an angel and a wise man and a star all put together.

Now I oughter turn on the cold water and simmer down.

21

Peter Murphy

I had to call Uncle Blackie to wake him up. Knowing him all my life, I know he went through the whole mystery once more before resting his eyes. He and that woman are so far ahead of me on this detection stuff that I hardly ever get out of the gate. I don't care. It's fun to be with them and watch them work. She hasn't caught up with him yet, but she will soon, and then it will be real fun.

She says she's afraid that when I find out the truth about her, I'll stop loving her. I can't imagine anything that could cause me to do that. Something must have happened to her when she was in her middle teens that made her feel utterly worthless. Whatever it was, it must have been something that others did to her, not that she did to herself. I'm sure the Coast Guard must have known about it when they recruited her. New London had to know it before she was accepted. She's been promoted more rapidly than is customary in that outfit.

Yet probably in her eyes it is something terrible, something that blights her for the rest of her life. When it finally spills out, I've got to be really cool.

And she has gorgeous breasts, even more gorgeous

than I had dreamed. She even half believes me when I say something like that.

I will not let her get away this time, that I swear. No matter how hard she tries.

22

Blackie

"She's gussin' herself for the party, as she calls it," Peter Murphy informed me. "I can't imagine what that means to her. But it will be interesting to see, won't it?"

"Doubtless."

"I'm being sweet and affectionate to her now. No pressure for the whole story. I figure that's the best strategy."

"Arguably."

"Following yonder star can get to be pretty complicated, can't it, Uncle Blackie?"

"Patently."

Peter Murphy was dressed in a conservative gray, three-piece suit with a white shirt and a cautiously striped red and blue tie. He looked like a junior partner in a very prestigious law firm. Not only was I unaware that he had brought such array with him, I was also unaware that he owned such garments.

Doubtless his good mother had insisted he bring it along in case he wanted to take someone special to someplace special. No names mentioned.

"You figure out what we know and we don't know about the mystery of the missing shrine?"

"Oh, yes . . . We know lots of things and we know absolutely nothing. We don't know who took the Shrine of the Magi, or why, or where it is."

"We can warn the cardinal about the dangers he faces, can't we?"

"We can, but I doubt that will bring the shrine back."

What would bring the shrine back?

I would have to figure out a new angle. Once again, a quick snapshot of the new angle sped quickly across my befuddled brain. I reached for it, but it slipped through my mental fingers.

Then our conversation was interrupted by a vision that appeared around the corner that led to the elevators. It was our ace marksperson, point guard, martial artist, detective, and girl guide.

In Coast Guard white dress formal, hair piled up on her head, very skillful makeup, glowing green eyes, and a radiant smile.

"Wow!" said her jularker.

My eyes blinked rapidly behind my windowpane glasses.

"I shonuff never reckon I'd be a-getting a chance to wear this hyar thin'," she said shyly. "Like to be only time in this here life I can do hit."

"I'm sure the Kardinal will be pleased, Cindasue," I said, for want of something more thoughtful.

"You the lasti'st, Cindasue," Peter Murphy gasped, "the killin'st sight I ever did see."

"Y'all don' think it's too extreme?" she asked hesitantly. "Will I shock the cardinal man?"

"Indubitably not," I said. "Bank on it."

"We'll take and drive the car out to that thar Lindenthal place. I ain't not a-riding the tram in this bodacious outfit."

Then, with a wicked glint in her eye, she added, "Happen I want to make a real impression, I'd better talk real shonuff English talk tonight, huh?"

"It won't make any difference, Cindasue," Peter Murphy told her, "what way you talk."

"As always in these matters," I agreed, "my nefoo knows what he's talking about."

"Nephew, Uncle Blackie."

So, straight into the setting sun, we drove out to the cardinal's modest house in Lindenthal, I in my clerical shirt with a touch of purple, Peter Murphy in his lawyer clothes, and Cindasue in her summer formal uniform.

I knew how the count cardinal would be dressed, but I kept my knowledge and laughter to myself.

When he opened the door, he was dressed in dark blue trousers and the vast red sport shirt that was his favorite (and of which I had argued that he had at least ten duplicates stored away).

"*Ja, ja,* it is like the middle ages when everyone dressed in their best when they came to visit the Prince Archbishop of Köln. Cindy, my dear." He bowed genially and kissed her hand. "You are always a beautiful young woman, but tonight you are dazzling!"

"Thank you, Cardinal," she said shyly.

"And Blackie, surely you were forced to wear that shirt. I don't know about you, Peter, but you look more like a rich banker than an academic."

All of this banter was punctuated by great, happy laughter.

He was not in the least embarrassed by his own attire.

"Rudi and Fritz are out saying Sonnabend Mass in parishes, and my usher has the day off. I have persuaded my cook to stay by promising her two extra days next week. I would not inflict my own cooking on anyone but Rudi and Fritz. Come, I will show you the chapel."

The chapel was a small room at the rear of the house, overlooking a well-tended garden. It contained a simple altar, a couple of kneelers, a wooden cross, and a full-sized copy of the Madonna of Limburg. Donatelli's work, I assumed.

"The vestments are over in this closet," he said. "I will put the water and the wine and the hosts on this little table, four hosts, of course."

He was urging the hard-shell Baptist to participate in

the Eucharist. Since Milord Cronin had given her Communion at Grand Beach on his insistence, this didn't faze her, though her eyes widened a bit. "You will, of course, preside, Blackie, and give the homily. . . . I will go and dress for the Eucharist."

"He surprise you, Uncle Blackie?" my nefoo, uh, nephew asked. "You have something ready?"

"I am not surprised," I replied, "and I do have something ready. I always have something ready."

Nor was I surprised when Claus Maria, Graf von Obermann, reappeared in his full crimson array: cummerbund, zucchetto, buttons, mantle, and even socks. All of us, save for herself, were upstaged. He knelt with the young lovers in a posture of intense devotion.

They sat comfortably on their chairs as I began to preach. I proposed to demonstrate to them all that Blackie Ryan is never unprepared to preach—well, practically never.

The Gospel was about Jesus proclaiming that the kingdom of God was near. I explained that by near, Jesus did not mean chronologically near, but existentially near. He had experienced more intensely than anyone before or since the closely lurking presence of God's love and thereupon urged all who would listen to him down through the centuries to seize, as rough children seized their toys, every opportunity that lurking love offered them in their daily lives and particularly in their closest relationships.

"I shall now tell you a story," I informed them. "A story told by the incomparable John Shea."

"The Kingdom of God," I began, "is like Patricia the Penny Planter. She is a young woman of some ten years who lives in a nice suburb near a large city, arguably Chicago, though I cannot testify to that with any certainty.

"Her house is a big old house with lots of oak trees in front of it. There is a wide street in front of her house down which each morning and night buses come bringing people to and from the train that takes them into the city to their jobs

"Well, last summer, life was pretty dull for Patricia. There were no children her age in the neighborhood with whom she could play. There was a *boy* next door who was a year older named Randolph. But he was so *awful* that Patricia could stand him only an hour or so (at the most) every day. She would spend another hour or two rearranging her rock and roll tapes. After that, there was just nothing to do. Life was *boring*. Patricia kept telling her mother how boring everything was. Finally, one afternoon, Patricia's mother said, 'Patricia, you are a very bright and creative young woman. Find something for yourself to do so you won't be bored.'

"So Patricia went to her room and looked out at the street and was more bored than ever. Then a bus pulled up at the stop in front of her house. Patricia watched the people who got out. They all looked so tired, heads bowed, shoulders slumped, faces frozen in terrible frowns. They dragged themselves down the street like they would never wake up in the morning again.

" 'Not a single smile,' Patricia remarked to herself. 'How awful!'

"The next morning, she watched people walking down the street to catch the bus. Still no smiles. How terrible!

" 'I've got to do something about them!'

"So early that afternoon, she went down to the street and began to write signs in chalk on the sidewalk. At the bus stop she scrawled, 'Treasure near' and added an arrow pointing down the street toward her house. The next sign said, 'You're on the right track!' Then she wrote farther along, 'You're getting close!' Then, right in front of the biggest, oldest oak tree in her front yard, she announced, 'Treasure this way!' And pointed toward the oak tree.

"Then she put her brightest, shiniest penny in a little hole in the bark of the tree and wrote above the hole in her biggest letters, 'Treasure Here!'

"Then she retreated to her room to await the results of her plot.

"Three buses stopped in front of her house. No one even noticed the signs they were so dull and worn out. Then, finally, a woman got off the bus. She was *real* old, maybe twenty-four or twenty-five, but she looked a lot older because her frown was so heavy and her walk so slow. She had to be a lawyer because she carried two briefcases. If she smiled, she might be very pretty, but she never smiled.

"Well, she saw Patricia the Penny Planter's sign and just walked away. Then she stopped, went back to the sign, looked both ways to make sure no one would see her (she never thought of looking up at the window of the house), and then she began to follow the signs to the treasure!"

At this point, I began to walk along an imaginary sidewalk in the cardinal's little oratory.

"She took the penny out of the oak tree and threw her head back and laughed and laughed and laughed. She kept the penny and put a quarter in the tree; then she straightened out her shoulders and strode briskly down the street with a happy smile on her face as a lovely young woman who had her whole life ahead of her ought to.

"Patricia, who was very pleased, went down to the tree, took the quarter, replaced it with another penny, and went back to her house, twenty-four cents ahead of the game. But she was a very honest little girl, so she put the quarter on her dresser in a separate pile where she kept the money she would give to the parish on Sunday—since in Patricia's country they didn't have a church tax like they do here.

"The next morning, an older man, like her daddy's age, slouched along the street. His clothes were rumpled, he looked kind of seedy, failure was written all over him. As he waited for the bus, he looked down at Patricia the Penny Planter's sign and grimaced like it hurt him. Then, after thinking about it, he shrugged kind of lifelessly and ambled down the street. He took out the penny, laughed and laughed and laughed, and then walked back to the bus stop like a man who was now a success. Then he returned to the treasure tree and put a dollar bill in the bark.

"By Friday, Patricia the Penny Planter had lost a lot of pennies (that was all right because she had two thousand of them) and earned fourteen dollars and twenty-five cents for the parish. She had seen a lot of men and women smile and laugh. Her life was no longer boring at all.

"On the last bus on Friday, a young man got off the bus who had to be a banker, he was so proper and prim. He wore a three-piece charcoal gray suit (although it was summer) and a starched white shirt and a dull tie and a hat.

"He looked both ways three times before he began to follow Patricia the Penny Planter's signs. He actually got as far as the sign pointing to the oak tree and had put one foot on the lawn in front of the oak tree before he turned around and walked away

"He didn't even look back!

" 'Drat!' said Patricia the Penny Planter. 'I wanted that one.'

"Well, that night, after Patricia the Penny Planter had said her prayers and turned off her light, she looked out of the window again. What did she see? You know what she saw! She saw the young banker in cut-offs and a T-shirt right in the front of the tree. Tentatively, he reached up to the treasure box, then he pulled back his hand like maybe he was afraid there was a snake or a wasps' nest in the tree.

"Patricia the Penny Planter threw open the window and shouted, 'Go for it!'

"Patricia the Penny Planter has a very loud voice.

"The young man was terrified. He turned and ran away as fast as his strong young legs could carry him.

" 'I'll get you yet,' she shouted after him.

"So, my friends, I ask you, how is the kingdom of

God like Patricia the Penny Planter and what are the treasures this ever lurking love offers us in our daily life?''

The count cardinal, who had listened with a thoughtful frown, applauded enthusiastically.

The two young lovers stared at one another in an agony of longing and confusion.

Having made my points, I went on with the Eucharistic celebration.

23

"Ja, ja," said the Herr Kardinal, *"*now it's time to get down to business, *nein?"*

I agreed.

At dinner the cardinal had removed his zucchetto and cape and cummerbund but retained the crimson-trimmed cassock. The conversation was delightful, because Cindasue had diverted our attention to the doctoral dissertation of her jularker (not called that in the given context). Peter Murphy had inherited his father's wit. (Mary Kathleen once said of him, "He makes me laugh every day; how can I leave him, even if he is from Boston and does talk funny?") The commodity markets are funny, anyway, and my nephew turned them into an ongoing romp. The funniest people of all were the FBI agents who bumbled and stumbled around the floor and among the pits of the exchange.

The wine had been excellent (though Cindasue sipped it cautiously because she had to drive back to Bonn), the food superb French cuisine, and the Black Forest torte for dessert so supremely tasty that I had to request a second helping, lest the cook be offended.

Then we had adjourned to a small, restful parlor (not

the Viking throne room of our previous session). We had enjoyed a tad of Baileys Irish Cream (which I had remembered to bring along).

Then the count cardinal had turned to the subject of the Shrine of the Three Magi.

"We have yet to find it, Cardinal," I began cautiously. "In the process of our investigations, however, we have discovered that its disappearance is inextricably tied to certain problems we have encountered at the dom."

"*Ja*, I was afraid of that," he said somberly.

"The first problem," I continued, "is that security at the dom is for all practical purposes nonexistent. Everyone seems to possess keys to the sacristy and to know the combination for the security system. It is quite impossible to determine who might have removed the shrine the night it disappeared—at least on the basis of who had access to the security structure. Instead of a three locked room mystery, there were in fact no locked rooms. Any one of scores of people might have done it."

"*Ja*, I told Freddie that we should modernize it, but he is quite stubborn, as you doubtless know."

"Criminally stubborn," I said. "Incidentally, at our dom we have several television cameras mounted in strategic places. Someone is always watching the monitors day and night. Moreover, we have also established electronic beams that cross the nave in random directions. Anyone crossing those beams will set off enough alarms to scare them beyond the city limits. It is, all things considered, a relatively inexpensive system."

"*Ja*." He made a note on a pad of paper. "That is very good. We must do that."

"Our second finding," I went on implacably, "is that Signor Donatelli is an excellent art forger, as your Madonna of Limburg in the oratory demonstrates. We make no accusations against him in regard to either the shrine or any other objects of art. But we would recommend that a careful survey be made of all the wondrous art in the dom by the most skilled experts to verify the provenance of everything. Given that the dom has been in effect wide open at night for some time, anything might have been taken and replaced by a copy. I grant you that stealing the shrine was a major operation that required many individuals, a highly effective logistic system, and a carefully devised plan. But smaller objects, to say nothing of the golden items in your treasury, which we must presume is as leaky as the rest of the dom, could easily be removed. There would be great temptations to engage in robbery, especially if the objects could be replaced with persuasive substitutes.''

"Donatelli," the count cardinal sighed. "I like him, you know, but he is, how should I say, unstable. Some things he might do for mere amusement. I will admit that I was frightened when he brought in the Madonna and told me it would look better in my chapel than in Sankt Maria am Kapital. Then he laughed. It was a big joke. Nonetheless, I had it carefully examined, just to make sure. The expert said that the man who made it was an excellent copiest.''

With another sigh, this one heavy, he made a second note.

"I agree," I replied, "that he is unstable. Moreover, he does not like Herrn Dompfarrer at all. It would be wise to make sure that he has resisted all the temptations that he might encounter.''

"Thirdly," I pushed ahead, "we have grave questions about the friendship between Bishop Heidrich and Herr Heinz Zellner. By all accounts, we hear the latter is a most unsavory man, both politically and personally. He is a thief, a torturer, and a sympathizer if not a financial supporter of the neo-Nazis. We do not have solid reason to believe yet that he is involved in the theft of the shrine, though we may learn about that soon. But the relationship between him and Bishop Heidrich, which seems to be patent to everyone, is a grave danger to the Catholic Church in this city.''

Claus Maria von Obermann's face grew grim. He tapped his pen on his notebook.

"I have warned Freddie often about this man. He does

not listen to me. He acts like the dom is his own little diocese. I do not want to fight with him because he has his supporters and because it does not seem right to punish one's political opponents."

"That is an admirably tolerant position, Herr Kardinal. Does not the situation change, however, when the opponent not only conspires against you but engages in behavior that is a threat to the welfare of the church and the faith of the people?"

"*Ja,* I cannot be too tolerant, as perhaps I have been. Tell me more bad news."

He smiled ironically and continued to tap his pen on the notebook but did not add any notes.

"It does get worse," I said, "as much as I regret it."

"Go ahead, Blackie, the truth will make us free."

"We also have excellent reason to believe that the Herr Dompfarrer is channeling money to neo-Nazi and anti-Turkish groups and doing so quite blatantly. I'm sure a routine check of his books will reveal that."

He dropped his pen on the table next to his ample chair.

"You are sure of that?"

"Sure enough, Herr Kardinal, to raise our suspicion with you. You can easily confirm it, we believe, by examining the records of the parsonage. An eyewitness we trust has seen the checks."

"You work very quickly, Herr Blackie."

He picked up his pen and made another note on the pad.

"Is there any more bad news?"

"Just one more point."

"I must hear it. I assume it is the worst?"

"By far. We have eyewitness testimony of the rape of choirboys by priests on the staff of the dom."

"*Mein Gott!*" He screamed, rising from his chair, a furious Viking prince, perhaps about to go berserk. "Are you sure?"

"We can tell you the witness's name, though we would prefer to maintain that person's complete anonymity so that we might protect the person from the very serious danger that person's courage might cause for the person's family.''

He sank back into his chair, his hands clutched to his face.

"You believe the person is not capable of lying?"

"Absolutely not."

"*Ja* . . ."

He removed his hands and sat up straight in the chair.

"I have heard rumors of inappropriate behavior between certain priests. I have worried about them. But I cannot do anything because of rumors. I listen carefully, I doubt, I hesitate. I am perhaps too political. You can tell me the names of the boys and the dates?"

"If necessary, but it might be much better if you set up a commission of proven and honest priests to investigate everything about the dom and to look into the sexual abuse matter."

"*Ja,* you are right, Blackie. It is good for us that you came here, even if you don't find the shrine. Freddie must go?"

"Absolutely."

"I must demand that he retire. If he does not, I must dismiss him, if I am to grab for Patricia the Penny Planter's treasure?"

It would be very difficult for this decent Rhenish democrat to fire anyone.

"Absolutely."

"*Ja* . . . Kurt is not involved, is he?" He asked, his face twisted in pain.

"Not as far as we know. As we understand it, Bishop Heidrich has tried often to replace him."

"*Ja,* that is true. Kurt has told you nothing?"

"Not at all. Only about his ME-262."

"Sometimes he is very complicated . . ."

"It seems unlikely that he is ignorant of the state of affairs. We have learned that he keeps his own young people away from the other priests at the parsonage."

"*Ja, ja,*" he said as he rubbed his hands across his

eyes. "If a commission is set up with my authority, Kurt will tell the truth, however obscurely."

He penned several more notes as though he were setting up the commission already.

"Well," he said sorrowfully, "it will all be done as you suggest. First thing next week."

"No," I said firmly. "It must all be done first thing tomorrow morning. You must assemble your commission and by noon tomorrow personally go to the dom and dismiss the Dompfarrer. He must leave before the sun sets."

"Is that not terribly harsh?"

"The question, Herr Kardinal, is whether it's necessary."

"*Ja,* that is the proper question. Is it?"

"Absolutely. Many things may happen tomorrow or the next day. The Church must be seen acting before they happen instead of after."

"What things?"

"You don't want to know. You want to be able to say you were not aware of these matters."

"That is true," he said, shaking his head sadly. "Even if these things do not happen, we must not waste any more time. I have wasted too much as it is. Perhaps I am too jovial."

"I don't think so, Herr Cardinal. Better a jovial democrat than a psychopathic authoritarian."

"*Ja,* perhaps."

I became aware that I was drained. My assault on this good man's serenity had been direct and brutal. It seemed to have worked, but only time would tell. Other churchmen have backed off from similar tough decisions when there was too much pressure.

"We are very sorry, Kardinal," Cindasue spoke up for the first time, her lovely face white and tense, "that we had to say these terrible things to you, especially after the pleasant evening with you."

"Ach, Cindy, you are all angels come to save us from catastrophe and not a minute too soon. I am grateful to all of you. I will act on these matters.'' He pounded the table with sudden fierceness. ''And I will act immediately! I will set up my commission tonight!''

Peter Murphy, shaded in the darkness in the corner of the room, rose and poured us all another glass of Baileys.

''Patricia the Penny Planter would be pleased with you, Cardinal.''

We all laughed to ease the nervous tension.

We chatted about other matters for a few listless moments and then rose to leave. The count cardinal needed every minute of his time to set in motion the wheels of his investigation.

Then we walked to the door of the house. The cardinal kissed Cindasue's hand again and shook hands with Peter Murphy and me.

''*Ja,* we search for a shrine and we find a mess. It is good we find the mess, even if we don't find the shrine.''

''We'll find the shrine, too,'' I said with no particular reason for thinking so, save for the picture that once again floated like a racing cloud across my brain. For a moment, I almost had it.

At the door, we met the returning Rudi and Fritz. They smiled at us, particularly at the U.S.C.G. person.

''Rudi! Fritz!'' the Cardinal said grimly. ''We have much work to do. Tomorrow there will be a *putsch* at the dom.''

''*Ja!*'' they shouted happily.

They, too, thought it was time.

We had also protected Helena Strauss and her husband. It has been a good night.

Outside on the side street that led to Dürnerstrasse, we paused in the pleasantly cool night air.

''You done right good, Uncle Blackie.''

''What if we're wrong?'' Peter Murphy asked.

''We are not wrong, Peter Murphy. Bank on it.''

''Shonuff,'' Cindasue agreed.

24

Cindasue insisted that she was perfectly capable of driving home by herself. It was late at night. My nefoo had drunk too much mountain dew. He and I needed a good night's sleep and a day off tomorrow on the Rhine River. He'd jest be a-falling asleep in the car and she would have to drag him to the train.

She looked pretty tired, too, face drawn and formal whites wilted.

But my nefoo apparently understood the signals better now and decided that this was not the night to push for the ultimate resolution of the Cindasue mystery.

So we rode down the elevator to the parking lot beneath the hotel and escorted her to her Benz. She bussed her jularker a quick good night kiss. He and I went back to the lobby of the hotel, where he proposed another sip of "Baileys Mountain Dew."

We reclined in comfortable chairs in the spacious lobby. Mine enabled me to face the street in front of the hotel.

"Do you think she wanted to get rid of me tonight?"

"Arguably."

"I'd say 'patently.' "

I remained silent.

"I reckon I've become too much for her now. She wants to escape for a bit, maybe needs to escape."

In the back of my head, a bell was ringing loudly, a fire station alarm bell. Something was wrong.

"You will permit her to escape?"

"Short run. I didn't figure that tonight was worth fighting about."

The bell grew louder. Whatever was going down was terribly wrong.

"Something wrong, Uncle Blackie?"

I had not seen something outside and then I saw something outside. I knew what was happening.

I jumped out of my chair with alacrity that I permit few to see and shouted, "The garage! Stairs! Now!"

We dashed down the concrete stairs at full tilt, myself in the lead.

As I had expected, there was a melee at the unattended exit gate. A skinhead was on the garage floor, moaning. Two others, armed with knives, were closing in on a bedraggled and furious Cindasue, who was wielding an iron pipe like it was a Viking battle-ax.

Everything went into slow motion, a fierce battle that, one way or another, could last only a few moments stretched out into what seemed like leisurely hours.

The skinheads were cursing in German, Cindasue was bellowing in mountain talk, "No-count male-hog pole-cats, I'll castrate the whole lunkhead lot of y'all!"

So saying, she ducked under one knife that was swung at her, jabbed the assailant in the gut with the end of her weapon, then as he doubled up, she hit him in the shins with it and stamped on his toes.

He fell to the floor and joined his buddy in a chorus of agony.

Martial arts, mountain style.

The remaining active skinhead grabbed Cindasue by the shoulder, pulled off the remnants of her white formal blouse, wrapped her in a stranglehold, and aimed his knife at her face.

She kneed him in the stomach, he grunted, and his grip on her weakened momentarily.

She squirmed, slipped partially out of his grip, and almost escaped.

Shouting triumphant curses, he recovered his strength, captured her again, strangled her, and, as she weakened, delicately touched her face with his razor and prepared to cut her face to pieces.

Just then, my nefoo hit him from behind, pulled him off Cindasue, hurled him to the floor, and jumped on him with a cry of fury.

Cindasue, gasping for breath, stamped on the skinhead's fingers, kicked his knife away, and picked it up herself. For good measure, she kicked the two wailing skinheads in the groin, notably increasing the sound level of their curses.

Don't monkey 'round with our mountain flower.

What was I doing all this time?

I was standing just inside the entrance to the up ramp, waiting for the man who had been our tail yesterday, whom I'd seen entering the garage while we were sitting in the lobby. I had possessed myself of a large push broom standing neatly in a corner of the garage as the only available weapon.

As he sauntered through the door, doubtless assuming that the cries of pain were from our side instead of his and preparing to enjoy the fun, I stepped behind him and banged him on the neck with the business end of the broom.

He dropped the small caliber revolver from his hand, staggered, wavered, grabbed the back of his neck, and then straightened up and pulled a long dagger from a sheath on his belt.

Meanwhile, with the quick move of a cougar, Cindasue jumped at the gun, grabbed it, and backed away from him.

"Pete, keep an eye on them singing varmints. Uncle Blackie, stand back; I'm a fixing to kill this here varmint, less'n he drop his knife thing."

The man chortled. This tiny slip of a girl could not possibly shoot a gun, even if she seemed to know how to hold it in both hands. Cutting her up would be fun; then, gun in hand, he'd go after us.

Mistake. Terrible mistake. The marksperson prize-winner had learned to shoot, by her own admission, before she was toilet trained.

She warned him again, he laughed again, and, only three feet away, he lunged.

The small gun popped, like a single firecracker on the Fourth. A blossom like a bright red mum opened on his shoulder. He dropped his knife, clutched his shoulder, and screamed.

I discreetly snatched the knife, though I had no idea what I would do with it.

"Ah aimed for your shoulder, varmint. You do what I tell ya, or nex' time, I'll kill you plumb 'tween the eyes. Now, git over by your friends. . . . Ah said *git!*"

He got.

"Pete and Blackie," she continued, "y'all stand back. I'll watch them polecats."

We did as instructed.

"Any of y'all move, and I'll shoot ya," she warned the wretched band of would-be assailants. "I'd jest love to kill y'all dead."

Despite this clear warning, one injured raider reached for a knife that neither Peter nor I had retrieved from the concrete floor.

She shot his fingers. He cried out again.

"Pete, you git that thar knife."

He done got it.

"Ah only got me four bullets left in this here gun," she warned our prisoners, "an' thar four of y'all. So next time you mule faces move, I'll plug him plumb 'tween the eyes. Y'all hear me?"

"Thank'ee, Peter Murphy, suh, for saving me from that there varmint."

"My pleasure, ma'am. You want me to hit him again with this pipe?"

"Only when I tell you to."

"Yes, ma'am."

My nefoo's voice was cool, even amused. But his black Irish face was as set in stone as the icons on Mount Rushmore.

At that time, like Major Reno riding to the aid of Lieutenant Colonel George Armstrong Custer, the *Polizei* arrived. Five of them poured in from the ramp and then halted abruptly at the sight before them: a Benz pulled against the wall, its bumper crushed and its door pulled off its hinges; three screaming skinheads on the floor; a cheap punk clutching his bleeding shoulder; a furious young man gripping an iron pipe; a hapless cleric, a knife in hand almost as long as he was tall; and a battered but determined young woman, holding a gun like she knew how to use it.

"Y'all stay out," she warned, brandishing her weapon at them. "Happen you look at that varmint, you see I done shoot straight."

"Polizei," said a young man, perhaps a sergeant.

"Ah don't give a hoot in hell who y'all are. How I know you ain't varmints like these mule faces?"

I retrieved our she-cougar's purse from the floor near the Benz, nodded politely to the cops, removed her cellular phone, and dialed Ernie's home number. I forget most phone numbers, but not important ones.

A green and white cop car with a green light whirling zoomed into the garage. *They look like ice cream trucks,* I thought. And these cops in their khaki uniforms looked like modernized members of the Afrika Korps.

"Y'all tell them varmints to stay in that thar car till we'uns find out you real cops."

The sergeant knew enough English to shout at his colleagues, who were emerging from the vehicle with a massive collection of highly dangerous automatic weapons.

"Schulteis," the voice on the phone informed me.

"Blackie . . . We have a situation here at the hotel. We have incapacitated a band of skinheads who have tried to attack us. To be more specific, the fräulein unterleutnant incapacitated them. A number of personnel purporting to be colleagues of yours have appeared, including a group in a car that purports to be one of yours who are well enough armed to storm the Bundesbank. Our Fräulein Unterleutnant is understandably disinclined to accept that claim at face value. Perhaps you can talk to the man who seems to be their leader.''

There was no doubt in my mind that the men and women who had swarmed down the ramp were authentic cops, summoned doubtless by a terrified hotel staff. However, Ernie would tell them who we were and thus avoid needless confusion as to who wore the white hats and who wore the black hats. Moreover, it was necessary to placate our intrepid boss lady.

''Obersuperintendent Schulteis,'' I informed the sergeant.

He snapped to immediate attention.

He was reduced to repeating the all-purpose German word, ''*ja,*'' while he nodded vigorously to Ernie. Then he described in rapid German what he and his colleagues had come upon, with periodic glances at the fearsome young woman who clung to her gun like she was ready to fire it at any moment at anyone who displeased her.

Finally, he gave the phone back to me.

''Formidable!'' Ernie exclaimed.

''Oh, yes.''

''She is unhurt?''

''Oh, yes.''

''Will you tell her to give the gun to my sergeant?''

''You tell her,'' I said passing the phone over to its proper owner.

Her face still cold and hard, she took the phone.

''*Ja, ja,* Herr Obersuperintendent . . . Ah didn't do nothin, jest fought off a few polecat varmints, like a woman has to do all t' time in McCloud's Holler whar I hail from. *Ja, Danke. Ja . . .*''

She motioned the sergeant toward her and lowered the gun.

He saluted, smiled, and bowed.

She handed the gun to him and actually smiled back.

"Sorry to be a-making trouble for you folks. Lawd knows, I'm glad y'all here to collect them thar monkeyshiners. They shonuff did mommick up this hyar garage floor. Y'all better do somethin' 'bout that varmint who's a-bleedin', 'less'n he done die."

The cop shouted instructions to his colleagues, punctuated with cries of *"Schnell! Schnell!"*

Meanwhile, she had returned the phone to my possession.

"Ja," said Ernie, "formidable! I will be there in ten minutes with Frau Schulteis."

I returned the phone to Cindasue's purse. Meanwhile, she had dissolved into the waiting arms of Peter Murphy. He was weeping, she was not. Not yet.

"Them durn polecats done ruin my formal whites," she protested.

Tears dangerously close to my own eyes, I said, "Mountain cougar woman, this h'yar Federal Republic fixin' to give you another uniform and, less'n I don't understand, them thar'll be some fancy new medal they'll put on it."

"Shucks," she said, smiling slightly, "I ain't no mountain cougar woman, much as I'd like to be. . . . Ah didn't do nothing, 'cept'n tame them varmints. . . . Peter Murphy, you the lastiest jularker in the whol' wide worl'."

Fifteen minutes later, we were in a corner of the lobby of the hotel, attempting to restructure our mission. Cindasue, wearing Peter Murphy's banker's coat over the ruins of her uniform, insisted first of all on calling the duty officer at the embassy in Bonn. She gave him, in her own style, an account of the event, in which she designed to minimize her activities.

No way that the duty officer bought that account. He must have asked a lot of questions, because Cindasue retreated behind hill talk to confuse him. Finally, it seemed, he pulled out the whole story.

"Durn fool say if theyz done hurt me, the Yewnited

States of Merica would be a-startin' World War III.''

Three armed young woman cops (younger even than Cindasue) stood close to us, their eyes bright with admiration.

She had yet to weep and had a lot of weeping to do. Most of the time, she cowered in Peter Murphy's all-too-willing embrace. Periodically, she would pull away from that protection to protest about something.

"Why they all a-treating me with so much respect? I no durn fool heroine!''

"Hero,'' I said applying the canons of political correctness to her speech. "And you are, young woman; you might as well get used to that.''

"Hmf . . .'' she snorted.

"Whar's my vehicle?'' she demanded. "What'd theyz done with hit? Them thar varmints done smashed it with that iron bar and then torn off the door.''

And she had snatched the bar to begin her defense.

"The *Polizei* will have it repaired for you by Tuesday. They'll have a substitute for you tomorrow morning, one of theirs, because as you told us, nobody does nothing here on Sunday.''

"I gotta go back to Bonn t'night.''

My nefoo recaptured her.

"You listen to me, Cindasue Lou McCloud. We have a room here for you. Maria,'' he nodded at a blond cop, "will be in the room with you. Heidi and Luci will be outside the door. You're staying here tonight and that's settled, you hear?''

"Ah don't have my nightie,'' she pleaded weakly.

"The thought of you in bed without a nightie, Cindasue, sends my fantasy life into orbit. But, alas, I won't be in the room with you. Not for a while, anyway.''

She giggled and blushed.

"Happen you ever be in that sityation, I a-doubting that you could cope.''

"We'll see about that.''

She giggled again and snuggled closer to him. I thought, however, that she was still semicatatonic. I wondered whether her problems in Stinkin' Crik were related to shooting people.

Then, having drifted inconspicuously (as I always do) away from our group, I called the count cardinal on her cellular phone, which I noted needed a recharge.

Rudi answered and assured me that Herr Kardinal was very busy. He yielded when I told him who I was.

"Ja?" the count cardinal said, a touch of impatience in his voice.

"A group of skinheads tried to attack Cindy in the garage tonight, a mistake they will regret for the rest of their lives. She is undamaged but, ah, somewhat rumpled. They seemed to be ordinary street punks, not effective fighters. They were led by an older street punk who is also a petty criminal. The last named began following us a couple of days ago."

"Ja," the Kardinal mused. "You think that Freddie might be involved?"

"We have no proof of that, Cardinal. Herr Schulteis will naturally try to link the event to our quest, I assume with his usual discretion. I cannot understand why anyone on the dom staff would want to engage in such terrorism, however."

"Only if they are crazy, Blackie," he said ponderously. *"Ja,* I think Freddie is crazy."

"I thought you should know."

"It is good that you called me. . . . Cindy is not hurt?"

"Only emotionally, but she will be all right."

At that point, Ernie and Frau Schulteis arrived. I had felt sorry for Ernie because he had such a tough job. He lost my sympathy when I saw Frau Schulteis. She was a slender, gray-haired woman, well groomed, lively, and with a smile that would melt all the ice around the North Pole.

Immediately, Cindasue was sobbing in her arms. We had crossed the first bridge toward her recovery from combat trauma.

I worried about the possibility that there was combat

trauma out of her past that might link up with the present events. I did not like that possibility.

Peter Murphy left the two women together and strolled over to the hotel desk. Our team had always been treated with great respect. Now we were greeted like special visitors from heaven—Peter Murphy and I because we were associates of the now-legendary Cindasue.

Ernie and I found another constellation of easy chairs. I ordered two glasses of Baileys. We began to talk.

"Street punks and petty criminals," he said contemptuously. "The skinheads said that Hans Steiner offered them money to beat up some Americans and rape and disfigure an American woman. They claim that they do not know where the money came from. I am inclined to believe them. Steiner is in surgery now. He will live. I suspect that he received the money from someone else, whose name he will say he did not know. Whether he will remember the name when he faces a long term in prison remains to be seen. Do you have any suspicions?"

"The dom staff," I said bluntly.

"The woman that we are protecting in Ahrweiler worked there once, did she not?"

"So I am told."

He cautiously sipped the brown liqueur that had been placed on the glass table next to him.

He raised his eyebrows in approval.

"*Ja,* I have never tasted this before, but it is very good. *Very* good. Irish, is it not?"

"The most popular liqueur in the world. One percent of the export trade of Ireland."

He drank another sip and nodded in approval. Due to the machinations of the evil leprechaun, most of mine had already disappeared.

"There's been no attempts on her, though we will continue our protection indefinitely as I promised. It is easy duty for us in Ahrweiler. And pleasant, from what I hear about the woman . . ."

"Arguably."

"I have other distractions, as you perhaps have noticed."

He smiled contentedly and finished his Baileys off.

"Indeed."

"I have often worried about the dom," he mused. "Perhaps I should have a talk with Claus—unless you already have."

"I have. I believe we will see action in the very near future."

"*Ja,* that is good. It is a very complicated situation. You think that the Dompfarrer is responsible for the attack."

"Certainly not directly. I would not want to eliminate the possibility that he lurks behind it. I believe that he is or more likely has become quite mad."

"I agree." Ernie nodded his head. "The Federal Republic is not inclined to indict a bishop, although he was once a Hitler Youth and, in my judgment, never stopped being a Nazi. There are those around still, Blackie. Even in the Church. Sometimes I think especially in the Church . . . But why would he steal his own shrine?"

"I have no idea," I admitted.

"You think there is no connection?" he raised an eyebrow.

I had noted that with Frau Schulteis watching him out of the corner of her eye, he was not smoking. Good for her.

"That remains to be seen. The security system at the dom is worthless, as you probably know. Almost everyone has keys and knows the combination."

"*Ja,* so anyone with a van, a few young men, an adequate plan, and some luck could have stolen the shrine."

"It would appear so."

"We will keep a guard—a substantial and well-armed guard—around you indefinitely, also. You may notice them. The young people will not."

"Cindy will," I replied, "but just now that is not a bad thing."

"I believe I will hear from Herrn Bundeskanzler later

this evening," he added. "I will inform you, naturally. You approve of my wife, *nein*?"

"What man would not?"

"*Ja*, she is a psychologist. She keeps me sane."

"And forbids you to smoke."

"*Ja*, she is a fine mother, as you can see, and an excellent wife, somehow better every year. That happens, does it not, Blackie?"

"More often than many people think," I said with my patented West-of-Ireland sigh, "but not, alas, as often as it ought."

I noted that my nefoo, whom a woman concierge had led over to the gift shop (closed at this hour of course, but open for the handsome young American) had emerged with an armful of packages.

I knew what he was up to, naturally; it would be a splendid show. Cindasue's degrees of freedom were diminishing, if only because she would miss him terribly this time. Loneliness—or the potential for it—is perhaps the strongest weapon against fear of intimacy.

I ambled over for the show; Ernie went to the telephone kiosk, perhaps to call the Herrn Bundeskanzler again on a line more secure than his own cellular phone.

"I brought some things to make your stay here in Köln more pleasant," he said to our heroine, as he unloaded his bundles on the couch next to her.

I noted the concierge lingered to watch the show. The three woman cops closed in. It was lucky that Blackie Ryan often fades into invisibility.

"Fust off," he said, " 'lessen your modesty be offended because you done brung no nightie 'long, I bought you one."

The red lace creation he removed from a bag, while artfully constructed, would provide not the slightest protective cover.

"Why you durty-minded polecat," Cindasue said with feigned dismay, "I'd never wear nothing like that."

"I'll take it back then."

"No you won't."

She clutched it to her chest (still amply protected by Peter Murphy's banker's coat.

"Happen I'll wear it someday."

"A wrap to go with it," he said removing a wispy garment of the same color that would add nothing at all to the protection the gown offered.

Cindasue abandoned her pretense of shock.

"Professor Peter Murphy, suh, you jest the sweet'st boy I never did meet."

"Here," he continued, now confident in yet another success, "are a couple of bags of things that Emma here says you might be able to use."

Tears appeared again in the traumatized young woman's eyes, tears of love.

"I assume we're going on our ride down the river tomorrow . . ."

"Up the river," she corrected him tenderly. "North is downstream, south is up."

"I bought you some things, happen we still go."

He produced white shorts, as short as modesty permitted, a purple knit shirt, and a red and white sweatshirt that announced in broad letters, Köln.

She was simply unable to answer, a rare enough sitiyation for our Coast Guard officer.

"Then, 'cuz your clothes all cut up, I got a few of these things, case you needed them."

He offered three cellophane envelopes of lingerie, which was almost entirely lace.

"Only a shameless hussy would wear them things," she protested as she hugged them. "You the lastiest, Dr. Murphy, suh."

It was all a sexual tease, of course, mixed with kindness and consideration. My nefoo was closing in on her. The escape hatches were clamping shut. Good for him.

Then he opened his most devastating surprise, a package with three swimsuits.

"Happen y'all wake up early and y'all want to go a-frolickin' in that thar pool, I bought these shameless things for the guards. Desk folk tell me that the pool doesn't open till ten on Sunday, but you'uns can use it any time y'all want. This hyar key will get you in."

For a moment, the three cops forgot they were cops on duty and became young women to whom an attractive man had given lovely presents. They swarmed around him and kissed him, the cops carefully, herself passionately.

"Oh, yeah," Peter Murphy said, "I forgot the last present. Cindasue, happen you stay around this h'yar hotel place, you'll need at least one more swimsuit. So I bought this 'un. Emma say you'll like it."

"It's only a few strings!" Cindasue cried out in fake dismay, tears flowing from her magic green eyes again.

"More than that," Peter Murphy reassured her.

Frau Schulteis winked at Peter Murphy. He winked back.

Then she gave Cindasue a packet of tranquilizers.

"This will help you sleep, dear, and it's not habit forming. You need a good sleep. And, young women, see that she goes to bed and sleeps, no all-night conversations."

"Yessum," Cindasue agreed.

"Ja, Frau Doktor," the three woman cops said obediently.

Apparently their generation did not call her by her correct title, "Frau Obersuperintendent-Doktor."

Egalitarianism had come to Germany.

I retired at that point to my own room to ponder possible new insights in the case of the mystery of the lost Shrine of the Three Magi.

I could find none.

25

Two phone calls disturbed my well-deserved early-morning slumbers.

The first was from Ernie, while it was still dark.

"The Herrn Bundeskanzler has given us permission to raid the *Schloss*. He seemed happy to do so, both because he wants us to find the shrine and because he has grown weary of Herr Zellner. If we find anything, we will arrest him this afternoon when he arrives at the Bonn-Köln Airport. If God is good, we will have the shrine by tonight."

It was no time to engage in a theological discussion about the goodness of Herself.

But it would not be wise to bet much on the recovery of the shrine.

I went back to sleep.

Then, when the sun had begun to rise, the phone rang again.

"*Ja,* Blackie," said the Herr Kardinal. "Today at ten-thirty we go to the dom and dismiss Freddie. You will come with us, *nein?*"

I pondered for a moment, bemused as I was by sleep, then made a decison.

"You bet."

Arguably, he had tried to disfigure a young woman who was virtually a member of the Ryan clan. That was intolerable. The ceremony would be like pounding a stake into the heart of a vampire.

Moreover, he might slip and say something about the mystery of the missing shrine.

I returned again to my well-deserved rest.

At nine-thirty, I was awakened by room service with a continental breakfast I had ordered before I went to bed. They did indeed provide grapefruit juice and a modicum of cornflakes, which I supplemented with dark chocolate. I called my nefoo's room. There was no answer. I assumed, correctly as it turned out, that he and his lady love were in the swimming pool.

I decided that I would return to my Blackie persona and attired myself in a white sport shirt, black jeans, and Bulls jacket.

Equipping myself with two more dark chocolate bars, I descended to the hotel lobby to encounter the younger folk in swimsuits and robes, coming up from the pool. All things considered, Cindasue seemed in good spirits and good health. I explained to them that I had a minor errand to attend to. I was ordered to be back by noon so we could do our Rhenish cruise while the weather lasted.

Our boss lady certainly did not look like a young woman who had engaged in mortal combat the night before. However, the traumas still lurked beneath the surface. Mere (relatively innocent) romancing in the pool with a jularker would not heal the new set of scars so quickly.

Shonuff would help, however.

As I arrived at the door of the hotel, a very large Mercedes limo arrived. Fritz was at the wheel, the cardinal, in full watered silk regalia, was next to him, and five very stern-looking young priests sat in the back. I was, however, constrained to sit next to the count cardinal of Cologne.

"*Ja,* Blackie, this time we do it right, *nein*?"

"You betcha."

As we navigated from the hotel toward the dom, which loomed peacefully over a peaceful autumn Sunday, I noted that there was a cavalcade of similar cars behind us.

"Who's the gang?" I asked with little diplomatic tact.

"Our investigation team, medical doctors, psychologists, retired police officers, art experts, accountants, lawyers, security people . . . *Ja,* nothing halfway this time!"

At least, I told myself, we're not using Mercedes Roadsters, like they do in the movies.

Then I reminded myself that we were on the other side.

And our weapons were briefcases and stethoscopes.

Five cars pulled up in front of the old, crumbling, Gothic parsonage. Some thirty priests and laity emerged, all in somber attire, as if they were going to a funeral. The cardinal put on his crimson, four-cornered beretta, Fritz screwed together his crozier, the cardinal took his place in the middle, with Rudi on one side and the Dompfarrer of Chicago, unaccountably on the other (appropriately, I thought, on the left). The men and women spread out in wings slightly behind him, like a flying wedge in the football of yesteryear.

We needed a cross bearer, a thurifer, two acolytes, and a choir in red cassocks singing "Vexila Regis Prodeant." However, for a sunny Sunday morning in a middle-class city in the German Federal Republic at the tag end of the twentieth century, it was not bad as ceremonies go, especially when the count cardinal's watered silk cape trailed out behind him like crimson contrails on a supersonic jet. Nonetheless, it was not up to Kenneth Branagh standards.

I found myself tempted to sing, "When the Saints Go Marching In!" In fact, I hummed it to myself.

What, I wondered, did the spirits of past archbishop electors think of our show? Probably they would have said they had seen better.

The cardinal hammered on the door with his croizer. A housekeeper opened the door and bowed out of the way, we piled in the door, filled the whole arched hallway, and spilled into a number of side rooms.

"Herr Dompfarrer!" The Herr Kardinal bellowed.

Bishop Heidrich appeared, also in full regalia, within a minute.

"*Jawohl,* Herr Kardinal!"

I thought for a moment that the count cardinal would give a lecture on why that was not a word that was approved in the BDR.

Instead, he shouted again in parade ground style, "Herr Dompfarrer, you will sign this resignation immediately."

He pointed to a document that Fritz was holding on a clipboard.

"*Nein,* Herr Kardinal!"

"*Ja,* then I will dismiss you, effective immediately."

Fritz offered a second document, which the count cardinal signed with a flourish.

"You are trying to destroy me! I will not leave!"

"Rudi is the new Herr Dompfarrer. He will take charge of this house immediately. You will leave or be taken to Saint Elizabeth of Hungary Hospital where you will be examined. If you are pronounced well and if we find no wrongdoing in our investigation, you will be free to leave."

"I forbid this," Heidrich shouted. "This is my house. You have no right to come in it like this. I will call the police. I will have you arrested. I will talk to the press. I will go on television."

"You will leave now!" the cardinal thundered. "Take him out of here!"

A couple of beefy guys in charcoal gray suits and a young priest grabbed the bishop and moved him toward the door of the rectory. The unfortunate man began to babble hysterically.

Later I would wonder if there were any other way to handle his removal besides this brutal putsch. I couldn't think of any, under the circumstances.

"You stole my shrine!" he cried. "You stole the Shrine of the Magi."

That stopped the count cardinal for a moment.

"You are a sick man, Freddie," he said more softly. "Why should I steal the shrine? You need help. We will give you help."

The question in my mind was why Freddie would make such a crazy charge. Momentarily, I saw the explanation again, but in the noise of our *putsch*, I lost it.

Now the former Dompfarrer turned on me. Apparently, to him at any rate, I was not invisible.

"Your young friend is not so pretty anymore, is she?" he ranted. "See what happens to spies."

Suddenly, everyone in the corridor was silent. So that indeed was where the assault came from. Apparently he had not heard of the outcome yet.

"She's fine," I shot back, perhaps too quickly. "You should see what your friends look like!"

"Freddie," the cardinal sighed. "Why?"

"Spies! Spies! They were part of the plot to steal my shrine! I will cut them all into little pieces!"

Foam began to flow from his mouth. He was becoming a raging madman.

The security people dragged him from the house over which he had presided for so many years.

There but for the grace of God goes Blackie Ryan.

"Why?" Cardinal von Obermann asked me. "Why?"

"I doubt that we will ever know."

Three of the four priests on the staff were also ordered to pack their things and depart for Saint Elizabeth's. They were terrified and all looked guilty. We had not asked Frau Strauss who the rapists were. We would find that out and pass on their names. Unless, as seemed likely, Cindasue had already done that.

The various experts distributed themselves around the parsonage and left for the dom.

"Nothing is to be destroyed!" the cardinal shouted after them. "Nothing!'

Then, suddenly exhausted, he slumped into a dining room that must have been built in the middle ages—and arguably had not been cleaned since then—collapsed into an ancient chair at the table and buried his face in his hands.

"I hate it all, Blackie," he sighed. "What else could I have done?"

"Not much. You could not have afforded to wait another day. Too many other things might happen."

Then again, they might not, and we might have been too harsh.

You have to make decisions and stick with them. There could be very little doubt that the men were guilty of terrible crimes, driven as they were by their various manias.

I looked at my hands. They were clenched in rage. Mess with our Cindasue, will he?

"*Ja,* Claus."

I looked around. Pastor Kurt had drifted into the room in his tattered old cassock. He sat next to the cardinal at the table.

The cardinal looked up and smiled.

"*Ja,* Kurt."

The ex-pilot nodded his head.

"*Ja,*" he said simply.

The cardinal smiled wanly at what was apparently the older man's approval.

"*Ja, ja.*"

I bid the two priests *guten tag* and slipped away. I still did not know what to make of Kurt. Yet the surprising bond between the two men showed me once again that for all the terrible things priests have done down through the ages, there is still power and glory in our office that transcends our horrendous human frailties.

I hailed a cab and in my clearest possible German asked for our hotel on the Hapsburgerring.

I did not want the young lovers going off on their Rhine cruise without me. They might do something dumb and get in trouble.

26

Peter

"Whafo you sleeping 'way the morning fo?" Cindasue demanded. "Why you not down hyar in the pool? We'uns have it fo 'noth'r hour or so."

She had awakened me about a quarter to nine with that challenging question. She sounded fine, but she was skilled at hiding her real feelings behind a mix of mountain talk and mischief. No way she could be feeling so bright and cheery after what had happened the previous night. My muscles and my head ached and I had not been involved in the rout of the skinheads nearly as much as she. I had slept badly because of the excess of adrenaline and because of nightmares about a razor cutting into Cindasue's face.

"You want me to come to the pool?"

"Shonuff!"

"I'll have to shave first."

"You can do that later."

"You're right, Cindasue, as always."

I put on my trunks and a robe and, still half asleep, stumbled down to the pool. The door was open. On the counter, a handwritten note informed me, "Peter Murphy, suh, close the door and it will lock and we'll have our own little private pool.''

Mother superior had planned for everything. She had thrown aside the top of her swimsuit and was waiting for me in the whirlpool, a shy smile on her face.

''Why fo, you looked so shocked? Happen you go t'any beach, 'cept'n it's Arsh, and you see tons of topless women.''

Her eyes were turned away from my open mouthed gaze. Cindasue's breasts, like everything else about her, were diminutive, shapely, graceful, challenging. A man would never quite get used to them.

''None like you, Cindasue.''

''Them wicked German cops done say we'uns should wait for you. I done tell them you like to die of shock.''

''I'd have eyes for only one woman.''

In a sudden movement she covered herself with her arms, grinned sheepishly, and moved her arms away. She wanted to reveal her beauty to me, but was embarrassed by her boldness.

''Wal, stop a-staring and come on in this h'yar pool.''

''Yassum.''

''You think I'm terrible forward, Peter Murphy, suh?''

She curled up against me, providing temporary cover for herself.

''I think you're wonderful,'' I said, stroking her back.

There was not much left to the remnants of her swimsuit. Truly, it was only a little more than a handful of string. Well, that's why I bought it.

''I'm not trying to seduce you,'' she said with a touch of guilt in her voice. ''Wal, not 'xactly.''

''That wouldn't be necessary, Cindasue. You did that the first day at Grand Beach.''

She looked up at me, her green eyes now unbearably fragile.

''Reckon?''

''Reckon.''

''If you want me after I've told you all about me, I like to be a good woman for you, Peter Murphy, suh.''

So that was the point of the splendid show.

I turned her over so she was cradled in my arms and I could kiss her breasts.

"Now don' you be a-doin' anythin' reckless," she warned me.

"Have I ever done anything reckless with you?"

"No, suh, you surely haven't. . . . Don't stop kissing me, not yet."

"You know what, Cindasue?"

"No, suh."

"I think you wanted to show me your breasts and let me kiss them as much as I wanted to."

"Maybe more, Pete."

No more moutain talk.

"Uncle Blackie says that most of the things men want to do to women, women want them to do. And most of the things women want to do to men, men want them to do. The problems are not in the actions but in such matters as tact, timing, sensitivity, patience, style, and honesty. Which are always serious problems, especially if people have hang-ups or are immature."

"I'm sure he's right, Pete. . . . Could you stop just a minute to give me a chance to breathe?"

"I think I can manage that."

I caressed the back of her neck.

"You'll never get away from me, young woman. You hear? Never."

"I'm not exactly running right now, am I?"

We both laughed.

"I always said to other women, I'd never go topless save for a man I really loved. So I guess I really do love you, which you probably know already."

"I kind of half expected that."

We both giggled.

I touched her breasts with my tongue.

She groaned happily.

"That's very nice, Pete. Promise me you'll always do that."

"I promise. . . . How are you this morning? I was too

distracted by the astonishment when I came in.''

"I intended to distract you and I guess I did. I'm OK. I'll have nightmares for awhile and a hard time sleeping. I'll talk to the psychiatrist over in Bonn and work it out. No great problem. I'm still in one piece and my face, such as it is, isn't cut. . . . I knew you and Blackie would come. I just knew it.''

What if we hadn't?

That was not a good question to ask.

"The face is unbearable, Cindasue.''

"Better than my boobs?''

"Breasts don't have eyes that glow, and lips that smile, and expressions that constantly change.''

Not bad, I thought, under the circumstances.

"Not bad,'' she said, "under the circumstances . . . Now, do you want to put my bra on so we can swim?''

"Glad to oblige.''

I fulfilled her request, slowly and carefully, with much touching and caressing in the process.

She twisted once and groaned, "Pete, you're driving me out of my mind.''

"I sure hope so.''

As soon as I had tied the last knot in the back, she sprang out of the hot tub and into the pool. I followed her quickly, as I was practically out of my mind, too.

"We done turn the water into steam,'' she informed me as she somehow emerged behind me and dunked my head.

I must have her by Christmas, I told myself.

27

"Uncle Blackie," Cindasue protested, "we'uns a-waiting on you. The boat ain't goin' to stay thar till we show up 'less'n we hurry."

"I had to attend a minor *putsch*. . . . I called my ne-foo's room. Since he did not answer, I assumed that you both were in the pool. Not wanting to interfere with the contemporary courtship rituals, I departed."

"We'uns done do nothing wrong, nohow," she assured me, a touch of pathos on her elfin face.

"I take that as a given. The critical question is how you feel this morning."

"Shucks, I'm tolable. Folks from McCloud's Holler pretty tough."

"The ambassador called her this morning," Peter Murphy informed me.

"He done worry about me, can you 'magin' that? I say to him, we mountain boomers are purty tough folk. And he say what's a mountain boomer? He he 'bassador man of the Yewnited States of Mericay and not know what a mountain boomer is!"

We were at this point hurrying to catch a taxi that

would take us to the Rhine embankment for our cruise upriver.

"Originally," I said, "it applied to the red squirrels up in the mountains who endure very difficult conditions. Then it came to apply to the descendants of the yeomen farmers who fought to make our country free."

I was patently showing off. But the little imp was trying both to trick and to distract me. Despite her glow from the swim and from romancing with Peter Murphy, she looked terrible. I wondered if somehow that scene in the garage was a repetition of whatever it was that made her fear intimacy with a man.

"Shucks, Uncle Blackie, you done know everythin'."

"Arguably."

"By the way, how did you know that something was going down in the garage?" my nefoo asked.

I sighed. It was not an easy question to answer. Only after reflection could I point to the signs. In the instant that the signs had flashed in my head I *knew* and began to run. Afterward, I realized that somewhere in the subbasement of my brain, I was aware that Cindasue's car had not come up the exit ramp, the end of which I could see from my chair in the lobby. At the same moment, I saw the shade that had been following us walking briskly down the ramp. Then the bells went off.

"Amazin'!"

"Elementary, my dear Lieutenant McCloud."

I can't help it. She did set me up with the line, did she not?

By this time, we were in the cab, racing toward the Rhine.

Both the young lovers were in white shorts, he with the inevitable blue and gold Notre Dame T-shirt, she with the white shorts and purple shirt he had bought the previous night. She wore the Köln sweatshirt tied around her waist and a white baseball cap (visor forward) which proclaimed United States Coast Guard and bore the Coast Guard seal and the single silver bar of a Fräulein Unterleutnant. Both carried Loyola sports bags.

"Do you have any suspicions, Cindasue," I asked, "about the origin of the attack last night?"

"I reckon," she said with grimace, "that it were that fella over to the dom."

"Precisely," I said, marveling to myself at the quickness of her insights. "You will be happy to hear that he and his associates are currently incarcerated in a mental hospital south of here, that a new team has taken charge of the dom, and that our good friend Rudi is now the Dompfarrer. There is every reason to believe that the police will soon apprehend the go-betweens."

"Why?" Peter Murphy demanded.

"That is not immediately evident. Bishop Heidrich is currently round the bend altogether. He did, however, make one interesting comment before being removed by the men in white who, incidentally, were not wearing white. He blamed the count cardinal for the theft of the Shrine of the Magi."

"Why?" Cindasue asked with a frown.

"I'm not sure, but I think it is an important clue, only I confess I don't know why. Cindasue, what do you think?"

Note that I was playing fair with my lovely young colleague. I told her the clue and asked her what she thought about it.

Then we disgorged from the taxi, ran frantically down the embankment, and scrambled up the gangplank of the *Düsseldorfer,* just before it was pulled aboard. In truth, if it were not for the shapely legs of the lieutenant junior grade, we almost certainly would have been left behind. Mind you, the crew were nothing if not respectful.

"Permission to come aboard?" she gasped, like a true naval person as she landed on the deck of the cruise ship.

"*Ja, ja,*" the handsome boatswain said with an appreciative grin and salute.

Cindasue snapped off a sharp salute in return.

Peter Murphy had to pull me aboard or I would have lost much of my minuscule dignity by falling into the Rhine.

We worked our way to the bow of the *Düsseldorfer*. There were relatively few people on the big craft because, as Cindasue said, it was past the cruising season, which ends on October 1, regardless of the weather. She passed shades like her own to both me and my nefoo.

"The Coast Guard teaches that we must take good care of our eyes on the water."

"Yes, ma'am," we said together.

She grinned—doing everything to pretend that the events of the previous night had no effect on her.

Only her eyes showed hints of terror and that only occasionally. Our brave young officer dare not reveal any fear.

Why not?

"Uncle Blackie," she asked, "why should the cardinal want to steal his own shrine?"

"I can think of no reason for it," I admitted. "Surely he wouldn't believe that he could outsmart such a resourceful team as this!"

"Including an ace detective," Peter Murphy said, "whom we almost had to pull out of the river."

I ignored that disrespectful and inappropriate sally.

"I think," our peerless leader said thoughtfully and in standard English, "that neither one trusted the other very much. The cardinal knew that the bishop was scheming against him and did not hesitate to take action when he finally had a good reason. The bishop suspected, wrongly in all likelihood, that the cardinal was scheming against him. In principle, either one could have stolen the shrine to discredit each other. So they both suspect that the other one has done it. Maybe neither of them did it, but they both think the other did it."

"Fascinating," I said. "But then who did take it?"

Patently, I had thought of that on the way back to the hotel from the dom. On the other hand, she had thought of it almost immediately when I had told her about the incident. The young woman could be a problem. Yet what if eventually the Ryan-Murphy genes and the McCloud genes be united in the same offspring as I thought not improbable? Not only would the battles of Culloden Moor and the Boyne be undone; we would also have a superb detective that would put both her mother and her great uncle to shame. Please note gender of projected child.

In any case, I didn't tell the Coast Guard person that I had thought of it, too.

"I don't know. Maybe no one wanted to discredit anyone else."

"Arguably."

"But then," she said petulantly, "who did take it?"

"Maybe no one?" Peter Murphy asked, struggling to get in the conversation.

"No one?" his love and I said in unison.

"Yeah, I know. It has to be missing, otherwise we wouldn't be here. The police, the cardinal, the ex-Dompfarrer, and the Herrn Bundeskanzler all say it's missing. They couldn't be conspiring to fool us, could they?"

"Holmes once said," I admitted, "that when the impossible has been eliminated, what remains, however improbable, must be true. I tend to disagree. I'm never quite sure what is impossible."

"Happen this h'yar varmint, Heinz Zellner has hit up in that *Schloss* place of his. Uncle Blackie, can we'uns please have jest a tiny peek at hit?"

"*Nein,*" I said firmly.

Then I decided that I had better tell the truth about the *Schloss* Zellner.

"In point of fact," I observed casually, "I have sound reason to believe that there will be a search of that place this very afternoon."

"What!" they said together.

"I only learned that this morning. When I first tried to contact my nefoo I believe he was in the pool with some young woman."

They both looked mildly embarrassed, but only mildly.

"Don't know who that thar hussy were."

"Then," I continued casually, "if you remember, we were pursuing this craft with some haste."

"Why they a-searchin' the castle?"

I did not want to give a bad example to my future niece by admitting the whole truth, which would have only reinforced her dangerous proclivity to risk-taking. I'm the one who will the primrose path of folly tread, kid, not you.

"I believe they discovered a van outside Herr Zellner's villa in Rodenkirchen, a suburb of Köln. It seemed to fit the description of the van seen outside the dom. There were canvas covers in the van that might have protected stolen art and that had, in fact, been in recent contact with paintings. This gave them the pretext for searching the villa. They discovered certain objects of art that were either missing works or were copies of missing works. . . ."

"Donatelli," she interrupted.

"Arguably, but who is to say? I believe that they are examining the provenance of these works at the present. Or more likely, tomorrow, when people in this country will be back at work again. They relayed the information about their discovery to the Herrn Bundeskanzler who apparently has grown impatient with Herr Zellner and was only too ready to permit a search of the *Schloss* when someone provided a reason to do so. Unless I am mistaken, that search will go down this afternoon, some hours before we arrive."

"Can we go?"

"Young woman, for all your charm and intelligence and insight, you are a hoyden."

"Yassuh, Mr. Preacher Man."

The *Düsseldorfer* was a handsome three-decker with sparkling awnings, bright colors, and resplendent flags straining in the light breeze. It plodded upriver at a pleasant pace through a continuous travel poster show created when the foliage on both sides of the Rhine was turning red and gold. After we passed Rodenkirchen, we left behind what might be called the suburbs of Cologne and encountered strips of postcard waterside villas and clusters of buildings, always with a church steeple towering

above them—hamlets that looked liked they hadn't
changed much since the mid-nineteenth century, save for
the BMWs, the Mercedes, the TV antennae, and the cabin
cruisers. Occasionally, a sail-boarder, with more courage
than prudence, rode the wakes of the river traffic. The
bright sun and the clear blue sky confirmed the travel
poster effect. On the far horizon, an occasional cloud, the
proverbial size of a man's hand, warned that this weather
would not last.

Although I watched carefully as the embankments
turned into hills and we slipped through dramatic gorges,
I caught no sight of Lorelei or similar creatures and heard
no Wagnerian arias sung by outsize blond singers of both
genders. Cindasue was humming something from *Göt-
terdamerung*, which was certainly not bluegrass music.
Better bluegrass, I thought, than Wagner. Better Puccini
than either.

I pictured in my imagination the many tribes that, even
before the beginning of recorded history, drifted down or
pushed their way up the river on missions of trade or
war, barbarians naturally, though they lacked such con-
veniences as automatic weapons, jet planes, poison gas,
guided missiles, and nuclear bombs. And other, equally
barbaric peoples, who surged across the river in either
direction, savages who killed only a tiny fraction of the
people who died on both sides of the river during the
early 1940s, often by bombs made in the U.S.A.

Despite my morose reflections, I could find nothing in
the peaceful autumnal riparian scene that suggested that
this was a sinister setting. The only trouble was in Cindasue's eyes, and that seen only when she removed her
shades.

"In point of fact," I said to her, "Herr Schulteis said
that if we should disembark across the river, he might
join us and inform us on the success or failure of his
search. He points out that they might well encounter
armed resistance. It should all be finished by the time we
arrive. And, I would remind you, young woman, that you
are an officer in the United States Coast Guard, not the

United States Marine Corps. You stay offshore; you don't land.''

If I were there alone, I would be in the forefront of the German feds as they closed in on the place. What I would do, however, was neither here nor there.

Her wicked green eyes twinkled with mischief.

''Yassuh, Mr. Preacher Man . . . leastwise I don't go cavortin' 'round them suburban villas, a-peekin' into vans.''

''Weren't there any guards at the villa?'' Peter Murphy asked with a grim face that suggested I was old enough to know better than to take such chances—an arguable position.

''Unaccountably there were not . . . or so I am told. Perhaps there is nothing really incriminating in the house, only forgeries. So Zellner wasn't worried about it being searched. It did not occur to him that even fakes could provide the DBR with sufficient reason to search his *Schloss*.''

''If'en I had a *Schloss* and an in-town villa,'' the Coast Guard person mused, ''I a-hidin' sumpin' like to get me in trouble in the *Schloss*, and not in no villa where a preacher man done slunk 'round and peek'd in the windows.''

''Precisely,'' I said, ignoring her gratuitous implications.

''No houn' dogs sprung on you and a-chasin' you outten that thar villa?''

We already have a strain of psychic sensitivity in the family—my cousin Catherine's son Jack and my cousin Brendan's wife Ciara. We could do without another one.

''There were two rather handsome Rottweilers in the yard, named Mutt and Mutta, I am informed. However, they very quickly made friends with me.''

''Houn' dogs?''

''My uncle charms dogs and little children,'' Peter Murphy assured her.

''And young women in their middle teens,'' I added.

"Thyz just plumb lay down, them Rottweiler houn's?"

"And rolled over on their backs!"

"Ah do declare, Uncle Blackie, that's right scary!"

"Especially if one is not sure that the dogs can speak English," Peter Murphy observed, still grim.

"As it turned out, they could."

"You don't think they will find the shrine up at the *Schloss,* do you, Uncle Blackie?" Cindasue changed the subject and returned to Standard English, a flash of terror shimmering briefly in her eyes.

Presumably, she felt again the touch of the knife on her face, before the rugby three-quarter-back hit her assailant.

She put her shades back on.

"I would be delighted if that were the case. We could then return to our respective bases and claim credit, with some justification, for recovery of the shrine and the reform of the Kölner Dom. However, for reasons that are not yet precise in my head, I rather doubt that the *Polizei* will find it in the castle."

"Reckon ah thin' so, too."

"How are we going to find it?" Peter Murphy, good social scientific empiricist that he was, demanded.

"Solutions," I said mysteriously, "tend to disclose themselves, eventually."

Once more, the solution did disclose itself, this time in more leisurely and tantalizing fashion. I grasped it, held it, and it slipped away. There was one piece of the puzzle, one element in the motherboard that was still missing. For the want of it, the rest was a jumble.

"Them hound dogs shonuff turned into puppies?"

"They were little more than puppies," I agreed. "Alas, human ingenuity had perverted them."

"Theyz got programs now that can change them back, so they jest bark," she mused. "Like to scare people but never done hurt them. . . . Ah jest dote on hound dogs!"

"Then there is hope for me," Peter Murphy sighed.

We'uns laughed. I'd have to discover whether Mutt

and Mutta might possibly bond on Cindasue. As I remembered, Peter Murphy done dote on hound dogs, too.

"I'll go fetch y'all some food," she announced and slipped away for a moment. I noted that as we walked aft, she kept a careful eye on all the passing traffic, a professional guard of water safety as well as a representative of the oldest of the nation's military agencies.

Doubtless she would have called it the Yewnited States Revenoo Cutt'r Service.

"She's hurtin'," my nefoo confided in me.

"Patently . . . and not unreasonably."

"Why does she have to pretend that she's not?"

"If we knew the answer to that, we'd have solved the mystery of Cindasue."

Peter Murphy's narrow black Irish forehead tightened. "It's the more important of our two mysteries, Uncle Blackie."

"Clearly. The wandering astrologers are long since dead. Herself is very much alive. As someone of some influence in Christianity once remarked, let the dead bury their dead."

We rounded a bend, a hill temporarily obscured the sun, the blue waters of the river turned gray, an appropriate color, given their pollution.

"Will we solve it, Uncle Blackie?"

"I have every confidence that you and she will."

She returned, carrying a tray on which one could see Kölsch beer, bratwurst sandwiches, a glass of red wine, and assorted apple and cherry strudels *mit Sahne.*

"Ah shonuff have to keep mah crew in vittles," she informed us. "Y'all want more, y'all a-chasing up them stairs youselves."

"Yessum," we replied.

We dug into our food with commendable vigor. Since there were five sandwiches, I assumed that two of them were certainly for me. Also one of each kind of strudel. *Mit Sahne.*

She frowned at a barge train that was passing us.

"That durn fool done cut it too close," she muttered.

"Them Romanians shouldn't be 'lowed on this hyar river. We'uns should take and ban 'em."

Before Peter Murphy and I could ask who "we'uns" were and what Lieutenant (J.G.) C. L. McCloud, U.S.C.G.'s role was, the church steeples of Bonn appeared on our right.

"The small town in Germany that Le Carré calls it looks different from the river, doesn't it?" she said. "It never was a small town. The university has been here a long time. Beethoven was born here. It's kind of a sleepy little middle-class city. It has come to mean a lot, however, in the world of the last half century, the place where a couple of postwar miracles occurred, the political one more important than the economic one. Konrad Adenauer created a new German democracy here. His most important decision was to abandon the old idea of a Catholic Center party and create something much broader—a Christian Democratic Union, political ecumenism before religious ecumenism . . . Peter Murphy, suh, you look surprised that this ignor'nt li'l hillbilly know so much?"

"I would have expected it, Cindasue."

Her sly "mountain flower" grin flitted across her face and her witch's eyes twinkled.

I noted that, whenever she looked at my nephew, she took off her sunglasses.

"Ya jest a-sayin' that. . . . Up there, right where my finger is pointing, is where Adenauer lived. And over there, that big place with the Merican flag, which looks like it's fit for a Roman proconsul, is the Embassy of the Yewnited States of Mericay. That's where I work, up there on the second floor from the top with one of those little windows overlooking the river."

"What do you do there, Cindasue?" Her jularker asked innocently.

"Jest set thar a-reading papers all day lon'."

"And watching the boats go by," I commented.

A mask settled quickly over her lovely face.

"That's right, Uncle Blackie," she said. "Lot more boats than ever went down Stinkin' Crik."

She seemed prepared to fend off further questions. We did not, however, need to ask them. Or want to know the answer. Our mountain flower was a member of a (probably secret) international task force watching for dangerous traffic on the Rhine. Toxic materials? Fissionable materials?

Arguably.

She must be very good at what she did to have received her silver bar so soon.

"Wonderful view," I said blandly.

"Shonuff do beat ole Stinkin' Crik," she said. "Don' hold a candle to that thar lake of your-un."

"Nothing does, Cindasue."

Just then, three black boats with *Polizei* in white on the side raced by us, weaving in and out of the slower river traffic like water skiers cutting across the paths of lumbering cabin cruisers.

"*Wasserpolizei*. Theyz sure in an all-fired hurry, ain't they?"

"Heading upriver to the *Schloss* Zellner?" Peter wondered.

"Arguably."

"When will we get there, Uncle Blackie?" she demanded impatiently. "I don't want to miss any of the action."

I turned from the apple strudel, which the leprechaun had substantially destroyed, to the cherry strudel before he could get at that.

"Young woman," I admonished her.

"Yassuh?"

"I remind you again that you are not here in the role of George Armstrong Custer and that you should not identify my nefoo and myself with the Seventh Cavalry."

"Or with Jeb Stuart," Peter Murphy added.

"That thar murderin' bastard," she said contemptuously. "Phil Sheridan was our man."

"Nonetheless," I said, "you take my point?"

"Yassuh," she said docilely. "I oughter be the aggressor only o'er to the basketball court. " 'Cept'n I like a good fight.''

"You've seen a dead body after a firefight, Cinda-sue?''

She turned pale. "I have not, Bishop Blackie. I belong in the Coast Guard, not the Marines.''

So. We slowly learn more.

We passed the famous glass-house parliament building in the government quarter of Bonn, a monument to a new country that wished to carry out its politics in the public eye.

"Your agency moving to Berlin when the government goes there in a couple of years?'' I asked her.

"Military and Foreign Policy offices are staying here,'' she replied, "at least for awhile. There'll be a lot of pressure to move them to Berlin, I think. But a lot more to keep them here as a reminder of where the New Germany began. My tour of duty will be over by then, of course.''

"And where will you go then?'' Peter Murphy asked, trying to sound nonchalant.

"Donno. I'm jest going along a-minding mah own busin's. See whar they want to send me. Maybe back to Benton Harbor, Michigan.''

Her green eyes flashed with mischief.

Three more police boats roared down the river, this time with sirens blaring.

"Flank speed,'' she said. "Theyz all the boats they have above Koblenz. Somethin' a-happenin', somethin' real big. . . . Theyz a-riding like they a-heading to the OK Corral. Uncle Blackie, what's goin' down?''

"We must assume that, if the government of the *Bundesrepublik* required our assistance, we would hear from Ernie Schulteis on your celluar phone.''

I was certainly as impatient as she was to find out what was occurring at the *Schloss* Zellner. Patently, the six fuzz boats (as African Americans in Chicago call police craft) were an indicator that Ernie and his merry men had encountered more resistance than they had expected.

"It will take another hour to get up there," she wailed. "They'll have found the shrine 'fore then."

"No way, Cindasue," I insisted, "it's not there."

28

The black boats stopped us above Remagen and the mouth of Ahr River. Lying sideways in the river, their green lights flashing, they blocked traffic like the white and blue patrol cars of the C.P.D. would interdict traffic at a Chicago intersection to facilitate either a parade or fire fighting or a crime investigation. An anxious file of barges, barge trains, and boats (one of the largest, filled with gleaming cars, defiantly announced Toyota in ship-size letters) waited on the right side of the river. A police craft pulled alongside the *Düsseldorfer* and asked for Fräulein Unterleutnant McCloud.

"Hyar ah be!" she yelled.

The skipper saluted and she saluted back.

We were taken aboard the fuzz boat with ceremony appropriate for a queen boarding her royal barge and whisked upriver. Ernie Schulteis doubtless had clout. So, too, did our diminutive Coast Guard person.

She and one of the cops engaged in somber, whispered conversation.

Looking deeply troubled, she rejoined my nefoo and me.

"I guess we weren't just joking about the OK Corral.

There's been a shoot-out at the *Schloss* Zellner. Ober-superintendent Schulteis has been wounded, though my friend Niki says it is not serious. Three other cops have been hurt. He says he believes they will all live. The folks in the black hats are holed up in a lodge outside the *Schloss*. He says that soon everything will be in order again. Apparently, the government forces have already secured the *Schloss*.''

"Yikes," Peter Murphy murmured.

"Ah don't wanna go 'shore, no way," Cindasue said firmly, "nohow. Ah done paid my dues for this h'yar weekend.''

I laughed as did my nefoo. Our would-be leatherneck looked sheepish and then joined our laughter.

The river ahead of us was ominously empty, just as a Chicago street on which someone has been killed looks when the police have cordoned it off.

We hurtled into a gorge with high hills on either side. The sun disappeared behind the hill on the right. Across the river, a huge castle loomed at the top of a tall hill, a vast pseudo medieval pile that might have made the manse of Ludwig the Mad of Bavaria look sane.

The fuzz boat skidded to a stop at a landing on the west side of the river next to a second boat. Two others cruised at midriver, periodically firing automatic weapons at a Gothic-style lodge in a small grove of trees a third of the way down the steep slope. In front of the *Schloss* what must have been half the police cars in the state of North Rhineland-Wesphalia were drawn up in battle array. From behind this wall, more automatic weapons were popping away at the lodge. To one side, a skirmish line of men in battle dress was easing its way toward the lodge.

The skipper of the fuzz boat conducted us across the gunwale to the second craft. Cindasue, as befit a Coast Guard officer, even one in dangerously short shorts, leaped from one boat to the other and saluted the skipper on the bridge.

Naturally, he saluted back.

Cops helped Peter Murphy and his aging uncle to make the transfer.

Across the river, the fireworks-sound of the automatic weapons continued.

The skipper, again with solemn ceremony, conducted us into the cabin. Herr Obersuperintendent Ernst Schulteis, his arm in a sling, sat at a TV monitor, a communication unit in his good hand.

"I don't need the holy oils yet, Blackie," he said, glancing over his shoulder at us. "However, when my good frau finds out the chances I've been taking, I might."

"She jest be happy you weren't hurt worse," Cindasue said.

"Ja," he said with a wry laugh. "What is the line in your American films? It only grazed me."

He shouted orders into his com unit.

I gathered he was warning the line of skirmishers to be very careful. Four wounded cops was enough—more than enough.

"The Herrn Bundeskanzler will have an insurrection charge . . ." he said. "I suppose you are wondering what's happening."

"It is a matter of some interest to us."

"Theyz a-fixin' to lob CS^2 inter that thar lodge?" Cindasue demanded.

Proper officers don't call it tear gas.

"Ja, they have to throw the canisters through narrow windows. It is complicated."

"Who them polecats in the lodge?"

"We're not sure. We wounded two of them in the *Schloss.* They are Slavs of some sort. Mafia. Belarus, possibly. Most likely former army officers trying to earn a living. Commandos."

Ernie winced and flipped a painkiller into his mouth.

"We approached the *Schloss* from the highway on the other side of the hill two hours ago. Three of Zellner's thugs saw how many of us there were and promptly surrendered. We entered the *Schloss* and encountered two men in black with black berets in the great hall. They asked no questions but opened fire immediately. They wounded four of us, including me." He shrugged. "It is fortunate that none of us were killed."

On the monitor, a young German in combat fatigues prepared to rush the lodge. The riverboats, the cops behind the cars, and the skirmish line poured a hail of bullets on the lodge.

"Careful!" Ernie shouted into his mike.

I found myself praying for the kid with the canisters in his hand.

"In the meantime, our men, who were exploring the river side of the *Schloss,* came under fire from the lodge down the hill. We retreated into the *Schloss* and summoned reinforcements."

The commando made a run for it, an automatic weapon in the lodge burped for a moment, the young man recoiled and fell behind a tree.

"Schwein!" Ernie yelled.

"She was wearing a flack jacket," Cindasue informed us.

She!

The TV camera picked up the kid hunched up behind the tree. She grinned and gave a thumbs-up sign. Only young people under twenty are crazy enough to fight in wars.

"She like to have some sore ribs," Cindasue commented.

The young commando raised her thumb again. Another fusillade rained bullets on the lodge, clipping away large chunks of rock and stone.

Ernie was shouting frantically into his mike.

The young woman dashed straight toward the house, feinted once, and then dove against the wall.

"She a brave 'un," Cindasue informed us, "but plumb crazy."

"Ja, ja," Ernie sighed. "Even you, Cindy, would not do that. Too old."

"Nohow, no way, never!"

I continued to pray to all available saints, especially those Irish monks who had once sailed down the Rhine.

The firing died down. Our young person hunched under the protection of the wall, twisted something on the top of a CS² canister, and, with an easy motion of someone tossing a softball, flipped it through a window a couple of feet away. Then she rolled along the wall and threw a second canister through another window.

Nothing happened for a moment. Then a dirty gray cloud oozed out of the first window.

Quickly, our commando sat up and slipped a gas mask over her face and slung an Uzi into firing position.

German commandos use Israeli weapons: there are a lot of ironies in the fire.

Then a door in the back of the house, facing the *Schloss,* opened, and four coughing men in black, hands in the air, straggled out. The commando stood up, her weapon on them.

Two more men emerged from a door on the other side and struggled up the hill.

"*Ja,* good," Ernie sighed. "Eight altogether. It is over. No one killed, thank the good God."

And the spirits of the Irish missionaries who lurked along the Rhine, doing whatever they could. Or so I had persuaded myself.

Men and women were cheering on the other side of the river.

"She jest a leetle slip of a thing, like me," Cindasue marveled. "Still, she plumb loony."

"Fastest sprinter they have," Ernie sighed and leaned back against his chair.

The skipper brought us coffee. No tea. Cindasue reached in her purse and produced four tea bags. The cop saluted and went to make tea.

"We found four young Turkish women over there," Ernie said weakly. "Heinz kept them in chains in the cellar for his amusements. They were not in good condition. We will repair them as best we can. None of them older than Frieda out there."

"He will not," I inquired, "get away this time, will he?"

"Our courts are very lenient." He sighed. "For example, the man who stabbed Monica Seles walks the street a free man. *Ja,* I think that Heinz will never leave jail, however."

"And the Shrine of the Magi?" Peter Murphy asked.

Ernie shook his head.

"It is a big *Schloss,* but we have not found it yet. We continue to search. We shall find it soon, I think. I am convinced that Herr Zellner is behind its disappearance. There is much treasure in there. Some of it stolen, I believe. We must investigate carefully. We want to have as many charges as possible against Herr Zellner."

"Varmint," Cindasue muttered. "Chain him up to a wall for the rest of his life. Hit would serve him right and proper."

"Are the Belarus in permanent residence?" I inquired.

"That we do not know for sure," Ernie said as he swallowed another pain pill. "We have no record of them entering Germany. These groups of skilled, high-priced, mercenary criminals do not stay in any one place long. It is like the Thirty Years War, *nein*?"

"So they may have been here for a spectacular robbery?"

"*Ja,*" Ernie agreed, his hand on his chest near his wounded arm. "In the Thirty Years War, we would have killed them with as much cruelty as we could. Now we will put them in jail for a few years. We progress, however erratically. . . . We will naturally question them about the shrine. They are professionals. They will tell whatever they know to save themselves."

"Do you believe, sir"—Cindasue filled Ernie's coffee cup and poured some tea for my nefoo and me—"that they stole the shrine?"

"I think it very likely. Tomorrow they will tell us, and the case will be over."

"If they know where it is," Cindasue said.

"*Ja*, I think they do. It will merely take time for them to realize that they must tell us."

A couple of medics appeared and insisted that the Herr Obersuperintendent must now go to the hospital.

He didn't fight the suggestion.

Later, we congratulated the brave Frieda, who was still on an adrenaline high. Having heard of the battle at our hotel the previous night, she insisted on hugging Cindasue. They bonded immediately, as women do, and wept in each other's arms.

"Shonuff," Peter Murphy said proudly.

Women, of course, are the braver of the two genders.

We saw the four young Turkish women as they were loaded into ambulances. Young women who had once been pretty and might be so again, but whose lives had been blighted by diabolic savagery, one hoped not irrevocably.

Cindasue cowered in Peter Murphy's arms. I invoked the resident Irish spirits.

We then transferred back to the *Düsseldorfer* for the completion of our peaceful Sunday cruise on the Rhine.

"What you think, Mr. Preacher Man?" Cindasue asked me.

"You mean about the curious affair of the absence of the Slavic commandos?"

"Yessuh, that thar curious 'fair."

"What was curious?" Peter Murphy asked.

"That theyz still thar."

"After they stole the as-yet-undiscovered Shrine of the Magi," I added.

"Plain, Mr. Preacher. Just plain."

"So, tomorrow we will hear from the hopefully recovering Ernie that Herr Zellner brought them in for a big heist that has not happened yet. They were waiting for his final orders."

"To steal the shrine?" my nefoo asked. "But someone has already stolen it, haven't they?"

"Maybe someone a-fixin' to steal it ag'in."

29

"Where did she go?" Peter Murphy, who had been sleeping, woke up, looked around, and, like the good jularker he is, noted that his lady love had disappeared.

Our excursion on the *Düsseldorfer* was winding down. Ahead of us, crimson in the setting sun, the spires of the dom were growing larger and larger. The dark clouds, which had massed in the western sky all day, were temporarily aflame as they prepared to bring the first sting of winter down upon us the next day. Most of our fellow excursionists were snoozing as my nefoo had been. Needless to say, they wanted an account of the shoot-out at *Schloss* Zellner, which our Coast Guard person supplied in simultaneous translation of Appalachian English, Standard English, and German in rich and exciting detail. She described the valiant Frieda as though the child were Brunhilde (albleit a slender version) reborn. Cindasue refused to permit unimportant factual details to interfere with the dramatic sweep of her yarns. Her jularker wisely did not try to correct such minor literary license.

Then she had drifted away, doubtless while I was resting my eyes.

"She's probably somewhere crying her eyes out to release the tension."

"I should go find her?"

"Arguably."

At first, she would want to be left alone while she wept. Then she would want someone there to sustain her.

Peter Murphy returned shortly with a woebegone child in a Köln sweatshirt tucked into his arm. She looked like she could be no older than twelve.

"I'm fine," she protested as she returned to her deck chair. "Nothing wrong with me. I'm all right."

She did protest too much. It was time to introduce some realism into the discussion.

"Young woman," I said sternly, "if you wish to assert that you will be all right in a reasonable period of time, no one would deny the truth of such an assertion."

"Awh-huh." She curled up and clung to her jularker's hand, prepared to listen, with just a glint of amusement in her enchantress's eyes.

"Patently, you are a talented and gifted young woman with enormous recuperative powers. Though your life has not been easy, you nonetheless managed to join the oldest of our services, to perform so brilliantly as a rating, that the USCG virtually forced upon you an appointment to New London, to perform brilliantly there both on the basketball court and in the classroom, and to become a senior cadet officer, to be assigned to very important work and to win an early promotion."

"You jest speculatin', Preacher Man. Purty good speculatin', howmsoever."

"In addition, you generate sufficient low-key erotic appeal to bring an appreciative smile to the other gender and to induce members of that other gender to do just about whatever you want them to do, present company not excepted."

"I don't call it low-key, Uncle Blackie, not in the whirlpool, anyway."

"Hush ya mouf, chile!"

I ignored this romantic interruption.

"In addition, you have also established once again on this return trip what was evident at Grand Beach some years ago: You are a superb storyteller who does not permit literal details to interfere with the flow of the story."

"All us mountain boomers thataway."

"Therefore, one cannot escape the conclusion—though you will try to escape it—that you are not only a remarkably appealing young woman, wearing or not wearing your Appalachian mask, but also an incredibly strong one."

"Awh-huh."

"Therefore you will surely be all right in a few days. However, at the present time, you are under considerable strain because of all the truly horrific evil you have encountered in less than twenty-four hours, especially since this evil is in some fashion not unlike other horror that has imposed itself on your earlier life."

"Awh-huh."

"One thus concludes that you are dispensed from the necessity of appearing in complete control at the present. It is permitted that you fall apart completely whenever you feel like it, especially when a respectful set of arms happen to be available."

She bowed her head and wept softly.

"Shonuff be nice happen a family 'round to take care of lettle loggerdly head girl chile."

Peter Murphy wept with her. For the second time in our venture to Köln and environs, I, too, felt my eyes sting for this wonderfully vulnerable young woman and her astonishing capacity to do what all humans must do and almost none are able to do well: surrender herself completely to the loving care of others.

Peter Murphy, I reflected, had found himself a keeper.

She dried her tears, put on her Coast Guard baseball cap again, and told us that she would drive back to Bonn in the morning with the car Herr Schulteis had loaned her. She would report to the ambassador and her superior officers, check her office work, see her shrink person, and come back on Tuesday morning.

Was that all right? She asked looking from one to the other of us.

Certainly, it was all right.

"Don't you go a-solvin' any mysteries till Tuesday, Uncle Blackie."

"Tuesday it will be, Cindasue."

With the grace of God and a lot of luck.

In my E-mail were the usual missives from the Lord Cardinal and my sibling/matriarch.

Claus tells me what went down there this morning, Blackwood. Remarkable. However, we still must have the shrine back.

To which I replied:

Shrine problem resolved Tuesday. Home Wednesday. Thursday at latest.

Mary Kate warned me:

Punk, don't you dare let Petey exploit that poor little girl.

To which I replied:

Signs are moderately positive. It wouldn't be all that far from wisdom to tentatively plan a Christmas wedding.

As I had remarked earlier, with the grace of God and a lot of luck.

30

Peter

"Ah jest wanna cuddle, kinda peaceful like," she informed me as I guided her into the whirlpool.

There were two swimmers in the pool despite the late hour. We could not have done much else.

"Fine," I said.

"I done called Frau Schulteis. She done brung her man home. She say she enjoys havin' him dependen't on her."

"As though we men are not always dependent on our women."

She held my hand even more tightly.

"Peter Murphy, suh."

"Yessum?"

"Will I ever be a woman like her?"

"What to you mean?"

"Happy and sexy and self-possessed and warm and loving?"

"Cindasue, girl chile, you must stop comparing yourself to older women who have lived a lot longer, had more experience, and are different from you. You are already all the things you just mentioned. When you're in your forties, you will be the same way, but in your own style.''

"Awh-huh," she sighed. "Guess so."

We said nothing for a few minutes.

"Peter Murphy, suh?"

"Yessum?"

"Happen you still want me after I done told you about . . . what I promised to tell you about . . .''

"Not a chance I won't."

"Happen you get me all nekkid and shivering on your bed . . .''

"No nightie at all."

"Ah understan'. Will you be a-taken care of me for all my life like you do now?"

That was a strange question. Or maybe it wasn't.

"I promise that with all my heart and soul."

I hoped that was good enough.

"Be a heap of carin'?"

"On one condition?"

"Wha's that?"

"That you take care of me, too."

"Shonuff," she bussed my lips ever so lightly.

I would never let her go.

Never.

31

Blackie

As I had expected, Ernie informed me first thing on Monday morning that (a) the shrine of the Magi was not in the *Schloss* and (b) the Belarussian commandos had no idea what it was they were supposed to steal and (c) Heinz Zellner had been taken into custody at the Bonn-Köln Airport.

"He's in jail now," Ernie concluded, "screaming about his rights and trying to pull strings. He'll never get out, not even in the BRD."

We had therefore accomplished many good works but not the one we had come to accomplish.

Had Zellner used other agents to steal the Shrine? Possibly. But why?

I didn't yet want to exclude the possibility that he was involved in some labyrinthine plot, even possibly one that would get him out of prison.

Would the Herrn Bundeskanzler and the cardinal free him—or maybe let him escape—in exchange for the return of the shrine? It would be hard to do that, especially since CNN already had the story of the Turkish slave girls who were innocents he had personally selected for slow death from a Turkish village. Feminists all over the world would rightly go crazy.

I encountered Cindasue and Peter Murphy in the dining room, staring dreamily at one another and eating breakfast. They had prepared a place for me with the usual appropriate ration of raisin cornflakes.

"He a-looking so sleepy 'cuz I made him take and swallow one of them pills Frau Schulteis done give me. Else'n he maybe a-trying to knock down my door."

"The dreams were wonderful," Peter Murphy admitted. "I wish I could remember them."

"I thought you were driving to Bonn."

"Woman gotta have her breakfast, specially her jularker set cross the table, eatin' her up with his purty blue eyes."

"A reasonable position."

"Uncle Blackie," she continued, "happen you search the basement of that thar parsonage place today, maybe you find the shrine thing thar."

It was an interesting idea, not very likely, but perhaps insightful.

"Ya see," she continued, her green eyes shrewd, like a cat in the mountain forests, "Herr Zellner plans to steal hit, but it's gone before he can get to hit. The cardinal man thinks the bishop man done stole hit to embarrass him, and the bishop man thinks the cardinal man done stole hit. And Zellner's commandos don't know who done stole hit and all the time someone else has hidden hit in the parsonage somewhere and when everyone gives up, this un a-takin' hit away."

Remarkably ingenious. Too bad I had to ask the crucial question.

"Who?"

A look of disappointment possessed her face.

"I donno."

"And why?"

"You a spoilsport, Uncle Blackie."

"Your theory does offer some interesting suggestions we'll pursue this morning."

We conducted Cindasue to her car, which was parked outside. No more underground garage. My nefoo held an umbrella over her head, fending off the driving rain. Autumn had left us, and the long darkness of North European winter had begun.

She and her jularker hugged modestly and then that worthy and I, equipped with umbrellas and raincoats, hiked over to the dom to interview again the cardinal and the new Dompfarrer.

Actually, I wore a maroon poncho with gold letters that proclaimed "Chicago! The City That Works!"

The cardinal and Rudi, in their ordinary Teutonic clericals, were waiting for us in a room with towering vaults, which must have been the throne room of the medieval archbishop-elector. Claus Maria von Obermann sat in a chair that, while not quite a throne, was almost as old as the room.

"*Ja, ja,* Blackie." He rose and embraced me. "You have caused great trouble in the BDR. That is good. Very good. They will give you medals. I will give you medals! *Ja!*"

"That will not be necessary," I said firmly.

Then he asked with great concern about Fräulein Cindy. I assured him that she was one tough lettle mountain boomer and was recovering nicely.

"Zellner is a monster," he continued, waving his hands as though he wished he could have done something long ago about Zellner. "He belongs in jail for the rest of his life. Those poor women."

"And those poor choirboys," Rudi added. "The priests confessed last night. We are trying to talk to the parents and see that the children get proper therapy."

"I will have a press conference this afternoon and admit the whole truth. We will establish a board like Herr Kardinal Cronin. It will not happen again."

"Rather, it will not happen so often," I cautioned. "As long as there is asymmetry in power, there will be abuse. The best we can do is to minimize it and to strive to heal. No easy tasks."

"*Ja,*" he said, slumping back into his chair as if the terrible weight of abuse by humans of their fellow humans wore him out. "*Ja.*"

"All the things you said we would find," Rudi continued, "we did indeed find. Financial and sexual abuse, oppression of staff, connivance with neo-Nazis, lax security, everything."

"I have already spoken with Sean," the count cardinal told me.

"I know. . . . He remains dissatisfied with our inability to find the Shrine of the Magi."

They both laughed at that.

"You didn't happen to find it lying around the parsonage, did you?"

They thought that was funny, too.

"Like perhaps in the cellar?" Peter Murphy asked, advocating his lady love's theory.

The two Germans glanced at each other.

"We go now to look."

There were, in fact, three cellars. A modern office was in the first. Under bright artificial light, accountants were working with laptop computers and huge account books, doubtless trying to straighten out the mess that the ex-Dompfarrer had left. Our old friend Helena Strauss seemed to be in charge, chic and low-key in a navy blue suit. We permitted the count cardinal to introduce us as though we did not know one another.

"*Ja,* she and her husband have a bakery in Ahrweiler, but she comes now to help us with the mess. We miss them both. He was the best baker in all Köln."

"Fascinating," I said.

Then I whispered, as the cardinal led the way to the *Unterekeller* "May we come again to talk late today?"

"*Ja,*" she whispered back. "Seventeen-thirty?"

"Good."

"We make supper for you."

"Excellent."

The *Unterekeller* was a storeroom for old candlesticks, vestments, chalices, processional crosses, altar cloths and other ecclesiastical material that was too good to throw out but too worn to use and had not yet acquired historical status.

"And the artwork in the dom and the treasury?"

"Signor Donatelli is beside himself with rage that we dare to doubt him. I explain that it is the Dompfarrer we doubt, not him. So far, however, all is in order, *nein,* Rudi?"

"Ja."

The cellar steps deteriorated as we went down. Sharply tilted rocks in a spiral corkscrew led to the *Untereunterekeller.*

"This room has been here for at least a thousand years, long before the dom was started. It is above a Roman bath, we think, though we have never tried to excavate it because the parsonage itself is too valuable a monument to risk."

"It leaks sometimes when the river is high," Rudi explained. "It is very damp, as you can see."

He shone a flashlight beam around the rough stone room whose walls dripped water.

"This was here when Saint Martin came," the cardinal exclaimed. "It was old even then, we think."

Rudi tapped his foot on the floor, also of thick stone.

"Right here," he stopped when the tap caused a slightly different reverberation, "we think is another staircase down to the Roman town. When we have finished restoring the dom—if that ever happens—we will explore down below."

Aggripina, Martin, Barbarossa, Nicholas of Verdun, Buonaparte—the shades gathered together again.

"Nothing here." Rudi sighed. "They would have had a difficult time carrying it down the steps, would they not?"

"Ja, and why hide it here?" the cardinal added.

"Just a stab in the dark." I sighed.

A flash of light, however, came from that stab in the dark.

I lost it almost at once, but it would come back.

"Is it haunted, Herr Kardinal?" Peter Murphy asked.

"In this part of Köln," the count cardinal laughed jovially, "everything is supposed to be haunted. It is said that a good priest once fell in love with a good woman, not the first time, surely. They loved one another down here and were caught once when the water in the river flooded in rapidly and drowned them. However, a friend, it is said, gave them absolution before they died. God, I am sure, loved them."

"As he does all," I added.

"You sense anything, Uncle Blackie?" Peter Murphy asked me.

"Not especially. It is too bad Cindasue isn't here."

"She'd climb the walls."

We retreated to the first floor of the parsonage.

"Many of my predecessors did not live here," the cardinal explained. "The citizens of Cologne loved their freedom dearly and expelled the archbishop-elector from the city. They built a castle up in Zons from which they were permitted to come on sacred days or on occasion tried to recapture the city by force of arms. Fortunately, those days are behind us."

The image of his coming in with an army to drive out the civil government produced a jolly laugh.

Some things do improve.

Coffee, tea, and sweet rolls appeared miraculously on the old table.

"Tomorrow I will reveal the truth of the missing Shrine of the Magi," the Cardinal announced. "Some heard poor Freddie's cry yesterday. The rumors will spread. We must tell the truth of our own free will before we are compelled to tell it."

"It will magnify the impact of Bishop Heidrich's sickness." Rudi lifted his hands in a sad gesture of powerlessness. "The Zellner scandal will involve us, too, because he and the Herr Bischof were known to be friends. But what can we do?"

"*Ja,* what can we do? It is, after all, not the first time the shrine has been stolen."

"If it has been stolen," Peter Murphy murmured.

We all turned on him.

"Ja, it has been stolen," the cardinal insisted. "I thought Freddie did it, Freddie thought I did it. We were both wrong."

"I know," Peter Murphy said. "Some people saw the empty place. Bishop Heidrich could not have imagined it, nor those who replaced the shrine. Yet no one seems to have it."

A valid point. But since it wasn't in the dom, it had to be somewhere, and someone had to have it.

"I saw the empty safe where the substitute was kept," the cardinal explained. "The then-Dompfarrer wanted to convince me that the shrine at the main altar was the substitute, not that I doubted it. Why would he want to deceive me, especially if he thought I was responsible?"

"I get a headache when I try to think about it," my nefoo shrugged. "Unless we can find out where it is, we will not know who took it or why, will we, Uncle Blackie?"

"Arguably." I sighed.

"I even spun the combination of the safe so that no one could open it and see that there was no substitute inside."

An idea wafted into my head and paused.

"The Dompfarrer suggested that you do that?"

"Ja." The cardinal was puzzled. What, he must have wondered, was I driving at?

"The safe was open when you inspected it? Opened by the Dompfarrer?"

"Not open, but unlocked. He had opened it so they could replace the real shrine. Then he had closed the door so that no one would notice that the change had been made. He summoned me immediately, so that I could see it was empty before Herr Donatelli and his workers arrived."

"Fascinating."

I had no idea why it was fascinating.

"Ja. So tomorrow we will tell the truth, *nein?"*

I crawled out on a very long and very thin limb.

"Tomorrow afternoon. Late."

"*Ja.*"

"I am confident that by then we will have solved enough of the puzzle to mitigate the damage of your announcement, if not eliminate the necessity for it."

"That would be good, very good."

Peter Murphy glanced at me like he thought I had gone completely over the top. How could I possibly make a wild promise like that?

With the grace of God and a lot of luck, I would be able to freeze the image in my head.

A lot of grace and a huge amount of luck—not that the two were theologically separable, or so it seemed to me.

"We have two small presents for Pfarrer Kurt," I said, searching for the model planes.

"I have them, Uncle Blackie."

"Ah!"

The Kardinal and the new Dompfarrer thought the gifts were wonderful.

"That is good, very good. Poor Kurt would never think of buying them for himself. . . . The one with the Iron Cross is the one he flew?"

"*Ja.*"

What had happened to the world when a cardinal priest of the Holy Roman Church did not know the difference between an ME-262 and a P-47!

Pastor Kurt was summoned and we withdrew to a small room that looked like a slightly oversized confessional with a high ceiling.

He smiled at us, his pleasant, abstracted smile, like he was trying to remember who we were.

"*Ja.*"

"We brought you two presents, Pastor Kurt."

"*Ja?*"

I removed the boxes from the plastic bag in which we had schlepped them around and presented them to him.

"*Ja!*"

He opened the first box—the Messerschmidt—with trembling fingers.

"My beautiful aircraft!" He cradled it in his hands like it was a rare chalice, studded with precious jewels. "So beautiful!"

"Yes, it is," said my nephew, the Knight with the Good Heart.

Actually, it wasn't nearly as lovely as my friend Megan's F-18 Hornet. But Father Kurt doubtless knew nothing about an F-18.

Then he opened the other box.

"*Ja! Ja!* My opponent. Not as lovely an aircraft. Fat. But very brave men. Very brave."

Then he demonstrated for us, mostly in German, how curtains of P-47s drove the German jets out of the sky. It was a confrontation between the oldest and the newest of technologies, the air-cooled Thunderbolts and the air-breathing jets. His demonstration ended with the ME-262 spinning earthward.

He sat with us at the tiny conference table, the size of a primary school desk, and rolled the two models back and forth, his simple face ecstatic.

"Much has changed since then, has it not, Father Kurt?"

"*Ja!* Much the same, too. Humans don't change."

A long philosophical statement from the former pilot. We would have to work hard to get much out of him.

"Many recent changes here at the Dom?"

His eyes lit up. "*Ja!* Good changes!"

"Bad things happened here?"

He nodded his head sadly.

"*Ja.*"

"Valuable things stolen, like the shrine?"

He looked at me shrewdly. "It has happened before."

"We must find out who did it."

"*Ja, ja!*"

I continued in this fashion for some time and made no progress. Either Pastor Kurt did not have any ideas on the subject of the theft of the shrine or he did and wasn't about to tell me or anyone else

"That old guy knows more than he's saying," Peter Murphy remarked as we raised our umbrellas and walked out of the parsonage.

The rain was slashing at the virtually empty *Platz*, furious at the long delay that had prevented its scheduled arrival. An equally angry wind swept across the *Platz*, stirring up scraps of paper left behind by the tourists and sweeping them toward the river, like a determined hausfrau. Only a handful of tourists, bending against the wind and the rain, straggled into the dom.

Peter Murphy and I huddled under a yellow umbrella at a table close to the Dom Hotel whose bulk broke the force of the wind. We would have our midmorning tea (and, in my case, cherry strudel *mit Sahne*) in an outdoor café, regardless of what the angels in charge of the weather thought.

"She seemed better this morning," he began.

"Arguably."

"I think she loves me, Uncle Blackie."

"Arguably."

"You are confident we can solve the mystery by tomorrow afternoon?"

The honest answer was no.

"Arguably."

"And we'll go home Wednesday?"

"Arguably."

"What time tomorrow?"

In for an inch, in for a mile.

"Morning."

"So she and I will have our conversation in the afternoon."

"Or evening."

"No way, Uncle Blackie. Afternoon. Do you think she will try to avoid the conversation?"

"Is the pope a Catholic?"

"I'll have to insist?"

"That is your decision, Peter Murphy."

"What will happen after the conversation?"

"That will depend more on you than on her."

"I let her get away the last time, didn't I?"

"So it seemed."

"I won't this time," he said, his face tight, his eyes hard. "No way."

I sighed loudly. The intricate diplomacy of shifts in the modalities of human intimacy exceeded the skills of most of humankind. Only erotic energy and extraordinary effort from the relevant angels had thus far preserved the species from extinction caused by fear of the intimate other.

"Let us review what we know about the events of the morning of the theft of the Shrine of the Magi," I suggested, changing the subject.

Peter Murphy removed a notebook from his black trench coat pocket.

"At six o'clock," I began, "Father Kurt entered the sacristy, routinely turned off the alarms, and admitted the verger into the dom. The verger opened the doors for the handful of faithful who participate in the six-thirty liturgy in the Lady Chapel. As far as we know, none of them noted that the shrine was missing, presumably because only a few lights were turned on in the dom."

"Why only a few lights?"

"Because clergy are afraid of wasting electricity. Some of my staff remonstrate with me about my, as they see it, wasteful habit of turning on all the lights in the morning. To which I reply that the energy consumed in such a God-like activity is much less than litigation costs occasioned by a broken limb of a devout Christian."

"I see," he said with his most charming Peter Murphy grin. He should save it for the young woman for whose lovely body he so patently (and virtuously) lusted.

"Pastor Kurt noted with some horror that the Shrine of the Magi was missing. He called the Dompfarrer on the intercom and informed him. Then he began the liturgy, lest he impose an unseemly delay on the people of God. At some point shortly thereafter, the Dompfarrer appeared on the scene and confirmed the loss. He summoned assistance, went to the workshop, opened the safe, removed with the help of his aides the substitute, and carried it to the large plastic box where the shrine normally rests—presumably after the faithful had left the chapel.''

"It sounds risky," Peter Murphy observed as he made several notations in his book. "The verger knew, the people at Mass might have noticed, others may have come into the dom.''

"Granted. But the Dompfarrer thought he had no choice but to take risks. I assume that the substitute was covered with canvas and that, given its weight, it was moved on a dolly which was at hand in the art workshop. As I remember, there was an elevator of some sort from the workshop to the floor of the nave. Presumably, they worked in haste.''

"Right. . . . Risky or not, they got away with it."

"Then," I continued, "he thought it appropriate to summon the count cardinal to witness what had happened. . . .''

"As you would have summoned Cardinal Cronin."

"Yes," I said ruefully, "to face his instant demands that I recover it half an hour ago.''

"Bishop Heidrich may even then have thought that he was being set up. Or he may merely have wanted to go on record that he had reported the theft instantly.''

"So, our good friend Claus Maria Graf von Obermann comes with all deliberate speed, sees the substitute in place, visits the workshop, views the empty safe, closes the door, and spins the lock.''

"Why that ceremony?" my nephew asked.

"Perhaps to assure the cardinal that there had not been some kind of switch and that indeed the shrine had disappeared.''

"Who had the keys to the workshop?"

"That is an excellent question, Peter Murphy. We shall pose it to our friend Nicolo Donatelli in a few moments. . . . We must assume that all of the actions we have described occurred before that excellent gentleman and his colleagues arrived at work at nine.''

"If the thieves were lucky, Uncle Blackie, then so were those that did the cover-up. Too much luck?''

"Arguably, Peter Murphy. Someone must have suspended the law to which the name of your revered family has been attached.''

"Does not the ignorance of Sr. Donatelli about the subject of the theft of the shrine strike you as curious, Uncle Blackie?''

"He was not ignorant of it,'' I said, stumbling into another trap that he and his love had set for me, hatched no doubt between them earlier in the morning.

"That was what is curious. Why should anyone tell him? Either the Dompfarrer or the cardinal?''

"Fascinating,'' I said, covering up my embarrassment.

"Yet it was assumed that he knew, wasn't it?''

Indeed it was.

In his whitewashed bastion, always secure from the weather, good or bad, Nicolo Donatelli slumped at his desk like a broken man.

"Because I paint excellent imitations I am not a forger,'' he wailed. "There are no imitations out there, except the shrine, and I didn't make that. That swine Heidrich blurted out that it had been stolen. There are rumors everywhere. It is demanded that I open the safe to assure people that the substitute is inside. I cannot open the safe. It is intolerable, a safe in my workshop that I cannot open!''

"You would open the safe?''

"Certainly not! I will protect the secret until the truth emerges in the press. But when the journalists come and demand that I open it, I will have to admit that I cannot!''

"Only the cardinal and the former Dompfarrer can open it?''

"Yes, so it is said. I don't understand why. It is in my workshop, is it not?''

''Most certainly. . . . Have you ever seen Herr Kardinal open it?''

''No, why should he bother? He has better things to do, doesn't he?''

He rose from his chair and paced back and forth. ''They will embarrass, ridicule, humiliate me. I, the successor of Henri de Verdun, am not the master of my own workshop!''

''The Dompfarrer did, however, tell you about the theft of the Shrine of the Magi, a closely guarded secret.''

''He had no choice.'' He waved his hands like an opera tenor who had been caught double-dealing (as in *Norma* for example). ''I arrived early to work that morning and saw him and Herr Kardinal at the door of the empty safe. He did not want to tell me what my eyes had already discovered. Herr Kardinal made him tell me.''

''Besides you, who has the key to this workshop?''

He sank back into his chair, exhausted, distraught, offended. ''Supposedly, only the Dompfarrer. Like all other security precautions around the dom, this one was absurd. I assume that many other keys exist.''

''But no one else knows the combination to the safe?''

''Who knows?'' He waved his hand to indicate that the question was of minimal interest. ''But I doubt that anyone else knows it, except the fools that service our security system. In any case, the combination is changed every six months. No one is supposed to know about the imitation of the shrine. That is absurd, too. Everyone knows that there was an imitation in place when they were repairing the original twenty-five years ago.''

''Of course.''

''I am a copyist, Monsignore,'' he exploded in another burst of rage and erupted again from his chair. ''Not a forger. I am perhaps the greatest copyist in the world. Now those so-called experts upstairs are examining every piece of art in the dom to see if it is a forgery. They treat me like a common criminal. It is not a crime to make copies, so long as you acknowledge that they are copies.''

''I saw your breathtaking imitation of the Madonna of

Limburg in the cardinal's chapel," I said in a placating
tone. "You do excellent work."

"*Si, si* Monsignore, but I did not forge it. Certainly
the Herr Kardinal showed you my signature on the bottom: *Hac imitationem Magistro Nicolo Donatelli fecit.*"

"Of course."

He had not, but that probably didn't matter.

"I put that on all my work. See!"

He removed Mona Lisa from the wall and shoved her
at me. I turned her around, with less reverence than she
deserves, I fear; sure enough, there was the copyist's signature.

"Of course," I said again.

"I am not a fool! If I made forgeries, I would be
caught, eventually."

"Did you make copies for Heinz Zellner?"

"Naturally. He wants to posses everything. He has a
Mona Lisa like this one." Tenderly, he placed his own
copy back on the wall. "The *Polizei* will find it while
they are searching the swine's castle. They will see my
name on the back and accuse me of forgery. How can it
be a forgery when you acknowledge that you have done
it? Bah!"

"Why did he want copies?"

"So he could tell his guests that they were originals!
He did not care, and they could not tell the difference!"

"He has no stolen originals?"

"I do not know. I was never invited to his castle, thank
the good God!"

"He paid well?"

"Well enough. . . . The Church never pays what someone is worth, especially if he is a great artist."

"That is true," I agreed.

"Who do you think took the statue?" Peter Murphy
asked bluntly.

"The swine Zellner! With the help of the Dompfarrer!
Naturally! Is it not obvious, especially after the revela-
tions yesterday? Why should there be any doubt?"

"It does not seem to be in the *Schloss,*" my nephew said.

"Only because they have not taken the risk of bringing it up there. It is hidden somewhere in Köln. They must be made to admit that they have hidden it." Tears emerged from his bleary eyes. "It must be returned here where it belongs, where Henri de Verdun created it."

32

Our next stop was the treasury, whose blatant display of gold and jewels in room after room I thought to be disgusting and vulgar and which, like all of its kind, deeply offended American tourists, including Catholics. The precious chalices, monstrances, reliquaries, and other objects represented a different approach to Church wealth than the one we favored. You gave the money to schools and hospitals and religious orders today. However, they probably brought more money into the Church's coffers today through admission charges than if they were sold and the money invested in the DJ. Nonetheless, I still find the treasuries depressing and vulgar.

Rudi, looking as dyspeptic as I felt, was patrolling the treasury. Various folks of both genders in white coats, naturally, were poking and probing at the objets d'art.

"Any problems here?" I asked.

He shook his head in the negative and smiled sheepishly.

"All is in order, as we like to say. Except that we have a treasury. I will put up a sign that says that the admission fee will go to support projects for the Third World poor. That may make these rooms more acceptable."

"That is good," Peter Murphy observed. "Very good!"

It occurred to me that my nefoo and Rudi were about the same age.

"Where is our Cindy today?" the new Dompfarrer asked.

"In Bonn, being hailed as a hero by her colleagues."

"You will marry her?"

"By Christmas," said nefoo asserted confidently.

"That is very, very good," Rudi agreed. "She is remarkable."

"You've noticed that, too!"

"Oh, yes. Naturally!"

They both laughed in complacent approval of Cindasue, body and soul. As well they might.

Having exchanged these encoded young male comments with Peter Murphy, Rudi turned to me. "We are putting in the television cameras and other warning systems tomorrow. It is astonishing that nothing else seems to have been removed. Many people could have come in at night and removed anything they wanted."

"What then would they do with the objects they took?" I asked. "There is not, I would imagine, a large market for chalices from the fifteenth century or for the Milan Madonna."

"That is true, but there ought not to be a large market for Shrines of the Three Magi, either. . . . Truly, you will have it back by tomorrow afternoon?"

"I'll at least know where it is. . . . Tell me, Rudi, do you trust Signor Donatelli?"

"*Nein.* He is very slippery and very clever. But he is too wise to steal from the dom and replace what he has taken with copies. Everyone knows, you see, that he is a copyist, so he is the first suspect. Our investigators will swarm all over his workshop this afternoon. He will scream and threaten resignation. They will find nothing. He will not resign."

"So you don't think he's involved in the theft of the shrine?"

"I didn't say that, Herr Blackie. He may very well be involved, but not directly and not overtly."

"My thought exactly. . . . Have you learned the combination to the safe yet?"

"The safe?"

"The one in which your predecessor secured the substitute shrine."

"That safe! No, I don't know it. I suppose only Herr Kardinal knows it, if he has remembered. I could never understand why it was so important to my predecessor."

"And speaking of that worthy hiearch, what news do you have of his current health?"

Rudi shook his head sadly. "They say now that he is quite mad. He believes that he is now the archbishop of Köln. They fear he will never recover."

"Sad," I remarked, thinking that if I were to go mad, I would find a role that would be a good deal more fun than being an archbishop.

"Very sad," Rudi agreed. "Tragic."

"So," I said to my nefoo later, when we emerged once again on the windswept *Platz,* "Rudi approves of your choice in brides."

"Arguably," he said with a satisfied smirk. "I won't let her get away this time, Uncle Blackie. No way."

I chose not to comment. The outcome of the relationship seemed to me to be very much in doubt. It almost certainly depended on my good nephew's persistence and determination. At the present moment, I thought that he protested a little too much.

In a small café down one of the side streets, we doffed our raincoats and dispatched several bratwursts and a variety of strudels *mit Sahne.*

"You still think you can solve it within the next twenty-four hours?"

"Unquestionably."

"Did we learn anything important this morning?" he asked.

"Little odds and ends that might fit into a pattern," I equivocated.

In fact, the pattern comes first in human knowledge, then the odds and ends that fit it.

"Anything more for us to do today—before our return to Ahrweiler late this afternoon?"

"I personally am returning to the hotel to rest my eyes for a brief period. You may do what you wish, though I would not suggest a run down to Bonn. Still, a phone call might well be in order."

"It might indeed."

So we found a cab that would take us back to the Hapsburgerring. Leaving Peter Murphy to his own devices, I retired to my room and pondered what we knew, not in the hope of solving the puzzle but rather in tentative expectation that the picture for which I was waiting would choose to descend into my brain, open the elevator door, and stand there grinning at me as my possible future niece-in-law would whenever she was one up on me.

Nothing happened.

I had learned one matter of considerable interest that morning: Apparently, nothing else had been removed from the dom, although it would have been easy to do so. No one had routinely taken advantage of the leaks in the security systems. This particular theft had been a special operation.

I thought again of Heinz Zellner's Belarus. They certainly were the kind of men one might summon for a major art heist. Moreover, they would have talked by now if they had participated in such a heist. Perhaps they had come for another bold theft, but why two within the same month?

Perhaps to show that you were powerful enough to do whatever you wanted?

I punched in Ernie's number. Frau Schulteis assured me genially that her man was feeling fine and would need only the rest of the week off before returning to work. How was Cindy?

I explained that the worthy and admirable young officer was in Bonn for the day and would return tomorrow.

Before I was permitted to speak to Ernie, I listened to several paragraphs of praise for Cindy.

Ja.

"I don't need a week off," Ernie protested when I obtained permission to speak to him.

"Nonetheless, you will take it."

"*Ja,*" he said. "I do what I'm told."

Sometimes.

He had little new information. In addition to scores of copies and forgeries and some dubious material, the *Schloss* had contained three famous treasures that art police had sought for years. No Shrine of the Magi, however, though the police had searched every inch of the property. The Belarus, once members of the Soviet elite Black Beret crowd, knew only that there was a plan for the beginning of the following week. No one had briefed them on it yet. They were frightened because of the newspaper headlines, which spoke of a "Russian invasion" and were certainly telling the truth. The Herrn Bundeskanzler would present a medal to Frieda and to Cindy, too. The Turkish young women would live. So would the men on both sides who had been wounded in the firefight, thanks be to God. What were my thoughts on the mystery of the shrine?

"I expect to have a solution by tomorrow at noon."

Politely skeptical, Ernie said he would be interested to hear it.

Never doubt Blackie Ryan, I said to myself with a good deal more confidence than I felt or the circumstances justified.

Not that I had not made such promises before and carried them off.

Before I turned to the essential project of resting my eyes, I sent off two messages on E-mail.

The first was to Milord Cronin:

Solution by tomorrow at noon. Home Wednesday.

And to Milady Mary Kathleen:

Nephew projects Christmas wedding. Keep your fingers crossed.

Then I gave my weary eyes the rest they so richly deserved.

I believe the solution came to me several times in my dreams. But I did not remember it when I awoke.

By now, the reader will naturally have seen the solution and deem it to have been patent all along. Said reader will wonder if I have grown senile in my advancing years or whether the arguably star-crossed romance between Peter Murphy and Cindasue had distracted me. More likely, I will plead in my own defense, I was still not over the malignant effects of jet lag.

The rain had stopped before my nefoo and I began our second pilgrimage to Ahrweiler. He seemed quite confident that he could find the town again. For all I could have done so, it might just as well have been in northern Alaska.

"You were right about the phone call, Uncle Blackie," he admitted once we had fought our way through the Köln traffic and entered the autobahn. "I was in deep trouble because I had not called earlier."

"So she missed you. That is to be expected."

"I don't know whether she missed me, but she did want to hear all the details of our messings around this morning. Fortunately, I am an anthropologist by training and can remember details."

"She wanted to know whether I had as yet solved the case?"

"Sure."

"And you told her?"

"That you claimed you would have a solution by tomorrow morning."

"She doubted this patent truth?"

"She said that she might have one by then, too."

Fascinating.

As a punishment for my sins, Lady Wisdom has insinuated a number of young women into my life who aspire to, as one put it, "Out-Blackie Blackie"—to solve my puzzles before I do—the senior Megan at the cathedral rectory, an Irish person named Nuala Anne, and now Cindasue Lou McCloud. From McCloud's Holler.

They all had come close on occasion—too close.

"Otherwise?"

"Otherwise, she said she was feeling better and had a long way to go."

"Ah."

So we had accomplished some good in our confrontation on the Rhine.

I soon found myself at the table of Franz and Helena Strauss in Ahrweiler, consuming white and then red Ahr Valley wine and a host of German food that would have preserved a man with an ordinary metabolism from hunger pains for several weeks.

Patently, my metabolism is different.

Helena wore a blue knit dress with gold buttons, makeup, and jewelry, the assembly of which left little doubt as to her sumptuous beauty should we have been in any such doubt. No Wagnerian matron, but someone from an older and more elegant and quieter era.

Yet she fluttered and flushed at every word her Franz said in praise of her work and stopped that work completely whenever he touched her arm. Lucky man, indeed.

Our conversation turned to the remarkable events at the dom the last two days and the scandal at the *Schloss* Zellner. Our host and hostess thought that Herr Kardinal had dealt skillfully with the questions on television and that the Church had escaped with more credit than perhaps it had deserved.

"The Kardinal called and asked if I would help out this week and next till Pfarrer Rudi put everything in order. My Franz said I should do it, and of course he is right. I will work there for two weeks and then become a consultant once a week. They will pay me for once a week what Bishop Heidrich paid for a whole week."

"Senior consultants," I agreed, "are expensive."

"*Ja,* it is good, very good," Franz agreed, with a hearty laugh and a quick caress of her flank. "I will be able to get some work done in the bakery. Women are often a distraction in bakeries."

"*Ja, ja,* Franz," she said, briefly crimson.

"Really?" Peter Murphy asked.

Much laughter.

Questions about Cindy interrupted the flow of our conversation. Her heroism in the garage had already taken on a legendary aura. Peter Murphy agreed with the common opinion around the table that he was a very fortunate man and he should take good care of her.

"She should take good care of me," he pleaded. "I need her protection more than she needs mine."

It was an assertion that was in substantial part true, more true perhaps than he had yet realized.

We turned back to the events at the dom.

Was the shrine truly missing? Everyone said that the ex-Dompfarrer had said someone had stolen it. What would happen?

In for a mile, in for ten thousand of them.

I assured everyone that the problem would be resolved by noon tomorrow. My nephew, he of little faith, rolled his eyes in dismay.

I then began to probe gently for hints.

"Was the Dompfarrer mad enough to conspire with Heinz Zellner to help him steal the shrine in order to discredit the cardinal?"

"Certainly, especially during the last months. Perhaps there was some physical sickness, but he seemed to everyone who worked there quite mad. Even the young priests who were his favorites feared his rage. He struck them often, as he had struck some of the women who worked for him."

"Do you think he was sexually involved with the younger priests?"

She hesitated, a proper, practicing Catholic Rhenish matron.

"I do not believe that he . . . he engaged in sexual fondling or intercourse with them. He did want them totally dependent on him, the way a woman is supposed to depend on a man.''

"Not in today's Germany.'' Franz glanced at his wife with adoring eyes.

She snorted. "Certainly *not!*''

"He loved pomp and power, Herr Blackie. He enjoyed snarling at men and women and forcing them to obey him. He especially reveled in humiliating them in front of others.''

She shivered, as well she might. Such men's sexual payoff came not from sexual intercourse with men or with women, but from humiliating humans regardless of gender. No wonder he wanted to become an archbishop and a cardinal.

"And Pastor Kurt?''

She frowned and pursed her lips.

"Pastor Kurt was unaffected by the Dompfarrer. He ignored him. Often he seemed not to hear him. He is a very complicated man. You can never be sure what he hears or thinks or even if he hears or thinks anything at all. Herr Bischof Heidrich sometimes seemed afraid of him. Once Herr Bischof was ridiculing a young woman from Pastor Kurt's youth group because of a dress she was wearing . . . too short, he thought. Then Pastor Kurt came into the room. Herr Bischof stopped and left the room. We used to say that Pastor Kurt was there representing the Kardinal. Yet he is so simple that it did not seem possible that he was a spy. . . . Always talking about his jet fighter.''

"You saw the models he has now?''

"*Ja,* all afternoon, he walks around showing them to us. He was as happy as a child with a new toy.''

Kurt was still an enigma to me. A thief he certainly was not. A saint he might well be. Or maybe merely a simple priest who had never quite recovered from that March day in 1945 when the curtains of P-47 Thunderbolts had caught up with him.

I imagined those vague eyes turning to steel again

when he caught Heidrich verbally assaulting one of his teenagers. Not quite as simple as he might at first appear. He knew a lot more about the theft of the Shrine of the Magi than he was willing to admit.

Who, I wondered, might he be protecting?

Or was he involved in some other game that was comprehensible only to his often befuddled brain?

I knew that I would never pry his knowledge out of his head. I had to get at it some other way.

"I have the impression that he sees everything," I said tentatively.

"Sometimes I think that, and sometimes I think it is my imagination. He certainly is very happy that Pfarrer Rudi is now the Dompfarrer. He follows him around like a worshiping puppy."

"Or like Rudi was a young pilot just assigned to his squadron?"

"*Ja,* Herr Blackie, just like that. . . . You don't think he stole the shrine, do you?"

"Hardly . . . he does not look at women, it seems to me."

"He looks at me often," she laughed. "He seems to enjoy that."

"He should," Franz agreed.

"It is young women he does not look at, especially those who remind him of his wife."

"Wife?"

That was the first I had heard of a wife.

"She died in one of the raids on Köln while he was flying his aircraft. Often he seems to confuse her with the aircraft. He carries her picture in his prayer book. A lovely child, hardly eighteen."

"If the shrine is really missing, Helena, who stole it?"

"The Dompfarrer," she replied promptly. "Everyone at the parsonage suspects him. He had been hinting for weeks that he would soon replace the Herr Kardinal. He knew the shrine would be stolen. He knows where it is."

And most likely he will spend the rest of the days of

his life in a mental hospital, firmly convinced that he is the archbishop of Köln.

I hope that they would provide him some crimson robes for the day he thought he had been named a cardinal.

The issue then seemed to be that I must determine where he or Herr Zellner or the two of them in some combination had hidden the shrine.

The only problem with that was that the ex-Dompfarrer, now turned archbishop, had accused the cardinal of stealing the shrine to discredit him.

We took our leave from the Strausses with profuse gratitude for a "real German meal" and for the bag of cinnamon raisin buns that Franz presented to us as we were leaving. They both hinted that they would like to come to Chicago someday, if there was a good reason to come.

They did not add, "like a wedding."

The rain had stopped, but the air was heavy with moisture, and fog shrouded the valley walls, perhaps, I fantasized, hiding the ghosts of warriors who in ages past must certainly have fought over this lovely little valley.

"When I'm his age," Peter Murphy informed me, "I want a woman who looks at me with soft, adoring eyes like she does."

"Such an outcome is not completely beyond the limits of a husband's ability."

"Yeah . . . Uncle Blackie, does she know how beautiful she is?"

"She knows that men find her attractive and that does not disturb her. In fact, she even likes Pastor Kurt's admiration. However, she sees herself as she really is only as she is reflected in her husband's adoration."

"Not bad, huh?"

"No, Peter Murphy, not bad at all."

"Like Mom and Dad."

"Arguably."

"I'd better call her at her apartment," he said when we pulled into the garage at our hotel.

"Yes, indeed. It would be most unwise not to."

I thereupon repaired to my room and, worn out from the exertions of the day and despite my interlude of resting my eyes in the afternoon, promptly departed for the fabled land of Nod.

Did I have a problem I had to solve before noon on the morrow?

Sufficient to the day, is the evil thereof, I told my drowsy self.

33

I woke up in the middle of the night, not sure where I was. A vivid picture lingered in my mind, a critically important picture. Only I wasn't sure of what it was a picture.

I stumbled over to the window, still not certain what the room was in which I had been sleeping. I pulled open the drapes, looked out the window, and saw the dom in the distance, its spires wreathed with thin fog swirling around in the floodlights that cut through the night and turned the fog a misty white, the cover of a paperback fantasy novel about some far-off and long-forgotten world.

Of course. *Colonia Claudia Ara Agrippinensium.* Only I wasn't a Roman or a German. I was a compatriot of Saint Martin, come from beyond the sea.

Then I knew what had happened to the shrine.

I dressed quickly, donned my poncho, which seemed appropriate for slinking around in the fog, found a sleepy cabdriver in front of the hotel, and persuaded him to drive me to the dom and wait for me.

The Domplatz at night was hardly medieval in aspect.

Bright signs announced the presence of Canon, Sony, Vuitton, Cartier, and Hermes products, ready to go on sale first thing in the morning, a retail marketplace eager to reopen. A green and white *Polizei* car waited silently in front of the dom, perhaps locking the barn door a little late, as they might have thought, wrongly it would turn out.

But the fog was thick, and if one squinted a bit, one imagined that it was 1242 and Thomas Aquinas had just been made a priest.

I walked around in the mists and the fog, circumnavigating the dom, glancing up at the steeples, marveling at the buttresses and the huge nave, dreaming of all the history that had surged and eddied around this holy place, thinking about the ragtag band of stargazers who came to Bethlehem and all those after them who came in search of their own star. During this admittedly excessive indulgence in pseudomysticism, I checked out my scenario—my interpretation of the image with which I had awakened—to make sure I had it right. Several times I did it wrong, making mistakes that violated the image. Finally, I got it just right and laughed to myself.

Precisely!

Fascinating!

Better late than never.

In a lonely bed in a small apartment up the river in Bonn, had C. L. McCloud, Lieutenant Junior Grade, the United States Coast Guard, also gotten it right?

Arguably!

But not the whole story, I was willing to wager.

I woke up my taxi driver again and bade him to convey me back to the Hapsburgerring. The cab might well have been a large (and tame) white charger. Blackie was returning victorious.

In my hotel room, I flipped on my OmniBook and composed an E-mail message to His Gracious Lordship Sean Cardinal of the Holy Roman Church Cronin:

Mystery Solved. Return Wednesday. Alert limousine driver, red carpet custodians, and trumpeters. Hold Michigan Avenue parade.

Regards, Blackie

I thereupon went to bed and slept the sleep of the just man.

34

Cindasue was waiting for me at the breakfast table. She wore a black dress with thin white stripes and a matching jacket. It was mid-thigh length and would have been quite modest if it wasn't for the slit in the skirt. She had tossed a black, imitation leather raincoat with a thick belt on the chair next to her. Sophistication today.

"You came up early," I said, offering her one of the precious raisin cinnamon buns that I had smuggled into the dining room.

"Reckoned ah'd get me an early start . . . missed the jularker, too," She said with a sweet smile, not unlike that of Helena Strauss minus a couple of decades of love.

"How you doing?"

"A-feelin' purty good. Ways to go. Shrinkin' lady say I a-doin' all right for lettle moutain boomer. . . . Uncle Blackie, Frieda and I went to see the young Turkish women yesterday. We made them laugh. We've made up our minds that they're going to be all right!"

"That settles it then."

"Uncle Blackie . . ."

"Yes?"

"You done figure out what happened to that thar shrine?"

"Yep. . . . You, too?"

"Yep. . . . Ah tell you what: Hyar's two pieces of paper. You a-writin' on one sheet and I on t'other."

We wrote down our solutions and exchanged them. Naturally, they were the same.

"Durnation!" she cried and clapped her hands. "I done knowed I had hit right!"

She looked around sheepishly, embarrassed by the noise she had made.

"Sorry," she murmured with notable lack of sincerity. "When you a-figurin' hit out?"

"About four A.M. . . . You?"

"Durn," she said, some of her enthusiasm gone. "A-ridin' up hyar from Bonn . . . You know who and why? Ah don't."

I told her.

"Wow!" She leaned across the table. "Uncle Blackie, you plumb wonderful."

"Arguably."

"You know what this means?" she asked with a smile.

"Oh, yes."

"Reckon you'uns a-goin' back tomorray?" She sighed and her shoulders slumped, all the vibrancy and enthusiasm drained from her. "Reckon I oughter tell my story to your nefoo man, huh?"

"Who am I to say, Cindasue?"

"You a-sayin' some extray prayers for a lettle she polecat from McCloud's Holler she do it right?"

"Certainly . . . though, Cindasue, no way you could do it wrong."

"I'm not sure, Uncle Blackie. I'm terrified. I don't want to tell him my story. But I have to, don't I?"

"Shonuff, Cindasue."

At that point, her jularker appeared and swept her up in his arms like he was tackling someone in a rugby scrum.

"Whafo ya a-stranglin' me fo?" she demanded happily.

"I didn't see you all day yesterday," he explained, still holding her above the floor.

"Uncle Blackie, make this hyar polecat put me down."

"Beyond my power." I sighed.

He kissed her again and then deposited her back in her chair.

The few people still in the dining room smiled at this dramatic manifestation of attractive young love.

"I declare," she murmured, flustered and pleased, as she reached for her purse and makeup. "You done mussed me up."

"We have," I intoned solemnly, "a ten-thirty appointment with the count cardinal and Pastor Rudi at the dom. It is time to clear up this little difficulty."

"You shonuff sound like that Sherlock Holmes fella, Uncle Blackie."

35

"I don't remember the combination," Claus Maria Count von Obermann admitted. *"Ja,* I thought I did, but I do not have a good memory for numbers."

"Ja," Rudi agreed.

"How can we get it open?" the cardinal asked. "Poor Freddie knew the numbers, but he is not well."

Over the top altogether.

Cindasue, her jularker, the two Köln clerics, and I were standing in front of the safe in the art studio. We had asked Signor Donatelli and his workers to vacate it for fifteen minutes. To my surprise, the successor to Henri de Verdun had not argued.

"No one else knows it?" I asked.

"Nein," the cardinal said sadly. "Rudi?"

"No one that I know of."

"Perhaps Pastor Kurt?" I suggested.

"Ja." The cardinal rolled his eyes. "Perhaps."

"I will find him," Rudi promised.

"Kurt?" the cardinal said. "Impossible!"

"Not necessarily."

A few minutes later, Rudi returned with the former Luftwaffe pilot, carrying his model of the ME-262 in one hand and a prayer book in the other. His normal vague smile was unchanged.

"*Ja,* Kurt," said the cardinal softly.

"*Ja,* Claus."

"You can open this safe?"

He put the plane and his prayer book on a table. One might imagine, if one was sad enough, that the twin engines were the breasts of a young woman and the plane the rest of her body. Poor Kurt.

"*Ja,*" he said, as if everyone knew he could open the safe.

He bent over the dial, spun it back and forth a couple of times, and then, as the lock clicked for the final time, turned the handle that opened the safe. He turned and smiled at us even more benignly, as if to say, "Naturally, I can open the safe."

The count cardinal walked to the door of the safe. Father Kurt stepped back gingerly, and the cardinal pulled the door open.

"*Ja!*" he exclaimed. "The shrine!"

I looked over him. I knew what was in the safe, but I wanted to be sure.

"Shonuff!" Cindasue agreed. " 'Cept'n it's not the real Shrine of the Magi. That's up thar next to the main altar, where hit belong!"

I watched Peter Murphy's lips. He came dangerously close to saying, "I told you so." But, good jularker that he was, he didn't. Good husband; no, great husband.

Pastor Kurt continued to smile inanely. Then he open his prayer book, took out what looked like a tattered holy card, and showed it to Cindasue. "Erika," he said softly.

I wanted to cry. So did everyone else.

Cindasue put her hand on his arm and admired the young woman, killed long ago by an English or perhaps an American bomb.

"How can this be?" the cardinal asked when he had regained control of his emotions.

"It was clear to me there indeed had been a plot to steal the shrine," I began. "Yet somehow the plot, while apparently successful, did not produce the publicity that it should have produced. There was some reason to believe from his ravings to the staff at the parsonage that the former Dompfarrer saw it as a way of discrediting you. Since he was hardly capable of stealing it himself, he needed an ally. Herr Zellner was the obvious choice for such an ally. He hoarded stolen art and stolen women for his own pleasure. He also would know how to plan, organize, and execute such a theft, especially since he perceived how ineffective was the security system here in the dom. He may well not have cared all that much about discrediting you, Cardinal von Obermann. However, once he saw a chance to seize the shrine, it would be an obsession to him.

"That was reasonably clear almost from the beginning. But where was the shrine? And why was not the theft revealed? If Bishop Heidrich's goal was to embarrass you, Cardinal, then he should have leaked the fact of the theft to his friends in the press in such a way as to embarrass you. He did not, however, do so.

"I began to wonder if something had gone wrong with his plot.

"Then the police raided Zellner's castle on that cliff overlooking the river and found no trace of the shrine. Somehow, I had expected that because, dullard that I might be, I had begun to wonder if something had gone wrong with the planned theft—like another theft intervening. Among the many things that became clear to me last night, however belatedly, was the notion that the possibility of such an intervention was the reason he blamed you, Cardinal, for the disappearance of the shrine. His sanity was already slipping away, you see. He had planned to do something to you and in his mania, he figured you had beat him to it."

"*Ja*," the count cardinal agreed, "Poor Freddie."

Kurt was murmuring softly to Cindasue in German about the young woman in the picture. Occasionally, he brushed the small photo against his old cassock, as if to sweep away the dust—and maybe the memories.

"This would explain why the Belarus Black Berets knew nothing about the theft. Herr Zellner had summoned them to steal the Shrine of the Magi and someone beat them to it. One can imagine his fury, which, when vented against the now deeply troubled Dompfarrer, drove him even farther around the bend."

"Someone stole it before poor Freddie was able to?" Cardinal von Obermann asked, his mouth hanging open.

"Precisely. Indeed, it was stolen so that poor Freddie would not be able to steal it."

Rudi got it. His face lit up in a sudden, manic grin. *"Ja, ja,"* he murmured complacently. "That is good. That is very good!"

"Oh, yes."

"Let us suppose," I continued, "that there is someone in the parsonage, someone who is more or less invisible, as I generally am, who senses the plot, that this someone has access to all the keys and combinations and security devices in the dom and also to a large supply of strong young men only too willing to try something that seems crazy. Suppose someone thinks that the best way to prevent the Belarus or whoever from stealing the shrine is to steal it himself first."

"Ja," said the Herr Kardinal, still not getting it, because for all his brilliance and sophistication, he was essentially a simple man. Unlike myself.

"That is very, very good," he conceded. "That is genius."

"Oh, yes," I agreed. "Shonuff genius; a little strange perhaps, but genius, nonetheless."

Cindasue, no longer interested in the solution of the mystery, which she already knew anyway, was explaining to Pastor Kurt that she would come up from Bonn tomorrow and help him make an enlargement. There were doubtless photo stores in every block of the Old City where such copies could be made instantly for less than twenty marks. No way Pastor Kurt would know this.

"To continue," I said, "suppose that one night, this virtually invisible man and his allies should enter the dom, liberate the shrine, place it on a dolly, take it down here to the workroom on the elevator, and secrete it under canvas over there in that corner where there is, I must assume, always a stack of gargoyles or such like waiting repair. Perhaps a rearrangement of the materials in that area makes it look like there has been no change.''

"Risky, arguably, but also daring. Very daring."

"Brilliant," Peter Murphy, a witness to many daring risks on the floor of CBOT, said in admiration.

"After that, things follow smoothly, though there is one more risky ploy. The Dompfarrer is informed that the shrine is missing. Terrified by the prospect of Herr Zellner's wrath, he covers up the disappearance and re-places the missing shrine with its substitute. Herr Zellner, gathering his Black Beret types, plans an attack this week, since he does not know that the substitute shrine is now next to the main altar. If the police had not raided his *Schloss* on Sunday, the second theft would have oc-curred—to solemn high whistles and bells and Bishop Heidrich's plan would have worked, though I doubt that it would discredit you, Cardinal, as much as it would discredit him. It would presumably take a long time for Herr Zellner to discover that his shrine was phony.''

"I begin to understand," the count cardinal said, though he really didn't; not yet.

"The difficulty for the clever plotters who stole the shrine so that it wouldn't be stolen is that they can't leave it lying under a canvas cover in the workroom down here. The strategy for them is simple. Perhaps the very night of their brilliant scheme, they return to the workshop, open the safe, wheel the real Shrine of the Magi into the safe, and close it. The shrine is perfectly safe and it has never left the dom.''

Pastor Kurt, his arm now linked with Cindasue's, con-tinued to smile inanely—and a little proudly, too, I thought.

"But how did it get back upstairs?" Herr Kardinal demanded.

"Sunday night, when it was clear that Zellner and his

crowd were out of action and there would be no theft, they simply repeated the switch. They moved the substitute down here and the original shrine back to its honored place. This was very risky, indeed, but since nothing ever left the dom, not too risky. No harm done. And much good. Even if the Zellner plot had gone down, they would have simply moved the original back into place the morning after. They were finally very bold and very brave—and doubtless loved every second of it. The young 'criminals' would have a story to talk about for the rest of their lives.''

"It happened this way, Cardinal," Cindasue tried to clarify for me. "Pastor Kurt and his young people done stole the shrine so hit wouldn't be stolen and hid hit in the safe in the workshop after we found the safe empty. Then, when hit was clear that hit wouldn' be stolen, they switched hit back. They like to stole hit to keep hit safe and then unstole hit.''

"Ja," the count cardinal said, rubbing his chin. *"Ja,* I think I understand. . . . But if we had announced late this afternoon that the shrine was missing?''

"That would have been a mistake. I suspect that our brilliant plotter hardly anticipated that a prince of the church, even one such as you, would have told the whole truth.''

"Ja," said the count cardinal, a jovial grin returning his face. "That is good. That is very good. Very . . .''

"Original?" I asked.

"Ja. . . . Kurt?''

"Claus?''

"Ja."

"Ja," the former pilot smiled, this time knowingly, and then explained how the Fräulein Unterleutnant would help him make a large copy of the photo of Erika.

"The Turkish women and now Father Kurt," I whispered into her ear.

"Like the Ryan family," she replied, "I collect strays.''

36

Peter Murphy

"You plumb generous, Peter Murphy, suh," she said as we sat in the bar of the Dom Hotel. "You never done said I told y'all so."

"It's enough for me to know that I figured out some of it before you two did."

"Right brillian'," she agreed.

Then the smile of approval (of me) fled from her face. She became somber and silent.

I ordered two Kölsch beers.

"I don't want to do this, Peter," she began.

"You have to, Cindasue. You know that."

She nodded grimly. "I have three conditions. They are not negotiable."

"Let's hear them."

"The first is that you tell Uncle Blackie about it. On the way home. I couldn't go through it twice. . . . He probably knows, anyway. If I ever become a Catholic, I'll go to him for confession. He'll know my sins without my telling them."

It was a funny and insightful remark, but neither of us so much as smiled.

"And the second?"

She sighed, causing her perfect breasts to move up and down sharply. I tried to restrain my desires.

"The second is that you let me tell you the whole story without interrupting me. You can ask questions after I'm finished if you want to."

"Fair enough. . . . And the third?"

"The third is that we make no commitments today. I need time. You will need time, too. We don't talk about the future today. Not at all. Is that clear?"

"How much time?"

"Enough time."

"I accept that condition," I said cautiously. "Except I promise you that it won't be long, nothing like seven years."

She looked steadily into my eyes, her own green eyes hard and cold.

"That has to be up to you, Peter."

I relaxed. In effect, she had agreed that the time would be short. In fact, it would be real short.

"Now, don't interrupt while I'm talking."

I nodded my head to indicate I was already silent. I think that won me a trace of a smile.

"My mother killed my father, Peter. She blew his head off with a twelve-gauge shotgun. I was present when she did it. He would have killed me and probably her, too. I would have killed him before she did, if she hadn't grabbed the gun away from him. She went to prison. I went free. It wasn't fair."

I stuck to my promise.

"She loved my father. I don't know why, but she did. Well, maybe I do. She blamed me then for his death. I think she still does.

"He was from McCloud's Hollow, a place where everyone has been no-account since as far as anyone can remember. Somehow, he managed to go off to college and come back a teacher. They hired him to teach in the grammar school in the town I call Stinkin' Crik. They got him cheap because he wanted to stay in town. She grew up in the town, her father owned a small farm supply store, but everyone reckoned she was too good for someone from McCloud's Hollow, even if he had gone to college. They ran away to get married when she was seventeen. That wasn't real young by Stinkin' Crik standards in those days. She was pregnant, so that made it worse. They fired Daddy from the school but hired him again because they couldn't find anyone else who would teach for what they were paying him.

"They had four kids: two boys and two girls. I was the last. She had me when she was twenty-five, what I am now. As far as I can tell, they were still happy and still in love."

I clamped my teeth closed as this story of tragedy unfolded.

"At first, they lived in town, but then with four of us youngsters around, they needed more room and they didn't have much money. So they moved into a cabin up in our hollow. It was a terrible place, but in all my early memories, we were happy. Moving up there was a mistake, however. The folks in the town were willing to tolerate a teacher from McCloud's Hollow as long as he didn't live up there where everyone was drunk before ten o'clock in the morning and lived off welfare checks.

"My daddy was a wonderful teacher. I certainly did love him a lot and was proud to sit in the classroom with him when I was in fourth grade. I was usually a pest in class because I thought, correctly, that I was smarter than any of the teachers. I was probably smarter than my daddy, too, but I loved him so much I didn't say anything much in his classroom. He was proud of me, too.

"He drank a little up in the Hollow; not much, compared to anyone else, but still some. My mommy was a hard-shell Baptist and didn't drink anything.

"Well, you wouldn't believe there was a class system in a place as poor as Stinkin' Creek, but there was. We folks from the Hollow were at the bottom of it, no matter how much Daddy knew and how many meetings of teachers he went to and how many articles he wrote. They just laughed. Then when the principal of the grammar school died, he applied for the job. He had all the credentials and they should have given it to him. They just laughed and said that no McCloud from McCloud's Hollow could ever be the principal of Stinkin' Crik School.''

I shut my eyes in horror at what I knew was coming. I opened them quickly because I knew she was staring at me with those blank green eyes, eyes filled with unbearable pain.

''That's when he started to drink a lot. He believed in the American dream, even for folks from McCloud's Hollow. He had worked hard, got himself an education, turned himself into an excellent teacher, paid all his dues. None of it made any difference. If he were a less vulnerable man, he would not have been hurt as bad as he was. If he didn't love the mountains and the critters in them, he would have gone somwhere else. But by then I guess there was just nothing left in him.

''Up in the Hollow, no one thought anything about a man beating up on his wife and kids. My daddy was the only one who didn't do it. The men thought it was good for the women and the children if they got pushed around every once in awhile. But we'd been raised differently. He started too late. My poor mommy never fought back. My brothers did when they were old enough and bigger than he was. They beat him up badly and he left them alone after that. He didn't push me or my sister around much. He took it all out on Mommy. They fired him from the school when he began to come in drunk. Mommy got a job in a general store in town. As soon as the older kids graduated, they went off to Cincinnati, got jobs, and married. They didn't come back. That left my mother and father and me in the cabin up in the Hollow.

''As you know, Peter, I have a mouth on me. I told him that if he ever tried to beat me, I'd kill him. Did I mean it? What does a fourteen-year-old mean? I think I kind of meant it, but in the back of my head, I didn't think I would. I just wanted to scare him.

''Mommy was your classic battered woman, always

ready to forgive him when he sobered up, always defending him, always saying he really loved us.

"I knew that he really did, but I had begun to hate him for what he did to Mommy, sometimes every day. She'd put on her makeup very carefully, but the people that came to store would whisper that's what they did to women up in the Hollow, even good-looking, intelligent women.

"I did very well in high school over in the county seat. The kids laughed at me because of my funny clothes and the way I talked, though they didn't talk standard English, either. But I was the smartest kid in my class and point guard on the girls basketball team when I was a sophomore. Some of the kids changed their minds about me and I made friends. I had never done that in Stinkin' Crik, so I was surprised that it was real easy to make people like me.

"That's when it all went wrong. No real reason, either. Mommy and I came home one day in her old rattletrap car, she from work and me from school. We had won a basketball game and I had scored twenty points and I was pretty full of myself. I didn't notice the look in Daddy's eyes. He was real far gone, drunker than I'd ever seen him.

"He took out after Mommy, beat her with a thick stick, told her that I was more boy than girl, and he was ashamed of me. I had been his favorite, too. But the drink had control of his tongue.

"I told him that he was drunk and that he should shut his big mouth up and leave Mommy alone.

"He came after me with the stick and beat me something terrible. I refused to cry or to beg like my sister had done before she ran away. Instead, I grabbed his twelve-gauge—no matter how poor a man in the Hollow was, he had to have a twelve-gauge or he was no man—and pointed it at him. To tell the truth, I didn't think it was loaded.

"He kicked the gun out of my hand and began to beat me like he was going to kill me. I curled up into a knot and waited till I would die and the pain would stop.

"Mommy shouted that he was killing me. He said something like I had it coming for pointing a gun at my papa. All the crazy violence in a hundred years of McCloud's Hollow was in his voice. He would have killed me. Then Mommy blew his head off. I looked up and saw that my daddy had no more head. Blood and bone and brains were all over the room, all over Mommy and me and everything."

She stopped for a moment. Her cheeks were dry, her face devoid of emotion, her eyes still blank. If only she would cry out in pain . . .

"The prosecutor over at the county figured this was a chance to make a name for himself, teach those savages up in the Hollow they couldn't get away with murder. He indicted Mommy on charges of first-degree murder. He wanted to indict me, too, but I was so badly beat up, covered with bandages and all, that he decided against it. Our lawyer finally got Mommy to plead manslaughter. She was sentenced to fifteen years and got out in seven, the same time I graduated from the Academy. She moved to Wheeling, found herself a job, met a nice man who was kind to her, and married him. She's still pretty . . . lost a lot of weight in jail and hasn't put it back on. She seems happy.

"I'm the only one who visited her in jail. I was the only one who went to her wedding. Funny thing, he is a Catholic, so she was married in one of your churches. He is a widower and has some teenage kids. They love her, unlike her own kids.

"Well, I think I love her. She didn't come to my graduation from New London because she was just out of prison, but she wrote me a real nice note. Kind of short but real nice.

"She still blames me, I think. She never says it, but I can tell.

"That's about the end of my little Walton's Mountain American tragedy. I finished high school with the highest marks, but they wouldn't let me be valedictorian. They threw me off the basketball team, too, and they lost all their games. When I was a senior, some of the girls begged me to try out, and I did, but I was cut.

"I lived with my mother's sister and her family down in the town. They thought I was the devil's seed, but at least they fed and housed me and clothed me, sort of. I earned a little money by working at the same store my mother had worked at.

"So, the day after I graduated, I got on the bus and rode into Wheeling. I thought I'd join the Marines. Then I saw the Coast Guard recruiting sign and I figured that it would be better to save lives instead of taking them away.

"I was surprised that they accepted me, with my background, but it didn't bother them. Not even later when they wanted me to go to New London. The name McCloud didn't mean I was dirt in the Coast Guard. People liked me a lot. I didn't even have to try to make them like me. I didn't want to accept the appointment to New London because I was sure I'd be a failure. They liked me more there, even the men who resented women at the Academy. I ended up first captain, like your uncle guessed. I spent a lot of time talking to a psychiatrist while I was there. I'm functional now, as you have seen. I expect I'll never get over what happened to me. I'm afraid of men. I don't like dating. I don't ever want to marry. If a man ever tried to beat me, I think I might kill him. I'm a poor marriage risk because I'm so afraid of letting a man get close to me. I'd probably break a man's heart. I'm sure I'm frigid.

"That's all I wanted to say."

Gulp.

What do I say now?

As Uncle Blackie would say, I needed the grace of God and a lot of luck—and a bunch of angels whispering in my ear.

"But you still love me, Cindasue?"

The question surprised her.

"Yes, I do, Peter, with every cell in my body. Ever since that first day at Grand Beach."

"You know I'd never beat you."

"I know that." She smiled slightly.

"You have at least kind of dated me and seemed to enjoy it."

She nodded. "Very much."

"We have engaged in, ah, only the first tentative movements toward intimacy, and you have not seemed exactly frigid to me.

She wet her lips with her tongue. "You set me on fire," she said simply.

"So there's a chance—mind you, not a certainty—that I'd make a good husband."

"I'm sure you would."

"I might be kind and gentle and sweet and tender, and, for a man, not all that dumb?"

She smiled, not much of a smile, but a smile.

"Not even really dumb at all—for a man."

"So I might be a good risk for a marriage?"

"Arguably." Her smile was bigger this time.

"All right, so long as that's clear . . ."

"I'm the one that's the poor marriage risk," she interrupted me.

"Maybe I'm the one who should decide whether a woman's a poor marriage risk or not."

She pondered that point.

"You're not reacting the way I thought you would."

"Isn't that clever of me? I repeat the question: Isn't that my decision?"

She looked down. "I suppose so," she said softly.

"Good, just so long as we got those preliminary issues out of the way. Now I will make my statement and I impose the same rule of no interruptions. All right?"

She looked up at me, shy, suspicious, but game.

"Fair is fair."

"I have heard nothing this afteroon"—I began to work on my beer—"that does anything but enhance my admiration and love for you, Cindasue. I want you more now than when we came in here. You went through horror and survived. Not only did you survive, astonishingly, what you suffered made you an even more attractive woman than if none of those terrible events had happened. You're a no-risk proposition for marriage, Cindasue, my love. End of statement.''

"You shonuff one clever arguin' man, Peter Murphy, suh. You done hog-tied me.'' She sighed again and once more, the movement of her breasts sent pain and delight through my bloodstream and nervous system.

"Fool you?''

"Yessuh, shonuff done fooled me.''

Then Mountain Flower disappeared and the reasoned product of extensive therapy returned.

"I don't know, Peter. I don't know. I expected you to argue, and you really haven't.''

"Right.''

Then I made a high-risk decision, the kind of decision a man makes when he has within his grasp the star he has been following.

"You said you want time. I said I was prepared to give you time, but not much time. I intend to live up to both my promises.''

She inclined her head in acceptance of our agreement.

"Ya shonuff one plumb clever polecat, Professor Peter Murphy, suh.''

She kissed me affectionately at the airport the next morning. Hardly a passionate encounter. Indeed, not much different from her first kiss a week before.

I told Uncle Blackie the story on the way home.

"What do you think?'' I asked him when I was finished.

"When you finish your night-school law course this spring, you will take the bar?''

"Why not?''

"That would be wise.''

"But what about my response to Cindasue?''

"Oh, I think the jury was convinced. It's all up to you now.''

I wasn't sure what he meant. Not exactly.

37

Blackie Finally

Milord Cronin did not provide the trumpets or the red carpets, but he did await us in the arrivals hall at O'Hare International Airport, an unheard-of event.

After greeting my nephew cordially, he said to me, "Blackwood, I am glad you are on my side."

"I believe you have made that remark before."

"Even more so now . . . It will take Cologne years to get over the hurricane you created in a few days."

"Hours," said Peter Murphy.

"In any case, the *Bundesrepublik* proposes to award you a medal, though not one of the same rank as is going to the, ah, young woman."

"I solved the mystery, Cardinal," Peter Murphy protested, "and I don't get any medal."

He then told the story, a remarkably accurate and well-balanced version of it.

"I'll be damned," said Cardinal Sean Cronin.

"One trusts not," I remarked.

"If ever I want to stir up a hurricane in this archdiocese, I'll hire the three of you. . . . Incidentally, where is the young woman?"

"Still in Bonn," I said. "That is her present assignment."

"It does not exceed the limits of probability, Cardinal, that we will see her in Chicago in the reasonably near future."

They both laughed. I was not amused—save at his confidence that the Coast Guard person would ever show up in Chicago. She was courageous, all right, but was it reasonable to expect that she would be brave enough to risk the total surrender that marriage would mean for her, much more than it would for most other brides?

There is not much else to tell. Heinz Zellner faces life in prison. The pedophile priests have pleaded guilty to charges and are doing time. What happens to the poor men when they are released, I do not know. Bishop Heidrich now thinks he is a cardinal. As Christmas nears, more pilgrims visit the Shrine of the Magi. Ernst Schulteis is planning to retire. I receive presents from the Strauss Bakery in Ahrweiler. I refused the medal from the BRD, only to discover that Milord Cronin had already accepted it for me. Pastor Kurt presumably has his enlargement of his Erika. I have no information about the young Turkish women, though I presume that Frieda and her partner have not given up on them and never will.

I distributed all the bottles of Kölnisch Wasser, which were accepted with considerable enthusiasm, most recipients insisting that I shouldn't have when patently I should have.

I still blame myself for my slowness in uncovering the solution. Patently, the Shrine of the Magi did not ever leave the dom.

I attribute my failure to jet lag.

Epilogue

"What do you think of these E-mail notes, Uncle Blackie?"

Peter Murphy, this time with no advance warning from the Megan. He was in a state of high agitation.

I read the first hard copy:

Cindasue,

I loved you that first day at Grand Beach. I have loved you ever since. I will love you all my life. I will never stop loving you.

    With that in mind, I ask you two questions:

1. Will you marry me?
2. Will you come to Chicago around Christmas or before so Uncle Blackie can preside over our marriage?

Deepest love, Peter Murphy, Ph.D.

"Direct enough," I said. "None of the usual Irish circumlocutions."

The second was, if anything, more direct:

Peter Murphy, Suh.

Sure enough!

Sure enough!

All my love!

Cindasue

Cindasue McCloud
Lieutenant, U.S.C.G.

"They have promoted her, I see."
"Huh?"
I pointed at the space where J.G. would have once appeared.
"Damn! I didn't notice. I've got to do a better job at noticing things that are important."
He didn't say "important to her," which showed great progress.
"Indeed."
"Well, I gotta rush up to O'Hare."
"O'Hare?"
He pulled a small box from his coat pocket.
"I'm flying to Bonn via London this eveing. Gotta hog-tie her with a ring less'n she change her mind."
"Small chance of that, Peter Murphy."
"I'm not taking any chance!"
And off he went, following his star.
It was well that he did, I reflected. She would be expecting him there tomorrow in her office overlooking the Rhine in that fabled small town in Germany.
The phone buzzed again. The Megan, as expected.
"Is that cute boy engaged, Bishop Blackie? He sure acts like it."
"I think that's a fair reading of the situation."
"What's she like?"
"She is the kind of young woman who follows her

star, no matter how great the risks or grave the dangers, through field and fountain, moor and mountain.''

"Gee, can I meet her sometime?"

"I think that not improbable."

I looked up at the ivory Madonna, much prettier than either the Limburg Madonna or the Milan Madonna and, as I often do when an affair of the heart arranges itself properly, I winked.

Books on Appalachian English

Dillard, J. L. *Toward a Social History of American English*. New York: Mouton, 1985.

Farewell, Harold F., and J. Karl Nicholas. *Smoky Mountain Voices*. Lexington: The University of Kentucky Press, 1993.

Fetterman, John. *Stinking Creek*. New York: E. P. Dutton, 1967.

Thomas, Roy Edwin. *Southern Appalachia 1885–1915*. Jefferson, NC: McFarland, 1991.

Williams, Cratis D. *Southern Mountain Speech*. Berea College Press, 1992.

Wolfram, Walt, and Donna Christian. *Appalachian Speech*. Arlington, VA: Center for Applied Linguistics, 1976.